Playing For Her

A Wearside Story – Book 1

Ellie White

Cahill Davis Publishing Limited

ISBN 978-1-915307-20-0 (eBook)

ISBN 978-1-915307-19-4 (Paperback)

Cahill Davis Publishing Limited

www.cahilldavispublishing.co.uk

For everyone who has ever been told they aren't enough.

Chapter One

Jordan

I groan and squint as dozens of blinding lights and the familiar snapping of camera shutters hit me the moment I pull up to the wrought-iron gates and into the players' car park at Wearside Academy.

It's no surprise we have press here—they're always present for the start of pre-season to get a first look at our new signings—but I had wrongly assumed that coming to work early would eliminate the potential of it being so crowded.

Or maybe the "first look" they want is actually of our new assistant coach, who starts today. In an industry where rumours fly freely, there's not even been a whisper of who we can expect to take the vacant position. It's disconcerting, to say the least, but Coach Davison has assured me that as captain, I'll have a good relationship with his new right-hand man.

"*Robinson, Robinson,*" one of the journalists shouts as I climb out of my car and make my way across the car park towards the entrance. This is the worst part—feeling forced to parade myself in front of them, unable to hide my side profile from their pictures.

I catch sight of the familiar-looking journalist calling my name out of the corner of my eye and offer a small smile in the hopes a simple picture will keep the piranhas at bay. My politeness is my first mistake.

PR rule number one: don't engage with journalists unless it's been pre-approved by the club.

Mistake number one leads to mistake number two: my hand is up in a casual wave before I can stop myself. Like I said, I should know by now that it's a mistake because you give an inch, then suddenly it's feeding time. I drop my hand quickly and let out a sigh. I blame my mistakes on my tiredness.

"Robinson, how do you feel about the upcoming season?" he calls.

"What can we expect you to bring to the team?" yells another over the top of the first.

All I have to do is ignore them and close the final gap to the entrance.

"What happened last season, Robinson? Is that the kind of legacy you want to leave behind?"

I stop in my tracks, that last question cutting through the others like a knife, reaching my ears with such clarity I could swear the reporter is right behind me. I know I shouldn't, but I turn to face the man who asked, looking at him as I process the meaning behind his words.

His menacing smirk tells me his question has nothing to do with the fact I'm retiring this season.

What happened last season, Robinson?

The question echoes in my mind as I look at the crowd, trapped in the blinding lights of their camera flashes I freeze, taking in their eager expressions. Their cameras continue to click and their mouths are moving, but I don't hear anything other than a low hum of blood pulsing in my ears and the million-pound question bouncing around my brain.

What happened?

The heartbreaking scene plays on a loop in my brain as I stare blankly into the distance. It hurts just as much now as it did when it happened. It was the ninety-fourth minute of a fierce relegation battle that had been brewing all season. I was exhausted and my knees hurt, but so did my pride, so when Coach wanted to sub me, I begged him to let me play on. We were nil-nil and four minutes into injury time when I misjudged the angle as I tried to kick the ball out of our box. Instead, I sent it careening past our keeper to the back of our net, securing an own goal and our relegation to League One.

I'll never forget the roaring sound of the opposition as they realised they were safe in the Championship. Every day, I make myself remember the distraught faces of our fans who had travelled an eight-hundred-mile round trip from Wearside to Plymouth Argyle just to see me fuck it all up. I'll never forget the heavy silence in the dressing room as we showered or the pity on my friends' faces as we boarded the bus for the torturous seven-hour-and-fourteen-minute drive home.

Is that the kind of legacy you want to leave behind?

Absolutely not.

But I'm scared. I'm scared that despite devoting my life to this club, winning countless silverware, and being the longest-appointed captain in Wearside FC history, I'll not be remembered for any of that. I'm scared I'll be remembered for how I hammered the final nail into our coffin last season.

The sound of a door opening behind me breaks me from my inner turmoil. I glance over my shoulder as I clear the emotion from my throat, relieved to see a friendly face.

"Save it for the press conference, lads," Bridget O'Leary, our club press officer and head of marketing, yells to them in her smooth Irish accent. She stands tall, with her hands planted firmly on her hips as she waits for me in the doorway as if she could sense I needed her.

"Bridgie, baby, you're breaking my heart," a creep shouts back at her before snapping her picture.

"Call me baby one more time, Pete, and I'll have your credentials stripped and placed in a jar with your balls before you can say another word," she quips back with a stern smile.

The crowd taunt Pete, whistling and ohing at him as he hangs his head low.

"See you later, lads." Bridget holds the door open wider to let me pass.

"They almost had you there, Jordan."

I sigh. "I know."

Bridget is like a swan, beautiful and graceful on the surface in her designer clothes and with her well-kept appearance, but underneath the surface, she's paddling furiously trying to keep the entire club and all its players, including me, in line.

"That guy is a prick," I tell her when the door is safely closed behind us.

Bridget's body is leaning towards me as she listens, but her eyes are busy watching some of my teammates crossing the car park through the floor-to-ceiling windows. "I'll have a word with his editor before the press conference this afternoon. Speaking of the press conference, I've sent the notes to your email, but I'll run through the key points after the morning's training session too."

"Thanks, Bridget. I don't know what I'd do without you."

"Morning, Skip." Aaron Milburn always has a grin on his face and a mischievous glint in his eyes. His phone lies forgotten on the bench next to him where he sits fully clothed, as though he's just arrived.

He pushes himself up and greets me with a hug, taking my right hand in his fist and clapping me on the back with his left.

"I thought you'd have got a lift in with Bailey?" I ask, looking around at the empty dressing room as I make my way to my usual spot at the bench next to Aaron, where my brand-new training kit sits in a neat pile. I inspect it closely, the red polyester flowing through my fingers as I run my thumb along the embroidered club crest. This is the last time I'll ever do this, so I make sure I appreciate every last stitch.

"I thought you would have too?"

Aaron, Bailey, and I all live in the same private cul-de-sac with two of our other friends, and on a normal training day, Bailey would drive us all together. But today is anything but normal.

"I couldn't sleep, so I went for an early run." This morning more than ever, I needed the thinking space that comes with a run along the sand at Roker. Retiring this season wasn't an easy choice to make. It's hard to accept that my muscles don't recover as well as they once did now that I'm thirty-four. It's hard to accept that I need a day or two to recover from playing a ninety-minute game. It's even harder to accept I can't play football for the rest of my life when it's all I know. But I can't focus on that now. I don't want last season to be my legacy, and I can't fix things if I'm distracted by my own depressing reality.

"So, where did you go last night?" I ask Aaron, his tired appearance and the fact he's definitely wearing the same jeans and T-shirt I saw him leave the house in last night not going unnoticed.

Bailey walks in, joining us on the bench in front of his locker on the other side of me, providing a brief distraction as we greet him.

Aaron and Bailey are in their late twenties and couldn't be more different if they tried. Bailey is a typical boy-next-door type with short black hair brushed to the side and dimples in his cheeks when he smiles. The ladies love his innocent look. I'm not fooled though, having shared a hotel room wall with him more times than I'd care to remember.

Aaron is more obvious with his extracurriculars. He parades around in the press, causing havoc and generally living up to his bad-boy appearance. His hair is lighter and much longer than Bailey's and always held back by his signature elastic headband. He's covered in tattoos from his neck down to his waist including both arms and hands. He'd be the first to say he loves the attention that comes with it. But underneath what he chooses to show people, he's actually one of the softest guys I know. He's one of the most loyal friends I have and has even been by Bailey's side since he found out he was going to be a dad at sixteen, helping him raise his twin daughters.

"Let's just say my date went well," Aaron says, wagging his eyebrows as he finally starts to strip off to change into his training kit—something I'm already in the middle of doing.

I open my mouth to respond, but before I can, Bailey reaches past me to high-five him. "Nice."

"The gaffer will have your guts for garters if he finds out you went out last night when he explicitly told us not to," I warn him.

"Come on, it's not like I was drinking or anything, I just matched with some lass, and she invited me over to hers. Technically, we stayed in, if you know what I mean."

Sadly, I always know what he means.

"That's even worse, mate, you don't even know who she is." I rub my hand over my growing stubble, the stress of team responsibility already creeping in. "You'll have Bridget on your back as well as Coach if the girl sells the story."

"What is it they say? All publicity is good publicity?"

I shut him down with a glare.

"Lighten up a little. This is going to be our best season yet. We all want to give you a good send-off, so let's get started." He secures his long hair back from his eyes with a thin elastic headband before tugging on a pair of shorts.

"Anyway, Skip," Bailey says, the look on his face telling me I'm not going to like where he's going with this, "weren't you papped hooking up with a supermodel last weekend?"

"No, that was last month; it was a popstar last weekend," Aaron explains unhelpfully. "The young one."

My eyes widen at the word "young". "She's twenty-five."

He waves my comment away with a flick of his hand. "That's not the point. I'm just saying, you probably hook up with more women than Bailey and me combined, so why is it a problem for me?"

"Because the women I hook up with don't sell sex stories to the papers. All eyes are on you"—*and on me*—"this season, mate. Don't fuck it up."

"You know I won't let it affect my performance. But if it makes you feel better, I'll be more careful," he tells me, placing one hand on his bare chest and the other in the air in a Scout salute. "I promise."

The rest of the team start to arrive, each offering sympathetic smiles and sombre back pats as they pass by me to their lockers. Unlike Bailey and Aaron, who I can't seem to escape most days, I haven't seen the rest of the team since our last debrief after our relegation. It's up there in the top five worst moments of my life. Hell, who am I trying to kid? It's a solid second place after... well, it doesn't really matter what the top is.

I still remember the disappointment eating through the atmosphere in the media room as we gathered to discuss our failings that day. Everyone tried to convince me it wasn't my fault, but it was.

The place is unusually silent as we change, as if everyone has forgotten how to interact around me. I'm half-tempted to bring back the subject of hook-ups just to break the silence.

Ten or so minutes pass in excruciating awkwardness and worried glances thrown in my direction until I've finally had enough.

"Right, lads. Can I say something?" Not waiting for an answer, I jump onto the bench to address the team, like I have many times in this very spot. Twenty-five men look my way, giving me their full, undivided attention as they stop what they are doing. I take in their expectant faces. I've known most of the guys in here since they were kids coming up through the academy programme. I've been there for all their big moments on and off the pitch. They rely on me as much as I rely on them. "I really appreciate your concern over my feelings today… but I'm retiring, not fucking dying, so can you all, for the love of god, stop pussyfooting around me like I haven't got long left to live, please? We've got a big season ahead. We need to focus on the game. We need to focus on winning. Okay?"

The door to the dressing room closes loudly behind me, putting an end to my impromptu pep talk. Along with the rest of my team, I turn my attention to the door. My breath catches as Molly Davison's rich brown eyes meet mine across the crowded room.

This can't be real. I must be hallucinating or at the very least I'm asleep and dreaming. But as I blink a few times, willing the image to disperse, Molly remains. *My Molly.*

"Nice speech, Robinson." Coach Davison stands proudly at his daughter's side, surrounded by the rest of his coaching staff, looking down at his clipboard.

I can't find the words to respond to him; there are too many thoughts and emotions running through my mind.

Shock.

Anger.

Confusion.

My mind is short-circuiting. Is this what having a stroke feels like?

As the captain of the team, I know I should say something to our guest. But what I actually want to say to her wouldn't be suitable in front of a room full of our peers. And what I *should* say somehow isn't registering in my brain.

I let my eyes drift down her familiar body as I take in the unexpected sight of her. Half her deep brunette hair is piled into a messy bun on top of her head with the rest tumbling down her back in waves. I watch her full rosy lips part slightly, vivid memories consuming me as though it were only yesterday she belonged to me, not three years ago.

I draw my eyes down her neck, of which I know every intimate freckle in detail and could probably draw a map of them from memory, then I reach her chest.

Printed on her navy-blue Wearside FC tracksuit, just above her right breast, are her initials in large white capital letters, underlined with the words "Assistant Coach".

Chapter Two

Molly

I told myself so many times this week that I could handle seeing Jordan Robinson, that I was strong enough to face him. Clearly, now that I'm standing in front of him, I underestimated the strength of that connection we once shared.

My skin tingles as his gaze tracks the length of my body, and I swear his light brown irises spark when they lock with mine again. Emotion flashes across his face so quickly I don't think anyone else notices, but it vanishes just as quickly and his face takes on a neutral expression, matching mine.

I break eye contact first, glancing at my dad, who is fixated on his clipboard holding the attendance sheet, marking off the names of the players he can see directly in front of him and then around the rest of the room.

"Give me another minute, lads," Dad tells them as he continues.

The players who don't know who I am or simply don't care resume a casual chatter amongst themselves while they wait.

Aaron Milburn and Bailey Airey are staring at me, grinning in disbelief, and Jordan… well… just because I'm not looking at him doesn't mean I can't feel his watchful gaze fixated on me.

Out of my peripheral, I see him jump down from the bench he used as a platform for his speech. Sitting with his forearms resting on his thighs, he eventually looks away and watches the floor instead of me. As much as I want to look at him, like really look at him, I know I shouldn't allow it. Three years later, he still looks good enough to make me weak at the knees, and that is not the reaction I need to have with the highest-value player on my new team. His hair is a little longer than it was when we were together and it's styled and coiffed to the side. The deep brown stubble he's sporting is new too, and I have to say, the change really works for me.

I mean him.

It works for him.

Oh, Christ.

Using my iPad as a shield held tightly against my chest, I pull up a wall around me and lock away any lingering feelings. I'm here for me, not Jordan.

"Right, lads," Dad says, tucking his clipboard under his arm, "welcome back. I hope you're all well-rested after the break because we're in for some hard graft over the next few months. None of us wanted to face back-to-back relegation, and now that we've had an overhaul of the team, I'm expecting better things from all of you."

Everyone murmurs their agreement except for Jordan, who looks away guiltily.

"Anyway, it's not just changes on the pitch this season. As we know, our previous assistant coach, Kevin Quinn, has retired from coaching and is living it up in sunny Spain. So, I'd like everyone to give a big warm welcome to our new assistant coach, Molly Davison."

The room echoes with applause and words of congratulations from familiar faces and new ones alike as I smile around the room at my new family.

"Thank you. It feels great to be back at Wearside."

"Molly, for those who don't know, began her career here playing for Wearside Women," Dad continues. "She has the third most England caps of all time, has helped her team become Premier League champions five times, has won countless professional accolades, represented Team GB in the Olympics, and is a six-time women's FA Cup winner. She did this all before she was twenty-eight years old, so I know she'll be a valuable asset to the team this season."

Like Jordan, I'm unable to tear my eyes from the linoleum floor as I listen to Dad reel off my achievements, leaving out the devastating incident that ended the glittering career he speaks so highly of. It's no secret why I retired, but it's also no secret that I don't like to talk about my accident.

"Most importantly, Molly is my daughter."

Although his words are simple, the meaning behind them is clear and everyone in the room knows it. Roughly translated: "don't mess with my baby girl".

"Thanks, Coach," I reply, feeling the heat of my blush stain my cheeks.

I thought about preparing a speech. One where I'd plant the flag as the first female coach in a men's professional league and promise them that I'd do the team proud in the face of the adversity that is sure to come. But no matter how many times I put pen to paper or opened Word documents, I always ended up staring at a blank page or screen. In reality, the speech should have been simple and easy, but nothing simple and easy comes with knowing you're about to spend your time trying to help a team achieve everything you once were and are now unable to. And I'm not about to give an unprepared speech, so another smile will have to do.

"Right, then, let's get out there and see what we're working with." Dad hands me the clipboard with a proud smile, as though he's passing the baton, before he walks briskly out of the room. Jordan leaves quickly too, not pausing to stop and chat with me like the others. He doesn't even glance my way, and I can't say I blame him.

"Fucking hell, congratulations, Molly," Aaron says, bounding over to me and pulling me into a bear hug, distracting me from the unexpected pang of longing in my chest as I watch Jordan leave. "Kept this quiet, didn't you?"

I give him a half-hearted laugh as I fall in step beside him, walking out to the training pitches. "I had to; you've got a big mouth."

"You're not wrong. Does Brooke know you're back?" He looks at me with an unreadable expression on his face. I wonder whether he's hoping she doesn't know, meaning his best friend didn't keep this news from him. Honestly, despite the fact Brooke is my younger cousin, I'm surprised she hasn't cracked and told him.

"Yeah, she knows. She was the first person I told when I got the news last week." My smile turns into laughter as I watch his face morph into shock.

"I don't know whether I should be hurt or impressed that she managed to keep a secret from me." He ponders for a moment before breaking into another wide grin. "Regardless of the secret squirrelling, I'm happy to have you home... Gaffer."

He gives me another warm hug before he jogs to join the others warming up in the centre circle of the high-quality 3G artificial pitch I would have sold my soul to play on.

I sit cross-legged on the soft turf and watch Dad and the other coaches run through a number of fitness and agility exercises before he splits the group into two teams for a short game. As part of my coaching qualifications, I coached a high-profile women's team who, as amazing as they were, didn't have access to this level of fitness tech, and although I saw examples as I earned my badges, seeing it first-hand is a whole other level. And with different fitness tech and different coaches comes different styles of coaching.

As I watch them play, I'm amazed that the data from their GPS trackers feeds through to the iPad in my hand immediately so I can analyse their fitness and stamina in real time. I'm so distracted by watching Aaron's and Bailey's stats run side by side on the screen as they push forward on an attack that, when a looming figure appears next to me, I double take. Covered in sweat under the midday summer sun, he bends down to grab a blue isotonic drink from the caddy on the ground next to me and takes a long pull from the bottle. His Adam's apple bobs in his throat as he swallows, and I can't tear my eyes away. He dabs the sweat from his forehead with the hem of his shirt, giving a glimpse of his flexing biceps and tanned stomach that look just as firm as I remember.

I quickly avert my eyes.

I'm not here for him.

He places his bottle back into the caddy and pauses, standing by my side so he's towering over my sitting form. Looking out to the group, he finally breaks his silence.

"It's been a while, Mol," he says, stating the obvious without so much as a glance my way.

"I stopped by your house this morning. I thought we should talk before… well… this."

"I was out. But don't worry, we're good." He flexes his hips to stretch them out.

"Good," I answer simply.

Without another word, he nods and jogs back to his position on the pitch.

Chapter Three

Molly

I didn't think I'd ever find myself living back at my parents' house in my thirties. It certainly was never part of my life plan before my accident. Strangely enough, I welcome being back here. The feeling of safety and security of living under their roof again is exactly what I need after so long in London living with uncertainty, clinging to a sporting career that I should have let go of as soon as my doctor told me it was over.

The delicious smell of burgers grilling on the barbecue wafts over the back garden as Dad tends to it with care and concentration. I've missed watching him in his element like this. Unlike his firm, no-bullshit attitude at work, when he's in his own little bubble in his garden, he seems so content.

"Have you finished unpacking yet?" Mam asks me, turning her head to face me as we lounge side by side with a glass of rosé in our hands.

I shake my head. "Still a few cases to go."

"Over the weekend, we can go shopping and get you some things to put your own stamp on the place." She reaches out, slapping my forearm with a giddy glint in her eye. "The Range has opened down the road. It's massive."

I laugh at her excitement. "Sounds like a plan."

I look across the manicured lawn and colourful garden beds to the back corner of the garden where Dad had a small granny flat built for my grandma. It's an adorable little stone cottage with a bedroom, bathroom, and an open-plan living room and kitchen. It even has little window boxes with a variety of pansies giving it a pop of colour. Grandma had mobility issues as she got older, so the place is decked out with handrails and an easy-access shower. It meant she was close to my parents but still had her independence of living alone.

Mam suggested I take the granny flat instead of my childhood bedroom to give me a little more privacy, but I know she feels more comfortable knowing there are no unnecessary hazards… like stairs.

My hand absently brushes the long scar on my knee, catching my mam's attention. It's soft and shiny and still a reddish-purple colour in places, with a row of dots on either side where my stitches were. I don't hide it like I used to—it's futile. Everyone knows what happened to me.

"Are you in pain? Do you need anything?" Concern knits her brow.

"No, I'm fine. Thank you." I flash her a reassuring smile.

Three years ago, I sustained a life-changing injury as I was playing for England. A bad tackle left me with a shattered kneecap and a torn ACL. It was an intentional assault and the player in question lost their place in their squad, but no legal action was taken and she got away with a slap on the wrist.

Despite multiple surgeries and my shiny new titanium kneecap, I'm left with lifelong issues, so as much as I hate to admit it, the accessibility of the granny flat will probably be a good thing.

"Grub's up," Dad announces, carrying a platter of burgers in one hand and corn on the cob in the other across the garden.

Mam and I jump up to help by making space on the patio table between the bread buns and potato salad. It brings back more fond childhood memories of growing up here. Dad grilling the meat and Mam spending the morning preparing far too many side dishes that we'd end up eating for lunch for the rest of the week. We take away the little net tents covering the food and sit down in our usual seats at the table.

"What did you think of the lads today?" Dad asks as he places a burger on my plate.

"They were great. It might take a bit of work to get them to bond with some of the new lads, but it's only day one."

Mam scoops a healthy amount of potato salad, coleslaw, and side salad onto my plate next.

"That's fine," I tell Mam as she goes to give me a second helping of salad.

"Are you sure?"

"Very." She'd keep going if I didn't stop her.

"They're good lads; they'll fit in well," Dad agrees, back on the subject of the team.

"Bailey and Aaron were incredible up front today," I say, thinking back to the stats I pulled from their GPS vests. "Their skills came together seamlessly."

"Bailey has spent a lot of time in centre midfield lately, but I was thinking about sticking them both up front this season with Robinson. What are your thoughts?"

Although my plate is full, I reach for a corn on the cob, trying to distract myself from the sudden increase in my heart rate. "Bailey can play in any position he sets his mind to. I've not seen a player more versatile as him since Luke O'Nien joined Sunderland."

"When Robinson leaves, I'll be reliant on the two of them up front unless I can sign another striker in January." Dad tucks into his food, dabbing his mouth with his napkin as he chews.

I nod, knowing none of the lads already there are suited to that position and not having had the chance to see the potential in the new signings for that position so far. "Speaking of Jordan, have you given a thought to who will replace him as captain?" I do my best to play my question off as casual, but in reality, the thought of him retiring makes my heart clench. I know what it's like to give your whole life to the sport to wake up one day and not play anymore.

"Aaron has proven he's a good captain when he's covered for Robinson over the years. He's liked by the team and the fans, and the others listen to him." There's an air of uncertainty in his voice.

"But?"

"You've seen him in the media recently. Bridget has a constant headache trying to iron out his public image. His face is splashed all over the gossip rags consistently for the women and the partying. He's a talented player and would be a great captain, but he needs to buck up his ideas if he wants to represent our club."

"You've got a whole season to decide. He might surprise you and clean his act up."

"I've missed this," Mam jumps in, grinning excitedly as her gaze flits between me and Dad. "It's like the good old days when I pretended to have a clue what you're talking about."

Dad chuckles and gives her an affectionate kiss on the cheek. They've been married for thirty-five years and he still looks at her as though she hung the moon.

"So, what was it like meeting with the team?"

Mam tops up my drink, but even then, her eyes don't leave me. Even though I've not said it out loud, Mam could tell how nervous I was this morning, and part of the reason was I had no idea how the team would react to having a woman on their coaching staff. It's not like they don't have women at the academy at all—there are plenty of female physios and nutritionists—but I'm the only coach, and, historically, women stepping into this world almost exclusively run by men haven't exactly been well-received.

"Everyone was very welcoming," I tell Mam, hoping to ease her concerns.

"I think some of them were a little starstruck," Dad jokes. "Robinson in particular seemed to lose his voice when he saw her."

My eyes widen, but I manage to just about hold every other potential reaction from showing.

Oh, god.

"Interesting," Mam says, giving me a knowing smirk as Dad looks down at his plate. I sharply shake my head at her, begging her not to continue her train of thought.

Mam and Brooke are the only two people who know about my past relationship with Jordan, and both wholeheartedly disagreed with my decision to end things. It didn't matter to them that it was for the best, all they saw was the shell of the person I was when I lost everything. They couldn't see the bigger picture like I could.

"I'm glad today went well."

I smile, sending her a silent promise that once we're alone I'll tell her everything.

Chapter Four

Jordan

In my career, I've led our team onto the pitch countless times in front of a packed stadium, I've presented awards to sporting legends, I've mixed with the who's who of the FA, and I've met the president of the FA so many times we're on a first-name basis.

I don't get nervous around people. At the end of the day, we're all human.

So why the fuck can I not bring myself to knock on Molly Davison's office door?

The rest of the team and most of the other coaching staff left about an hour ago, and since then, I've been working myself up to talk to her.

Determined, I stride down the corridor to her office but as soon as I reach her door, I turn quickly on my heel and pace.

Come on Jordan.

It's not like she hasn't made herself approachable this past week either. It's the opposite. She's formed great relationships with the staff and the players love her. Team morale is the highest it's ever been and it's all because of her and the positive atmosphere she brings to the club.

It's why I feel so guilty about not trying to mend our broken—for lack of a better word—relationship before now. I need to do it if we're going to stand any chance at working together effectively this season, but fuck, this is hard.

As I continue my anxious pacing, Molly swings open the door, a surprised "oh" falling from her lips as she catches sight of me. We both freeze for a split second, neither of us remotely prepared to see each other. Which is ridiculous since I was the one who intentionally came here.

"Hi." The word comes out higher than normal with a slight shake in her voice. She clears her throat. "Sorry, hi." She adds sounding normal.

The first thing I notice is her hair. She normally wears it up and out of her face for work, but now it's loose, falling in long waves down her back. I want to reach out and twirl a strand around my finger like I used to. I want to bury my fingers in it as I pull her close to me. My eyes drop to her lips, and before I can help myself, I'm imagining how soft they would feel if I kissed her.

She must realise the avenue my mind has wandered down because she blushes and tucks her hair behind her ear, exposing the smooth skin of her neck.

Fucking hell, I'm a mess.

"Do you have a minute?" I ask her quickly before I change my mind and dash back down the corridor.

"I have a few minutes before my physio appointment."

"You're still in physiotherapy? For your knee?" I don't know why the revelation surprises me.

"Yeah." She doesn't elaborate on the subject, and we fall into another awkward silence, both of us hovering uncomfortably in her doorway. My eyes drop to her knee, as if I have X-ray vision and can see through her tracksuit.

"Are you okay?" I ask when she shifts her weight onto her other leg. It's a stupid question considering it's been three years since the incident and she's still seeing a physiotherapist.

The memories of that day flash in front of me as clear as if it were yesterday.

The fans are electric as England women face off against Germany in the European Championship final. Their chanting and singing easily drown out the noise from the away fans. Both Davison girls have scored by the time we're thirty minutes in and they're riding on the high of playing together for the first time on the national team. This tournament is Brooke's first time playing for England at a senior level, whereas Molly is celebrating a different milestone: it's her one-hundredth appearance wearing the captain's armband for England.

My chest fills with pride as I watch her tear down the pitch. She's calm and composed as she weaves in and out of the German defensive line. She's too quick; they can't keep up.

She passes the ball to Brooke, who passes it forward again, freeing up some of the pressure on Molly.

"Here," Molly calls out, wanting the ball.

My racing heart has lodged itself into my throat as I jump to my feet in anticipation. Her positioning is perfect; there's no way she won't score in this position.

The ball makes it back to Brooke, who catches Molly's call and lifts her foot to pass it to her.

"Ahhhhhhhh."

A blood-curdling scream rips through the stadium, silencing both sets of fans.

I hold my breath as my eyes flit straight to Molly, praying she's okay, hoping…

No.

I leap up from my seat, accidentally kicking over my coffee cup as I barrel through the crowd, towards her, unable to look away from her leg and the unnatural shape it's bent into. I reach the advertising boards, grabbing the cold metal bar above them to jump over when Brooke meets my eye and holds my gaze. My hands are still clenching the metal, but I pause, still poised ready to hurl myself over.

Brooke leans down to Molly and whispers something, her hand covering her mouth from the media, the fans, and, subsequently, me.

Molly shakes her head quickly.

"I'm sorry," Brooke mouths to me. And a sliver of sympathy does flit across her face before it's back to concern and back to full focus on Molly.

My heart shatters and helplessness washes over me as her team and some of the opposition form a shield around her as an ambulance pulls onto the pitch. A few of the girls cry uncontrollably, but most are composed and in control.

I fucking hate this. I should be by her side.

But Molly and I, we aren't public. Coach has no idea that I'm madly in love with his daughter. He has no idea that one day, I plan to marry her. And as much as I want to say fuck it and go to her, I can't let him find out like this. Especially not when I know Molly doesn't want me there.

I watch as the paramedics get her onto a board, an oxygen mask covering her delicate features, and load her into the back of an ambulance. My chest tightens and my shoulders drop knowing there's nothing more I can do other than watch as she leaves me.

That was it.

The last time I saw Molly until earlier this week, and yet, the pain of losing her is just as raw as it's ever been. But I can't tell her any of that, not when she's doing perfectly fine without me.

"What was it you wanted to talk to me about?" she asks.

I need to put on a brave face. I need to do this for my team. I can't let the fact Molly broke my heart without a care in the world ruin my final season. And so, while I promise myself that one day I'll tell her how I feel, I swallow whatever pride I have left.

"I just wanted to say I'm sorry if being around me makes you uncomfortable. It's not my intention. I let my personal feelings get in the way this week, and going forward, I will be professional."

Her face morphs into an expression of complete disbelief. She opens her mouth, but the creak of a door opening at the end of the corridor stops her. She looks in the direction of the noise and then back at me. Her lips part ever so slightly.

"You ready, Molly?" Physio Phil asks, popping his head out of the door, his gaze bouncing between us.

Well, this went fucking well.

"Yeah, I'm ready," she says to him before turning back to me one last time, her eyes swimming with regret. "I'm sorry, I've got to go."

Chapter Five

Jordan

"Are you going to tell me what's bothering you? I mean, I know you're shit at golf, but you're never normally *that* shit."

I flick a cardboard coaster across the table at my stepbrother, Callum, as I let out a snort. "I'll have you know I'm nearly as pro as I am at football."

Callum rolls his eyes. "In all seriousness, what is wrong?"

"Nothing. I'm fine." Usually, hurtling golf balls into the dark abyss serves as good stress relief, but even that didn't take the edge off earlier, as proven by missing more shots than I'd like to admit.

I take a long drink from my pint, hoping he forgets and moves on. We've been coming to this small country pub, complete with worn leather armchairs and scratched-to-hell wooden tables, since we were kids. Every birthday meal or family celebration is still held here. We even had our first legal pints at this very table by the window of the snug with Callum's dad, Tony.

There's always a warm welcome waiting for us here among the regulars and the staff, and despite Callum also being a celebrity in his own right—an ex-Olympian and world champion boxer—the usual patrons don't treat us any differently from anyone else.

When I put my glass down, he's still watching me intently.

"We've got a new coach."

"I saw…" He pauses to study my face. "Molly Davison is back on Wearside."

"Yeah." I let out a groan, rubbing my hands roughly across my face. I don't know why I'm so reluctant to talk to Callum about this, being one of the few people who knows about our past relationship. Maybe I'm just reluctant to talk about her in general, reluctant to feel the hurt and anger I was left with that I had to learn to bottle up. Nothing good will come from dragging the cork out of that one.

"This season wasn't supposed to get complicated. The last thing I need is to lose focus because I can't stop thinking about Molly."

"I thought you were over her. Weren't you dating that actress?"

I sigh again, lowering my gaze. "We went on two dates a few months back. It fizzled out quickly." I don't answer the other part of his question. I knew the moment I saw Molly that my feelings for her were still very much alive.

Callum watches me pick at another beermat for a few minutes, leaving pieces of shredded cardboard in a pile. Judging by how he sits back in his chair and rests his chin on steepled fingers, he's planning his next move.

"Sally, could we have another drink, pretty please?" He waves to the landlady of the pub who smiles at him with stars in her eyes as she puts down the cloth she was using to clean the bar. "Thank you." He adds, shooting her a charming smile.

"Okay, so what's the deal? If you're over Molly, why are you so bent out of shape?" Callum asks, getting to the crux of the matter just as two glasses of neat whisky are dropped off at the table along with a quarter-full bottle of the same amber liquid.

"You look like you could use the bottle," she says patting me on the shoulder.

Christ, is it that obvious?

"Thank you, sweetheart," he says, brushing the woman's arm.

I take my first sip, savouring the smooth heat of the Macallan. He places his elbows on the wooden table, resting his chin against his interlocked hands once again, as he stares into the depths of my eyes as if he can read my mind.

There's a reason he makes such a good teacher—his stare can bring out the truth from anyone.

"You're not over her." He fixes me with a tight smile, shaking his head and silently judging me.

"What? What's that look for?"

"Nothing, mate."

"No, go on, say it."

"She ghosted you, man. She took the coward's way out and had her cousin dump you. And you're still in love with her after all that?" His cold reaction doesn't surprise me. Since he was one of the few people who knew the true depth of my feelings for Molly, he was left to pick up the pieces when it all crumbled.

"I'm not in—"

"Your face right now says differently."

"Feelings like that don't just disappear. She was the one." My shoulders slump with the weight of my confession. I should be mad. I should hate her for the pain she put me through. I shouldn't be pining after her like a lovesick puppy.

"Until she wasn't."

I groan and drain my glass, setting it on the table between us.

"I take it your reunion this week has been less than perfect."

"She waltzed in there as if nothing ever happened. It was… fuck, I don't know what it was, and I don't know what I expected from her. It felt good to see her, like, just having her close to me lights up something inside me. Then, on the other hand, she didn't even tell me she was coming home for fuck's sake. I was completely caught off guard." I pick up Callum's drink and drain it in one, placing his empty glass on the table with more force than I intend. "The least she could do after ghosting me is give me the fucking heads-up that she's my new boss, you know?"

God, it feels good to get that off my chest.

"Yeah, that sucks," he agrees, nodding vigorously enough to make the amber liquid slosh around as he pours another generous measure into our glasses. "Why not tell her you're pissed off at her, then? Have an honest conversation with her. Either way, you need to find a way to deal with this; otherwise, this is going to be the longest season of your life."

"I wanted to talk to her a few times this week, but I think she's avoiding being alone with me. When I finally got her alone today, I clammed up and she had to rush off to see the physio. I ended the conversation apologising."

Callum rears back in his chair, his face distorted as though he's eating something rotten. "You apologised? The fuck you did."

I nod, taking another long drink of whisky. I'm pretty sure this is intended to be sipped, but the burn in my throat dampens the one in my chest.

"I said I'm sorry if I've made her uncomfortable since she returned."

"Fucking hell." He shakes his head. "You've got her number still, right? Call her or send a text or whatever. You need to talk to her, and if she won't give you the time, you've got to take it."

"Yeah, but she blocked my number when she ghosted me. Even if it is the same number and I do text her, she probably won't see it anyway."

"Then you have nothing to lose. If you're still blocked, then fine, she doesn't get it, but you still get it off your chest. If she does get it, then good. After the way she ended it, you deserve to have your say, and she needs to hear what a shitty thing she did."

Chapter Six

Molly

For as long as I've been friends with Brooke, Bridget, and our other friend Natasha, Friday nights have been reserved for us to meet up to put the world to rights over dinner and wine. Even after I moved away, I tried to make the effort to visit every month or two. Of course, that stopped after my accident—I refused to travel further than North London despite being invited.

When you look at the four of us, we're a bit of an odd bunch. A group of friends you wouldn't usually put together but oddly work, like the Spice Girls.

We've got Bridget who is exactly like Posh, impeccably dressed all the time; in fact, I couldn't even tell you if she owns a shoe with less than a four-inch heel. Her rich brown hair and make-up are always perfect, and she has a fantastic resting bitch face that would give Victoria Beckham herself a run for her money.

Natasha is definitely Scary Spice. Loud, swears a lot, and generally doesn't give a fuck what anyone else thinks about her. She's also the group protector; if someone ever started a fight with one of us, she'd finish it for sure. Luckily, things have never gotten that far.

Brooke is a mixture of Sporty and Baby Spice. She can go from tomboy to pop princess in a matter of minutes. She has long blonde locks like Baby but loves a tracksuit like Sporty.

And then there's me, the Ginger Spice of our group. The one who broke up the band to better her career and comes crawling back in the end right in time for the reunion ten years later. I will have you know I've never worn a Union Jack dress with my knickers on show, but when I was a teenager, I did have an incident with a bottle of blonde hair dye that turned my chocolate-brown waves ginger for a little while. Safe to say I now embrace my natural colour.

"How are you finding the job? Have you settled in?" Natasha asks as we unpack glasses and crockery from a box into my kitchen cupboards. I couldn't face unpacking without wine or my friends.

"It's great." I take a long sip of my rosé, trying to hide my true emotions.

"Well, that didn't sound all too convincing." Brooke puts down the pile of plates she's unpacking and turns to look at me, leaning on the breakfast bar that separates the kitchen and living room with her hands behind her back.

"Everyone has welcomed me with open arms at Wearside. The backroom staff have been amazing and the lads are great, of course. But the rest of the country just has a stick up their arse over it. Like grown fucking adults are crying over the fact I coach men as if I don't have relevant coaching qualifications and a sports science degree." I huff out a breath, tossing aside the tea towels I was folding. "I had to get rid of all my social media accounts and I don't dare watch sports news on TV anymore."

"Yet if a man coaches a women's team, no one bats an eyelid. A woman's health and fitness levels have so many changing factors depending on the stage of her cycle, what contraception she is or isn't on, and her age. It's such a fucking double standard."

I clink my glass against Brooke's in silent agreement with her statement.

"It doesn't help that Mike spoke out about me getting the job. He told Footy AM News the only reason I got the job is because my dad's head coach and my godfather is co-chairman. I mean, how does that make it look that one half of the club's owners doesn't even want me there?"

"Firstly, that's rubbish, you applied for that job and got it fair and square, and secondly… Mike Rodgers is a sexist fucking creep," Bridget says, venom coating her words. We all turn to look at her, but she waves off our concern. "You aren't letting it get to you, right? Because Mike and the media are wrong; you are more deserving to be in that job than anyone else."

"It's hard not to let it get to me, but every time one of those sleazy reporters says something, I get an urge to prove them all wrong." I pause, pressing my lips together. "But on the other hand, I also can't help wondering if they're right. What if I did only get the job because of Dad and Jason? What if I'm just an impostor, pretending to be something I'm not."

"You're not an impostor." Natasha places a gentle hand on my arm. "And I know you won't believe us because we're biased, so why not come with me to the academy one day? The girls talk about you all the time—you're like their idol—let their reactions prove to you that you belong."

"They don't think I'm just some washed-up footballer?"

"Are you kidding me?" She looks at the others in disbelief, shaking her head as though I've said the most absurd thing. "I'm there on Sunday. Come with me. You'll see."

After more than a few wines, Bridget and Natasha stumble out of my cottage around midnight, but Brooke decides to stay and help with the final few boxes. I get the feeling she's hanging around to check how I'm really doing because although Natasha and Bridget are two of my closest friends, my baby cousin can read me better than anyone.

"Has Aaron forgiven you yet for not telling him I was coming home?" I ask when it's just the two of us.

Brooke is sitting cross-legged on the island countertop, a glass of wine in one hand as she assembles my new air fryer because "air-fried chicken nuggets are the best idea for a midnight snack", apparently.

"Oh yeah." She laughs, pulling up a picture on her phone of the pair of them dressed in laser tag outfits. "I took him to play laser tag and let him beat me for the first time."

"You two are not normal." I shake my head with a grin.

"Meh." She shrugs before getting back to the task at hand. "So... can we talk about how you really feel?" She looks at me silently with a raised eyebrow, and I know she'll continue waiting until she drags the truth from me.

"I..."

Buzzzzzzz.

Brooke's eyebrow drops back in place as she snatches my phone off the counter before I'm even halfway to it. Her eyes widen as a grin spreads over her face. "Uh, Molly… Jordan Robinson has messaged you."

I ignore the way my heart skips a beat at the mere mention of his name. "Jordan?"

"Yeah, wanna look?" She holds my phone in her outstretched hand.

I stare at it unusually, the cardboard box from the air fryer remaining half-ripped in my hands. Over the course of the evening, we've made our way through six bottles of wine between four of us; what good can come of looking at this message right this second?

None, probably.

But then again… what if it's important? What if it's an emergency?

No. If it were, he'd call Aaron or Bailey or his parents.

"*Take it.*" Brooke touches the screen, and it comes to life.

"It's a voice message," I say, staring at his name, my heart thumping in my chest.

"Then listen to it."

"I can't. You do it."

"There is no way I'm listening to that message." She thrusts the phone at me.

"Please, Brooke, I can't do it." I push it back to her, determined to win this game.

"For fuck's sake, Molly."

As we play hot potato with the phone, she accidentally presses play, filling the room with his voice.

"Molly," he starts, an intense longing washing over me as he says my name with his raspy tone, "it's Jordan."

I'm hurtled back in time, back to the hundreds of voice notes we shared when we were together. Some were sweet and loving; others, hot and spicy; Most, random thoughts we'd have throughout our day.

"I'm really fucking pissed off at you. I was doing fine without you. I was over you and… fine…" There is a pause before he adds, "I was fine."

The vulnerable tone and slight slur of his voice hit me right in the heart in a different way. He's drunk, he's got to be, there's no way he'd send this sober.

Brooke shoots me a sorry look, realising that we probably should have waited until the morning to hit play. She jumps down from the countertop to stand by my side, wrapping her arm around my waist and resting her head on my shoulder.

This time, the pause is longer, about ten seconds or so, and I check my phone to make sure it's still playing.

"Keep going," Callum, Jordan's stepbrother, encourages him from the background.

"Now you're back, and I'm not fine anymore. I'm far from fine. Callum, what's the opposite of fine?"

"Angry," Callum suggests. "Furious, offended, exasperated."

"Hurt… I'm hurt you didn't think to give me a heads-up that you were coming home, I'm frustrated that you're avoiding me when we really need to sort this out, and I'm *fucking angry* because I'm not over you. Not one bit… shit…" his voice trembles.

My nose tingles as tears spring to my eyes. I did this to him.

"Anyway, that's all. You probably won't get this because you've blocked me, but whatever. I'll see you Monday."

I stare blankly at my phone for what seems like an eternity as I process the emotional roller coaster of the message.

"Oh. My. Fuck," Brooke says slowly, her glass of wine held in mid-air, as if she's forgotten she's holding it.

Chapter Seven

Jordan

A doorbell ringing penetrates the foggy unconsciousness I seem to have fallen into. It grows louder and louder until I have no choice but to open my eyes and accept the fact it is *my* doorbell ringing incessantly. Wearing just a pair of shorts and still half-asleep, I climb out of bed and stumble towards the door, the thundering headache of a hangover intensifying with every step I take down the stairs.

"I'm coming," I shout to the person on the other side of my front door seemingly standing with their finger glued to the doorbell. It's times like this I regret not getting a door with a window instead of the solid oak one I chose, forcing me to pull open the door to see who is there instead of having the chance to choose whether I can walk away and ignore.

My eyes blur as they struggle to adjust to the bright sunshine that beams down and into my house. I rub the sleep from my eyes and then use my hand as a shield against the blinding yellow.

Oh shit.

"Molly?"

Molly bites her lip and struggles to make eye contact as she stands on my doorstep, bathed in golden light that gives her a sun-kissed glow. She's not wearing her usual work tracksuit, because why would she if she's at my house on a Saturday morning? No, it's much worse because although she's gorgeous at work, right now, with her hair down and wearing denim shorts, I can barely focus on anything other than the intense desire building within me. It's quite inconvenient really. My heart rate spikes and my dick springs to life as though he hasn't got the memo that she isn't mine. I let my eyes trail down her body, drinking in each curve.

She clears her throat, pulling my gaze back to hers.

Shit, my boss quite literally caught me checking her out.

"Can I come in?" she asks, looking nervously towards the other houses in my gated complex belonging to Aaron and Bailey. I never did tell the lads we were dating just in case it got back to Coach. The less people who knew, the less chance of it blowing up in our faces.

"Yeah, sorry, come in. It's early, are you okay?" I open the door wider to let her through.

"It's lunchtime."

I glance at the clock in my hallway. Well, shit, so it is.

"Here, I got you a coffee." She passes me a takeaway cup from the coffee shop down the street, and I stare at it bleary-eyed before I take it from her. The heat is almost too much through the cardboard, but it feels good to focus on anything other than my pounding head. And the smell of caffeine is definitely something I don't mind waking up to.

"Figured if you feel anything as close to hungover as I do today, you'll need it."

"I must be still drunk or dreaming? One of the two."

"I can't comment on if you're still drunk, but you're not dreaming."

She looks around the entrance hall. Despite the large size, I tried to make it homely and intimate, with warm-coloured walls that have pictures of my family and friends on and polished hardwood floors throughout the ground floor.

"Your place is beautiful." She stops to look at a picture of me, Aaron, Bailey, Sam, and Kieran back in the early days when we all played at Wearside together. Next to that hangs a picture of Mam and Tony at their wedding. Molly smiles as she takes in a much younger me and Callum standing on either side of them.

Out of habit, my eyes drift down her body again, marvelling at the way her denim shorts hug her curves. She turns to look at me, catching me staring. Thankfully, she gives me an effortless smile and lets her own eyes drift down my shirtless torso, my skin humming as the air becomes heavy between us.

"Let me take your jacket." I hold my hand out for her jacket, then hang it on the coat rack, by the door, that's never been used in the three years I've lived here. "Shall we?" I point to the kitchen at the back of the house.

"Lead the way."

Silently, she follows me through to my kitchen, taking a seat at the white marble island as I rummage around for some painkillers in the drawers.

"Assuming you're looking for something in particular?"

"Mhm." I push another drawer closed as silently as possible. "Anything to take the edge off the pounding in my head."

"Thought you might need that too." She pulls a pack out of her bag and throws it at me. "Guess you're lucky I needed some too today."

"Thanks." I waste no time tossing back the painkillers and taking the seat opposite her, where she cradles her cup in her hands. I take the plastic lid off my cup and inhale the coffee, already anticipating its effects as I stare into the black liquid.

She remembers I like black coffee.

"So, you and Callum had a good night, then, I take it?"

I lift my gaze slowly from my coffee to meet her eyes. How does she know I was with Callum last night? Did I do something stupid like—

Oh… oh no.

No, no, no.

My horrified expression does nothing to deter her from swiping at her phone, and soon, my voice fills the kitchen as the memories of last night rush back to me.

Why on Earth did I think listening to Callum was a good idea?

I cringe as the closing lines of my message play out.

"I'm so sorry, I can explain… I—"

Molly reaches over, placing her soft hand on top of mine, stopping me mid-sentence. It's been three years since she's touched me. Three long years. But the feel of her warm skin on mine feels like home.

"Let me start. This past week has been difficult. We don't know how to act around each other anymore, and I know that it's completely my fault. When…" She pauses, taking back her hand and slowing her pace. "When I ended things, I didn't give either of us a chance to get closure, and your anger towards me is justified. We're also in a unique situation right now."

"What are you saying, Mol?"

"You came to me yesterday to clear the air. Well, how about we put a pause on real life now and talk about stuff as us, just Molly and Jordan? I mean, last night, you seemed pretty angry. Maybe it would help to get out all that anger, fight it out maybe? Then Monday, when we return to our real lives, I'm your coach and you're my captain."

"We've never fought, Mol, and I don't want to start now."

"You seemed ready to fight with me last night."

"I'm not going to fight with you." I rake my hand through my hair, the tension growing between us overwhelming me.

"Why not?" she argues, getting to her feet and rounding the island so she's closer to me. I stand too, not sure what else to do. She plants her hands firmly on her hips, her face stoic as she stares up at me through her thick black lashes. "You want to, I can see it in your eyes."

Can't she tell it's not a desire to fight with her? It's a desire *for* her, and now we're here, standing so close I can almost touch the wisps of dark hair curling at the nape of her neck and peeking out from behind her ear, that desire has only heightened.

I step closer, pushing my luck. She's not that much shorter than me with heels on, so now I just need to tilt my face down and we're almost nose to nose with a perfect view down her tank top. I watch as her gaze drops to my mouth. "I know what you're doing, Mol. It's not going to work."

"I know what you're doing too." She raises an eyebrow at me, her eyes locking on mine, unaffected by my closeness. If I didn't know her better, she'd intimidate me for sure. But I do know her, even after all this time, and while she doesn't intimidate me, she has determination by the boatload. It's what made her a great footballer and a terrifying sparring partner.

"You're impossible. You know that, right?"

"Yep." She grins, knowing she's won this battle.

I step away from her. "Fine, but sit down. I want to enjoy my coffee first. Then we can fight."

Chapter Eight

Molly

For the first time since I returned to Wearside, the silence between Jordan and me isn't awkward or uncomfortable, it's peaceful. The radio plays Courtney Sanderson singing a love song about second chances quietly in the background, and Jordan hums along.

He's still shirtless as we sit facing one another across the marble island in his stunning kitchen, and while it's distracting being able to count his abs up close and personal, it's also not weird, which is weird because surely it should be weird.

Now and then, we exchange familiar glances and small smiles that quickly morph into beaming grins. This is how it always was between us—it would start with those glances and happy smiles, and soon enough, we'd be naked and connected in ways I've never felt with any other man, as if not only our bodies but our souls were tethered too.

"Ready?" His expression is tentative when he places his empty cup down next to him. He wants to do this less than I do.

Am I ready to revisit that time in my life, to bring up the memories of life before my accident and the events that led us here? Am I ready to accept responsibility for how broken and disjointed we are now?

I have no idea, but Jordan needs this closure, and so do I.

"Yeah."

Jordan's eyes flash with concern, as my voice sounds less than convincing. "We need to do this."

I nod and wait for the first of many questions, wondering whether he'll start with something easy or chuck me in the deep end. He draws the moment out, standing up and walking slowly across the kitchen to turn off the radio at the wall before making his way back to me, sitting sideways next to me rather than across from me. He reaches forward to turn my stool too so there is no barrier between us.

"Okay, why didn't you tell me you were coming home to coach the team? You said you came to my door and I wasn't there, but you could have called."

Thankfully, this question is one I can easily answer.

"I had a week between finding out I had the job and moving back to Sunderland. I wanted to tell you, but when I picked up the phone to call, I chickened out. I didn't know how you would react, so I told myself I wanted to wait until I could see you in person, but really, I was just being a coward. I'm so sorry for that. I should have warned you. It wasn't right for me to put you in that situation."

"Thank you." He shifts uncomfortably as he thinks about how to word his next question, and I can tell from his face that it's a deep-end one. "I want to know what happened between us. How was it so easy for you to walk away? You were it for me, Mol. I thought you felt the same."

Hearing his broken voice last night was tough, but it was nothing compared to seeing the hurt in his eyes. I look away, unable to take the guilt. "It wasn't easy." My words come out as a whisper as heartbreak floods me.

"I need you to look at me, Molly," he says. "It looked easy from where I stood. You couldn't even tell me yourself. No discussion, nothing. You just walked away without even looking back to acknowledge the devastation you left me with."

"I'm so sorry." The words don't feel enough, but they're all I have to offer.

"I don't want an apology, I want an explanation. Surely, I deserve that? Please just tell me what I did wrong." He leans back on his stool, rubbing his hands down his face before the anger in his eyes is replaced with regret. "Is it because I wasn't there, in the hospital? Because I didn't think you'd want me announcing our relationship like that." He stops and shakes his head. "I didn't know what to do for the best."

"It was hell," I say quietly.

"What was? Tell me, Molly." He stands from his stool to pace, frustration and impatience radiating from him as he grabs his hair with both hands. His biceps tense as he composes himself, then he lowers his arms.

"Recovery was hell. *Life* was hell. There was no way I was going to drag you through it with me."

"Drag me through it? Molly, losing you was hell," he shouts. "You told me you loved me. We hadn't exactly discussed our future or where we were heading, but I never for one second pictured a future without you."

He moves around on the kitchen tiles, and I stand too, not knowing what else to do with my body and the nervous energy running through it. Tears prick my eyes as I try to defend my reasons.

"As I was waiting for surgery, they told me there was a high chance that I'd lose my leg, but even if they were able to save it, I'd need constant care as I recovered. I wouldn't be able to shower myself or go to the toilet on my own or do anything other than sit around in my misery."

"I would have stepped up. I would have been there every second of the day."

"I know, which is *exactly* why I had to end it," I shout back.

He takes a step back, his mouth dropping open as he digests my words. "You didn't think I could manage it?" His voice falters, the vulnerability seeping in.

"Never for one second did I think you weren't capable," I say, taking a tentative step forward, closing the gap between us again ever so slightly. "Jordan, I know you would have given everything to be by my side. But there's no way you would have been able to juggle caring for me and playing. You would have had to choose."

"You took the choice away from me. Don't you think I should have been consulted?"

"I was scared." I meet his eyes, the true reason behind everything finally coming out, the honest answer I've never even been able to admit to myself before. "You were at the height of your career, not just at Wearside but England too. If I had given you the choice and you chose to leave me..." The words choke me and the tears that have been threatening to fall spill down my cheeks.

"Fuck, Molly." His voice softens, and he takes my hand, pulling me into his warm chest. The comforting scent of his bare skin washes over me as I bury my face into him.

"Can you forgive me?" Each word is punctuated with a small sob or hiccup. If the roles were reversed, If he were the one who was injured, I would have given everything up and stayed with him. But would I have grown to resent him over it?

He has to understand, right?

"Losing you was one of the worst things I've ever had to deal with," he tells me softly. "I've spent three years trying to figure out what went wrong with us. I've spent three years trying to get over you. I thought you didn't want me anymore. I thought I wasn't enough. Knowing what I know now, I'm angry at myself for letting you go, I'm angry I didn't fight for us. And now… it's too late for any of that."

"I've always wanted you. You were the best thing to ever happen to me." My chest feels as though it might crack open at my confession. Jordan holds me tighter.

"What do we do now?" I ask eventually, tilting my head up to look at him as I stay wrapped in his arms. His eyes brim with unshed tears.

He clears his throat. "We try to be friends, I guess?"

I nod reluctantly before returning my cheek to his chest, savouring the last few moments of this embrace before we have to return to real life.

I thought once we had this conversation, things would feel instantly better, but somehow, it feels even worse. As if the heartbreak we've both been suppressing is out there in the open hanging over us for everyone to see.

Chapter Nine

Molly

No one notices me when I enter the Lauren Ramshaw Training Academy on Sunday afternoon until the door closes loudly behind me. A dozen teenage girls, who are all busy training, swing their heads around to face me, silence falling suddenly in the sports hall.

I brush my hands down my Wearside training top as I attempt a genuine smile. I wasn't this nervous walking into a room of grown men, so why does my stomach flip and my hands tremble at the prospect of meeting these girls?

Because I remember what it was like to be them.

"Hey." I give a little awkward wave.

"Hey, Molly," Natasha says, smiling proudly back at me from where she stands on the sidelines of the indoor sports hall. "Welcome to the Lauren Ramshaw Training Academy."

One of the girls gasps, her jaw dropping as if her eyes deceive her. "It's Molly Davison."

"That's me." I offer her a bashful smile.

"Are you staying?" one girl asks me excitedly.

"Oh my god, are you—"

"Okay, girls," Natasha commands, blowing her whistle for good measure. "Let Molly come in and get settled while you lot clear up."

The girls let out a collective groan as they start to pick up the countless plastic cones littered around the sports hall.

Battling her way through the group as they tidy, Natasha links her arm through mine and leads me to a small seating area in the far corner of the vast sports hall. It's not overly fancy—a wall-mounted whiteboard, some red plastic chairs, and a few wooden benches that you'd usually find in a school assembly, but it's more than we had. We used the boys' facilities, and if the boys' teams were training at the same time, we couldn't use the facilities at all; instead, we had to go to the local park and hope one of the pitches there was free.

"This place is incredible."

I look around the rest of the room, taking it all in bit by bit with gradually widening eyes.

What I didn't see when I came in here is that the walls are lined with bespoke exercise charts for women targeting the various positions they play on the pitch and what areas of their body they need to work on to achieve peak fitness for that role. There are two sets of double doors at the far side, one labelled recovery room and the other a gym.

It's the stuff I would've killed for as a young player.

"Isn't it just. Lauren would be so proud if she could see it."

Natasha's eyes fix on something on the wall, and she smiles, her eyes turning misty. I follow her gaze to a photo of Lauren Ramshaw dressed in Wearside Red, proudly holding a ball in gloved hands. "Yeah, she really would."

Lauren Ramshaw is a Wearside legend. She mentored a lot of young girls in the academy, including me and then Natasha a few years after that. She died on the pitch while playing in goal, and one of her biggest dreams was to open an inclusive training facility for women and girls from all around the country. She'd talk about it to anyone who would listen. To see her legacy makes me both proud that her dream came true and sad she never got to see the impact it's made on so many young women. It's one of the reasons Natasha spends every free moment she has mentoring the girls too. She'll make a great coach when she retires from playing in goal for Wearside Women.

"What do you think she'd say if she knew you fell in love with her son?"

Natasha laughs. "I'm pretty sure she dropped him off directly on my doorstep."

"Natasha, we can't find the key to the cupboard," one of the girls calls out, her arms full as she stands by a set of locked double doors.

"Two minutes, I'll be right there," she says, jogging towards the other end of the hall, her dark brown ponytail swinging behind her.

When I pull out my phone for something to do, I'm surprised to see Jordan's name on the screen. I bite down on a giddy grin as I open the text message.

Jordan: Morning, Mol. Have fun today! The girls are going to love you.

Molly: Thank you. The girls were
speechless when I arrived.

His reply comes through quickly, as though he was waiting
for me to respond.

Jordan: You have a habit of
making people speechless. Can you
remember the day we met?

A laugh escapes me as I think back to it. We were on a
sporting comedy panel show as opposing team captains. He'd
probably say it was embarrassing, but I found it endearing how
he struggled to get his words out as we hung out in the green
room that morning. He seemed so genuine, which is one of
the reasons I was attracted to him from the beginning. Not to
mention he was so funny, my stomach was aching by the time
we'd finished filming.

Molly: As much as I'd love to get
into that conversation, I've got
to go, we're about to get started.
Wish me luck!

Jordan: I'm really proud of you, Mol. You'll be great. Text me later and let me know how it goes.

"Who's made you smile?" Natasha asks as she sits back in her seat and wiggles excitedly at the first sign of gossip.

I put my phone away, quickly taking the goofy grin off my face. "What smile?" Feigning innocence has never worked for me, especially with Natasha.

"Oh, come on, who were you texting?"

"No one…"

She crosses her arms and raises her eyebrow.

"Fine. It was Jordan."

She sits bolt upright, leaning in closer with wide eyes as she whispers, "Robinson?"

"Do we know anyone else called Jordan?"

"Henderson, Pickford, Nobbs…" She checks them off on her fingers, and I roll my eyes. "I didn't expect you to be sexting with Robinson. Good for you." She shrugs as though it's not a huge deal and shoots me an appreciative smile.

"It's not like that. We're friends, or at least we're trying to be. It's complicated."

"That's a little ominous, have you two got history or something?"

"We…" I stop and sigh, knowing my blush has already given me away.

"Oh my god, you do." She shakes her head, attempting to wade through the information overload. "How have I been so blind?"

"You're not mad, are you? That I kept it from you?"

"No, of course not. You could have told me though. I would have kept that secret safe." I can see the hurt in her eyes, but she quickly hides it.

"I know. Things with Jordan and me have always been complicated, it was easier to keep things hidden."

Things didn't seem so complicated yesterday. After I pulled myself together, he ordered us some lunch to be delivered from a local deli as a fresh start to mark the beginning of our renewed friendship. We both know it was an excuse for me to stay.

We talked and talked for hours on end about anything and everything, catching up as though no time had passed. By the time I left, it was late and getting dark outside.

Despite spending the entire afternoon and evening with him, I wasn't ready to leave.

And it seems the feeling was mutual, as when I was lying in bed, he texted me a goodnight text with three kisses. It really hit me how much I've missed him over the years, and even at that moment, I missed him again. I thought about him right until I fell asleep, remembering the way he'd held my feet in his lap as we sat at his patio table in his sun-drenched back garden and the way he'd lingered as he hugged me goodbye, my longing mirrored in his eyes as we finally pulled apart.

The dreams that followed make things even more complicated for me. The dreams in which we were together again, and by dreams, I mean the X-rated kind that woke me up at two a.m. with no other choice than to finish the job myself.

"Complicated," Natasha repeats in a hushed tone. "I'd say so since you're now his coach. Is that going to be a problem for you?"

"No. I didn't come back for him. I came for the club and the team. I came for the countless women who have ever been shunned from the men's game or laughed at or ostracised because they don't fit the typical mould."

Jordan and I's relationship should be simple, and on paper, it is: I'm his coach and he plays for me.

As his coach, I'm the one with the upper hand in our situation. Dad might be the head coach who puts his final stamp on things, but I'm in a unique position with a lot of influence. I could tip the scale so Jordan is named in the starting eleven. I could tip it so he's benched. Not that I ever would use that influence, but still, to get involved romantically would be a huge conflict of interest.

"I agree, you're representing every woman who has ever dreamed of being taken seriously in the men's game. The world has its eyes on you, so as much as I love the thought of you both finding love, you need to be careful."

"I know." It's something I've thought of constantly since I took the job. Some people are desperate for me to succeed and others are just waiting for a scandal or something to happen to prove their dumb theory that women can't be involved in the men's game. A scandal like me taking advantage of one of my players.

The sound of the girls returning to the sports hall breaks me from my thoughts, a stark reminder of who I'm doing this for. They bound back into the room and sit on the benches spread in a semi-circle around Natasha and me. When they're all seated and silent, Natasha speaks.

"So, I thought it would be cool to bring Molly in today to give you a chance to pick her brilliant brain," she says to the girls. "Who wants to start?"

A dozen arms shoot in the air.

"Isla?" Natasha points at a blonde girl who is bouncing in her seat.

"If you could only give us one piece of advice, what would it be?"

"Oh, that's a tough one." I pause to think, crossing my legs in my chair as I lean back. "If I could only give you one piece, I would say learn how to take rejection and constructive feedback. Your coaching staff are experts and will give you the best feedback and advice you'll ever get, so listen and learn from that. They'll also make decisions that are right for you, and if that means putting you on the bench for a week so you can recover for a tournament or bigger game, then know they're doing it for the good of you and the team."

Isla nods happily and takes notes in her small, fluffy notepad, using her legs as a rest. A sense of pride fills me because I remember being like her when I was around twelve too, absorbing every little detail given to me like a sponge, bringing a notepad to every coaching session, scared I'd forget something if I didn't write it down.

"Phoebe," Natasha says, pointing to the girl next to Isla whose hand has been permanently raised since she took her spot on the bench.

"Did you always know you wanted to be a footballer?"

"I did. I was playing football with my dad as soon as I could walk. It never occurred to me to plan for another career, but Dad told me I should study sports science at college and sports and nutrition management at university all while playing professionally. It was tiring and at times really hard to keep going, but I'm glad I did, as it gave me the chance to coach after I stopped playing." I leave out the part where I reluctantly fell into coaching at first. At the time, I was still healing both physically and mentally.

Natasha points at one of the girls closest to us. "Summer."

"Is it hard to coach the men?"

I look around the semi-circle at this group of impressionable young girls ranging from twelve to sixteen years old. I try to think back to my days in the youth academy and what answer I would've wanted to hear. Back then, it never occurred to me that this was even possible and yet here I am some fifteen years later changing the landscape of the game.

"Honestly, coaching the men is the easiest part," I say with a smile. It's true, there's a set standard for coaching that has to be met regardless of the team or league they play in. "The hard bit for me is the mental toll of being a woman in a men's league. I know I'll never please everyone, and everyone has an opinion on me, but hopefully the pressure will wear off with time and then women in more prominent leadership positions will become the norm. The challenge is reminding myself that I don't need to please everyone, which for a chronic people pleaser is easier said than done; instead, I need to focus on inspiring the right people because I know I'm just the beginning."

"You inspire me, Molly." Summer has her chin resting on her clasped hands as she watches me with glossy, bright eyes.

Her statement, along with the echoing appreciation from the rest of the group, makes me feel as though I'm walking on air. As though I'm looking at my life through a clearer lens.

My job is coaching the men's first team, but my purpose is to prove that women can do this job just as well as any man. It's so women and girls like the ones staring at me with an innocent doe-like gaze know that they're capable too.

They're the reason I'm here.

This responsibility is heavy, that's for sure, but it's a responsibility I'm willing to carry if it means that just one of these girls also dares to break the mould.

"Thank you," I stumble, choking on the emotions lodged in my throat.

The girls continue to pepper me with more questions and tell me the stories of their lives and the games they've played together for the next hour until their parents arrive to collect them. With my revelation in mind, I take it all in and answer as best I can. I see so much of myself in these girls, and my heart feels so warm and full as my new sense of purpose washes over me.

As if three years haven't passed by, my first thought is that I can't wait to tell Jordan.

Chapter Ten

Jordan

A month after training begins, we're scheduled to play our first pre-season friendly away at Wessington Allsports Stadium against Wessington AFC.

From the outside, the team bus is nothing special, just a bog-standard black Mercedes coach with blacked-out windows. But inside, it's the height of luxury. Sleek leather chairs sit in twos with the odd group of four around tables until you reach the back of the bus, where there is a communal lounge area complete with a microwave, a fully stocked fridge, and cupboards full of snacks and pre-workout nourishment stocked by our team of nutritionists.

"At this rate, we'll get there hours before we actually need to. I could have had another hour in bed," Aaron complains through a yawn as he takes the seat opposite me, plonking his head down on the table between us.

"You know this fixture always gets heated. Coach wanted to avoid the inevitable abuse when we arrive," I explain, glancing to the front of the bus as Molly steps on board, dressed in her Wearside tracksuit, with her long hair pulled back into a French plait that ends in a swishy ponytail. I let my eyes linger a little longer than I should as she talks animatedly to one of the other coaches while she finds a space for herself.

We'd never tell her, but everyone is nervous to see the reception she gets at Wessington. She's had it tough so far with the press taking shots at her at every opportunity.

As if he can read my mind, Aaron looks towards the front of the bus where Molly sits at a small table by herself, headphones already on as she continues her analysis of previous games against Wessington AFC both at home and away, looking for anything she might have missed, which is unlikely, as I know she's been staying late in her office watching the same footage over and over again.

Although this is a friendly and doesn't count towards our league positioning, the first pre-season game is arguably the most important. It's an early indication for the fans and other teams how this season is likely to go for us. It's also Molly's first chance to prove herself to those who doubt her.

Traffic on the roads is minimal, and the drive only takes two and a half hours, although I already can't wait to stretch my legs properly. As the bus pulls into the Wessington Allsports Stadium grounds, the outside noise is loud. Too loud. All the lads exchange worried glances until, finally, we round the corner to the players' entrance.

Every direction I look, fans are lining the road as we drive the final stretch.

They're loud and obnoxious and I can hear their sexist catcalling from the safety of our bus already.

"If we let them score, maybe she'll get her tits out," I hear someone yell and the crowd descend into raucous laughter as they sing 'get your tits out for the lads.' Rage surges though me as I grit my teeth so hard my jaw might even shatter.

Judging by the green-grey hue of Molly's face, she's heard them too despite having her earphones in. Everyone is silent, the air inside the bus so heavy with anticipation it's becoming increasingly difficult to breathe normally.

How I manage to stay rooted in my seat for as long as I do, I'll never know. The bus stops with a shudder and I'm on my feet pushing my way down the aisle towards her. She looks up at me, her eyes wide as I sit down to face her across the tiny two-person table.

"Are you okay?" My voice comes out grittier than normal as I try to keep my cool. The last thing I need is for Molly to see how on edge I am. Coach looks back at us from where he stands talking to a couple of security guys, with his brows tightly knitted together and as much anguish on his face as I feel. I'm not sure if Molly notices, but if she does, she ignores it. He turns back around when he sees me sitting with her.

She pulls on the cord to her earphones and plasters a smile on her face that we both know is fake, yet neither of us acknowledge it.

"I'm fine," she lies as she looks out of her window at the sea of people, analysing the path she'll take into the stadium. The noise level of the crowd increases as we linger at our drop-off point, and she takes a deep breath, letting it out slowly to steady herself.

Although our fans are thrilled to have Molly at the club, the papers and the pundits continue to give her a tough time. If they only knew the impact she's had on the team already, there would be no question that she's the best coach for the job.

The fans bang on the bus with their fists, and she flinches ever so slightly. Molly's good knee bounces rapidly, banging against mine under the table.

"It's just an intimidation tactic," I tell her. "They're trying to psych us all out and they're targeting you because they know we're protective of our own."

"Is it always like this?" A brief flash of fear crosses her face that she recovers from quickly, hiding it away and hoping I didn't notice. But the vulnerability in her voice is unmistakable. It makes me want to wrap her up and hide her from the horrible world outside. "I never had this experience as a player."

I want to lie, to make her feel even the slightest bit calmer about the situation, as if this is some sort of "norm", but I know she'd see right through me and I know even more that she'd rather face the complete truth than settle for a lie to make her feel better. "No, it's not," I finally admit. "I don't know why this is happening now; there should be no fans here. We're earlier than anyone would have expected. If you don't feel safe, all we need to do is get the police to move them along. There is no reason you need to face that."

She draws back her shoulders, sitting taller in her seat. Her hardened face morphs into the same mask she's worn for the press since she joined us. "I've got this. If we get the police involved, they'll have won. They don't scare me." This time, her conviction is better, as if she's locked away her vulnerability in a box.

"It's not about being scared. I can help—"

"*I said* I've got this."

I hold my hands up in defeat, leaning back in the seat. She's hitting fight or flight and I can tell that the tiniest knock will switch her to flight. "Okay, we'll be right there beside you the entire time. All you have to do is give me a signal and I'll get you out of there."

Finally, a stadium official boards and tells us it's time to make our way in. There's a small roped-off area creating a narrow walkway through the crowd. If any of them were to reach out, they could easily grab her, and the thought makes me uneasy. Molly picks up her bag and gives me a tight smile.

I reach out to her and grip her arm, stopping her from rushing off. "For my own peace of mind, can I stay close to you?"

"If it makes you feel better, then yeah." Her face flickers with something that looks a lot like relief.

A rumble forms deep in my chest when I hear the fans start chanting at our players as soon as the doors open. Targeted insults fly through the air as each player steps off and makes his way down the walkway.

Bailey is standing ahead of Molly and turns to smile at her reassuringly before he steps off the bus, standing tall and protective in front of her like a bodyguard.

"You need to relax, Skip," Aaron says quietly to me, gripping my shoulder firmly as he meets my eye. "This reaction, they'll eat it up and it won't be you they throw it back at."

My heart is pounding as Molly steps off the bus. When her feet touch the tarmac, a mix of paparazzi and Wessington fans with iPhones pointed at us target her with more sexist remarks. Molly doesn't seem phased at all, unlike me. My fists clench so tight my knuckles could burst at any given second, the warning Aaron gave me a minute ago forgotten as instinct takes over.

Molly spots the small group of Wearside fans huddled next to the door, and her eyes light up with excitement when she zeroes in on a group of young girls, maybe fifteen or sixteen years old, all proudly wearing their Wearside kits.

She skips over to them as though she can't hear the insults flying at her and joins the girls at the metal barrier. I join her, shaking hands with a coach I recognise from the academy and posing for a selfie with one of the young girls.

The longer we stay out in the open, the rowdier the crowd gets and the more uneasy I become.

"Molly, we should go," I tell her quietly, trying to subtly tug her away.

She pulls her wrist from my gentle grip. "Is it just the five of you?" Molly asks, looking between the group and the increasingly agitated crowd.

"Yeah, I think we better make a move though and find somewhere else to wait, I didn't expect it to be this hostile," their chaperone confirms.

Molly turns and waves over one of the security guards at the door. "Excuse me."

He slowly ambles over, not looking overly concerned by any of this judging by the blasé look on his face.

"Yeah?" He asks, chewing on his chewing gum.

"Would you bring this group into the players' lounge, please. They're my guests today." Molly turns to the young players, their eyes beaming up at her as though she's their hero.

"Oh my god, seriously?"

"Thank you so much." The girls squeal in delight as the guard lifts the barrier to let them through. They skip towards the double glass doors, linking arms and holding hands.

I'm momentarily distracted by the elation radiating from the girls so much so that I manage to block out the abuse hurling around until one fan takes advantage of the open barrier and leans over to grab Molly. She dodges his grasp and moves towards the doors. Glancing back at me, her carefully curated mask slips, doing nothing for the rage that continues to build inside me.

"Look at her, such a stuck-up bitch she can't even look at us," one of the Wessington supporters yells.

"Even the sight of her pisses me off. This is a man's job. You complain that the women's game has too many men, yet you're here trying to do the same."

"Who'd you have to fuck to get this job, gorgeous?"

Molly flinches at the question thrown at her as though it's a punch to the gut.

That's what breaks me. I turn, my glare locked on him as my feet carry me forward in determined steps.

"*Jordan*," I hear Molly shout firmly from somewhere close by, but everything around me fades to black except the guy in question—he's crystal fucking clear.

The cheap polyester of his jacket gathers in my fist as I pull him to me by the scruff of his neck.

"Jordan, *stop*," she shouts again.

I'm vaguely aware of a commotion by the doors as more security appear outside.

"You want to try that again, prick?" I growl at him before Aaron grabs me, pinning both my arms down. He's strong, but right now, I've got enough adrenaline racing through me to take on the entire crowd if I wanted to. I let him hold me back. I don't let him move me though.

"You wouldn't dare touch me." He smirks, knowing full well I'd face a suspension and potentially criminal charges if I did. I toed the line grabbing him the way I did, but thanks to Aaron, it isn't as bad as what it could have been.

"Jordan." Molly's small hand holds my forearm, cutting through the thick atmosphere.

"You should go inside," I say through gritted teeth.

"Not without you."

Her determination is something I admire, but her stubbornness will be the death of me. I have no choice but to drop it if I want her to get back to safety, and she's more than aware of that.

"Fine."

Satisfied I'm not going to flip out, Aaron lets me out of his hold, and I start to walk with Molly again, placing my hand protectively on her lower back. She doesn't fight me on it even though I know I'm pushing it.

"Was it you, Robinson? Was she good?" the same guy yells as I finally get Molly inside.

My spine stiffens as I let go of the door, it's as though I've been struck with a bolt of lightning. Turning towards him, he smirks. Rage overcomes me, fire flushing through my veins and replacing all rational thoughts in my brain.

I'm too quick for Aaron and Bailey who are now inside, they don't have a chance in hell of stopping me before I charge over to the guy protected by nothing more than a metal barrier.

"Talk about her like that again and I will fucking end you."

This time, it's Coach who stands in my way with a firm hand slamming into my chest before Aaron and Bailey grab hold of me. He's practically breathing fire as the vein in his neck protrudes through his skin.

"*Get inside, now.*"

Chapter Eleven

Jordan

"Get him out of here," Coach orders one of the police officers who has finally been able to battle through the crowd, and I watch as the prick is dragged away still smirking as if he's won. I guess in some ways he has; I'm sure footage from a dozen or so mobiles will already be online.

As I burst through the sturdy wooden doors, leaving the mayhem of outside behind, Molly is standing with her arms crossed tightly across her chest. Her face is neutral as she watches Aaron pat me on the back before following Bailey and the rest of the team through to the players' area.

My chest is heaving as we stand staring at each other, neither one of us ready to talk, for what feels like a lifetime, until Coach slams his way through the doors to join us.

"What the hell were you thinking?" Coach snaps at me once it's just the three of us, his eyes full of rage as Molly stands to the side. If it weren't for the adrenaline still pumping through my veins, I'd be terrified; but instead, I use it to fuel my stubbornness and stand firm. "You're supposed to be leading by example, not starting fights before we even get in the place." He blows out an exasperated sigh, combing his hand through his thick hair. "What's gotten into you today? This is not like you."

He looks at me expectantly. He's right, this isn't like me at all, but I can't exactly tell him why I'm so defensive over his daughter. And I won't bring myself to regret it either. At least until maybe later when this alpha adrenaline wears off.

"They were saying things. Things about Molly, questioning her right to be here. Questioning the way she got her job."

"That's no excuse for violence, and I'll not tolerate it," he tells me, his booming voice fills the room as his face transitions from red to purple. . "She's a big girl; she can defend herself. We talked about this extensively before she joined the club. You think I haven't made sure my own daughter is prepared for this?"

Well shit, of course he did. And now I feel like a dick.

"I'm sorry, Coach."

"You're team captain, you don't need to be a white knight too." He says finally before stalking off towards the dressing rooms, leaving me, Molly, and stadium security standing in the lobby. Unlike her dad, Molly has kept a calm composure throughout the exchange.

"Is there anywhere we can go for some privacy?" Molly asks the hospitality host sitting behind the reception counter.

"There's an office just through that door," he tells her, pointing to the other side of the lobby at a door that reads "Merchandise".

Without question, I follow her, closing the door behind us. For the first time since last month, we're alone again. Just me and Molly.

It's a tight office space with a small desk and floor-to-ceiling shelves stocked to the brim with merchandise. There is more stacked in boxes too, giving us barely a couple of metres of space between us.

Molly gives nothing away as she stares me down. She used to be so easy to read, but this version of Molly is impenetrable unless she wants to let you in, and since that Saturday afternoon last month, she's been locked up tight.

"I'm sorry, Mol. I didn't mean to cause a scene." It's a battle to keep my voice calm when rage and adrenaline are still coursing through me.

"I told you I could handle it." She pinches the bridge of her nose before looking at me.

"Did you hear what that guy said?"

"The one asking who I had to fuck to get my job? Yeah, I heard it."

"Then why did you do nothing about it? Why did you walk on by without standing up for yourself?" I move to lean on the edge of the small wooden desk, giving her more room to pace the floor. She's barely containing her rage now.

"Because I'm used to shit like this happening, Jordan. I'm used to misogynistic comments. But the whole narrative since I got this job is that I got it because of nepotism or because I'm fucking someone important. I could yell from every rooftop at Wearside that I got my job on my own merit, but it wouldn't make any difference. I have to show them I'm capable, which is what today is all about." Molly's hands tremble as she tries to rein in her emotions.

"Well, you might be able to ignore it, but I can't just stand by and let them degrade you like that. I won't allow—"

"*You're only going to make things worse by reacting,*" she shouts, finally breaking from her controlled façade. "Every fucking person out there had a phone in their hand pointed at us. I don't even want to know what the fallout will be for me after that footage gets out, never mind you."

"No matter what that footage looks like, at the end of the day, they'll see I was protecting you."

"I don't need you to protect me." She throws her arms up in the air.

"I know you don't."

I reach out, holding on to her wrist and pulling her to me. After a moment of shock and hesitation, she leans into me. Hooking my finger beneath her chin, I tilt her face up so I can look into her eyes. It still feels so natural to hold her like this even though I'm crossing every line that exists between us now.

"I'm sorry I didn't listen to you and I'm sorry if I've made things worse. If we need to do damage control, I'll do whatever you need me to, no questions asked. I'll do anything for you. I care about you, Molly. It feels natural to want to protect you."

"You shouldn't say things like that, Jordan," she whispers as I twirl a piece of her hair around my finger. She runs her hand up my chest until she reaches my shoulder, her other on my waist.

"Like what?"

"That you care about me." Her eyes swim with emotion.

"But I do. I care about you as my coach, as my friend, as—"

"Don't." Her breathing slows. "Don't say it."

"As more than a friend."

"We shouldn't do this," she whispers, and yet, she doesn't remove her hand from the back of my neck, where her nails scratch along my hairline.

"I know, but that doesn't change how I feel about you." I caress her cheek with the palm of my hand, letting my eyes drop to her parted lips.

"You should get to the dressing room," she tells me, reluctantly stepping away, putting as much distance as physically possible between us in such a small space.

"You're not coming?" I lean past her, reaching for the door handle.

She shakes her head. "I need a minute."

Chapter Twelve

Jordan

I never thought I'd say this, but working with Molly is torture.

Don't get me wrong, the team is performing better than we have for years, but as summer blends seamlessly into autumn, it's as though my life is suddenly a game of *Bullseye* with a miniature Jim Bowen perched on my shoulder uttering those immortal words every second I spend with her.

"Jordan, let's have a look at what you could have won."

And I do, I look at her every single day and curse the version of me who failed to come close to the real reason she ghosted me and consequently let her go, believing it was her letting me go.

Fucking idiot.

I glance over to where she paces the touchline, watching carefully and shouting new orders to our defenders as West Hylton United change tactics and push forward on an attack.

A moment later, our longtime friend, neighbour and fellow England and ex-Wearside star striker, Sam Henderson scores past our keeper, Kieran O'Leary, in one of the most spectacular goals I've ever seen. When the referee's whistle blows, I'm almost certain it'll be called offside, but the call for VAR gives us a chance to regroup at the touchline.

"You need to be faster," Molly says in my ear, then places a bottle in my hand, lingering slightly as she leans into me. She covers her mouth with her hand so her words aren't picked up by the other team as her breath brushes my ear and neck. "Sorensen is right up your arse the entire time. Go in and go hard. Watch your left—that's where he's strongest. Aaron and Bailey will set you up."

I nod, keeping my attention on the pitch as I take a long pull from my drink.

"Do it exactly like we practised. Stay ahead of Sorensen. Find some space. Let the others take care of the other defenders."

The stadium is loud today, and it's been a particularly gruelling match for all of us with neither team seeming to dominate the other, which for the fans, I suppose, makes it exciting, but for me, it's exhausting. Not to mention, West Hylton United are a Premier League team, we were just one of the unlucky League One teams to draw an FA Cup game competitor two leagues above us.

With three goals apiece and eight minutes to go, the pressure is on.

"You look good out there, Jordan," Molly says when I hand her the bottle back.

"Yeah? Good as in good or, you know… *good?*"

She shrugs, a smile attempting to pull at her lips. "Get back out there." She sends me back to the pitch with an encouraging shoulder pat.

It's pathetic how much that one tiny back pat makes my heart thump a million miles faster as I jog back to my position, relaying the tactics to Bailey and Aaron. A moment later, the whistle blows with the confirmation that Sam's goal was offside, and our fans go wild in celebration.

When play resumes, everything drops into place. We take quick possession of the ball and keep it until Bailey receives a cross and moves up the middle. I remember the advice Molly gave and glance at my left. Sorensen is right there, with Aaron holding off another defender.

"Push faster, lads, go on," Molly encourages from the touchline.

"Yes, Bailey," I yell, throwing out my hand, indicating where he should send the ball. I sprint faster than ever to meet his pass. As soon as my right foot connects with the ball, sending it soaring through the air, it's obvious it's a goal.

I take off in celebration, running to the east stand, where our fans sit, and slide towards them on my knees. Each one of them is on their feet, cheering so loud they drown out the West Hylton fans, their faces mirroring my sheer elation as I pump my fists in the air. These are the moments I'll miss when I'm done, being able to connect with the fans in such a raw emotional state. When I slide to a stop, I take in the noise and passion of the crowd letting it flood my veins, embracing the electrical current surging through me. That is until I'm knocked onto my back by Aaron. He and Bailey throw themselves at me, screaming in my ear with joy, followed by the rest of my team.

We still have four minutes to go, and as they have proven today, West Hylton United is more than capable of scoring in that time.

Before the referee has a chance to resume play, an official holds up a board. Number thirteen, my number, flashes up as a substitution for Will Dixon, number nineteen. I breathe out a sigh of relief, subbing me for a defender at this stage of the game will give us a better chance of holding on to the lead.

"Well done, mate." Will says as we swap places over the touchline, he gives me a pat on the back as he replaces me.

"You did great, cool down and get yourself a rest." Molly gives me a double high five as I cross the touchline, falling in step beside me towards the dugout. "I'm so proud of you," she adds, and I feel as though I could go on and do another ninety minutes.

"Fuck, I'm exhausted," I tell her as I flop down into her seat with a sigh.

"Get up and cool down; otherwise, I'll force you into the ice bath myself later." She whacks me with her notebook. I let out a sarcastic groan, heaving myself up again as she takes her seat, returning to her match notes.

"You'd love that, wouldn't you?" I joke.

"Wait until you hear my plans for the cryogenic chamber we're installing at the academy this week." She punctuates her threat with an evil laugh without looking away from her notepad or the game in front of her. How she can concentrate on the game, make detailed notes, and still have a conversation with me is baffling.

My muscles protest as I stretch, and a movement on the pitch has Molly jumping to her feet. Her notepad falls to the black rubber floor of the dugout, forgotten.

"*Go on*," she calls, and I turn to see Bailey and Aaron pushing forward again, this time as a pair. Aaron sprints up on the right finding a pass from Anderson. Defenders swarm him, but to his credit, it doesn't faze him one bit. Keeping his cool among the added pressure he crosses to Bailey with precision.

"It's in," Molly predicts, her hands resting on her head in anticipation.

Bailey is exactly where he needs to be to accept the ball with his left foot, controlling it nicely before shooting hard towards the goal. He scores the fifth and final goal of the evening with barely a second to spare and everyone in the dugout jumps to their feet. It's pure carnage. I'm pulled from pillar to post by my team mates on the bench, cheering as we hug. When I eventually pull myself away, I turn to find Molly and I can't help the grin that spreads over my face as she jumps up and down on the touchline with her dad, cheering loudly.

The ref gives three sharp blows on his whistle, and the small stand of West Hylton's Exhibition Stadium that houses our fans erupts into celebration.

Although we conceded three goals today, for the first time this season, we're miles ahead in points, and the three points from our win today means we're a little more secure going into the second half of the season after the upcoming winter international break.

"Get out there and see the fans, Robinson," Coach tells me, grinning from ear to ear as he celebrates with the others in the dugout, and I jog back to the pitch to meet my teammates.

We huddle in celebration, jumping on each other's backs as everyone grapples with Bailey. A deep sense of pride settles over me as we stand united with the fans who have travelled to the opposite end of the country to watch us today.

Looking out towards the fans, I notice a little girl on the bottom row with bright blonde wild curls pulled back into a ponytail jumping up and down and holding a sign that reads: "There's Only One Molly Davison"—a chant that has become popular with our fans in the last few months. Grinning, I turn back to the dugout, where Molly is laughing and celebrating with her dad.

"*Mol*," I shout, lifting my arm in the air, signalling for her to follow me. She gives me a nod and starts walking my way.

I jog over to the little girl, who is still bouncing on her toes. Her eyes widen as I approach.

I cross my arms on top of the metal barrier between me and the little girl and her mam. The coldness of the metal is a welcome feeling from the heat coursing through me from the long game and adrenaline from the win. "What's your name?" I ask.

"Ella."

She glances to my left, and her wide eyes fill with pure unadulterated excitement. I follow her gaze to see Molly waving at fans as she passes, making her way over to where I stand.

"Hey, oh wow. I love your sign," Molly says to Ella, who squeals, unable to get any words out. It's even more heartfelt close-up, seeing that she's clearly spent a lot of time and effort on it. Each letter is a different colour and there are star sequins and glitter-glue hearts all over it.

"Molly, I'd love for you to meet my new friend Ella."

"I want to be just like you when I grow up," Ella rushes to tell Molly, her words tumbling out of her now. Her cheeks flush pink and her hands tremble.

"Oh really? You want to be a footballer?"

"Not really. I'm not very quick when I get the ball, so people tackle me easily, but I'm very good at bossing my brother and his friends around when they play at the park at the end of the street. They always win when I'm in charge too," she brags, puffing her little chest out with pride.

Molly is silent for a beat, tearing up as she processes the little girl's words. "You… you want to be a coach?"

The little girl nods vigorously. "I'm going to practise all the time, and one day, I might be good enough."

Warmth spreads through me as I watch the interaction.

"Of course you will be," Molly tells her with complete assurance. "You just have to put your mind to it and work hard. If I can do it, anyone can."

Ella beams up at Molly, and I'm glad to see her mam manage to catch a photo of the intimate moment.

"Would you mind if I take a quick picture?" her mam asks, and Molly nods, helping the small girl dip beneath the barrier so she can stand next to her with her arm around her.

I step aside and watch as they both grin for the camera and then Molly envelops Ella in a big hug before helping her duck back under the barrier.

"Thank you," Ella's mam says appreciatively, moisture shining in her own eyes.

"Would you mind sending me those on Instagram?" I ask her quietly so Molly can't hear me as she says goodbye to her biggest fan. "Molly doesn't have social media, but I know she'd love a copy of those. We won't share them or anything, I just have a feeling Ella has made her day."

"Of course. I got some really sweet ones." She smiles down at her daughter, then guides her away.

With one final wave to the remaining fans, the last of us on the pitch make our way towards the tunnel.

"Thank you, that really means a lot to me," Molly says as we walk side by side, emotion still shining in her eyes. It seems as though she wants to say more, but before she can continue, Bailey bounds up to us.

"What a game," he exclaims. He falls in step with Molly, wrapping his arm around her shoulders.

Her effortless laugh drifts through the air, and the way she grins at him has jealousy coursing through my veins. I know there is nothing in the gesture, they're just friends and have been for years, longer than Molly and I have known each other, but I want to be able to act like that with her. Instead, due to my own stupidity in Wessington, I only get high fives on the touchline now.

Chapter Thirteen

Molly

Instead of showering and changing at the stadium, as soon as we've finished our post-match analysis in the dressing room, I head back to the hotel alone. Usually after an eight p.m. away fixture, I go back to my room, devour a room-service pizza, and fall asleep watching reruns of comedy shows on E4.

But tonight, I can't stay away from the hotel bar even if I want to.

It's dangerous, I know.

I shouldn't flirt with Jordan, especially not in the dugout in front of a sold-out stadium, but the more time goes on, the harder it is to resist the chemistry that pulls us together. It's why I've attempted to put a little distance between us over the past couple of months.

His text from a few minutes ago replays in my mind:

Jordan: We're in the bar, are you coming?

After Jordan's reaction in Wessington, the press got a whiff that something might be fishy and they really ran with it. My worst fears started to come true. One reporter wrote: "*This is why we can't let women into men's football. Instead of focusing on the game, she already has Robinson fighting the battles she isn't strong enough to fight herself. It's his final season; he doesn't need this distraction.*"

It didn't matter that we won the game three-nil or that the team showed real grit and determination that day, setting up what has turned out to be a record-breaking season for us already. All that mattered to the press was a sliver of potential gossip.

If this isn't reason enough to stay away from him, I don't know what is.

But I'm also not going to miss the opportunity to celebrate with the rest of my team. So, now, I'm going downstairs to the hotel bar and I'm going to order *one* drink and one drink only. I'm going to sit with my team and enjoy our celebration. I have complete control over my impulses. The cheeky glint in his eye and his raging sex appeal will not break me.

"Molly," Bailey calls when I enter the bar area. "Over here." He waves to where my friends are waiting.

"Are we celebrating something, lads?" I ask, and their cheers roar throughout the bar. "You'd think we just won the FA Cup or something."

I shrug off my leather jacket and hang it on the back of the chair at the head of the table, taking my seat as Jordan arrives, setting down a tray of drinks he's brought over from the bar so he can hand them out. Our eyes meet, and my racing heart quickly becomes the least of my worries.

I watch as he swallows hard, allowing his eyes to drop to my cleavage as he takes in my outfit. I can practically see the memories of that night playing behind his darkened, lust-filled eyes as he looks at me as if I'm a meal good enough to devour.

I wore this outfit on our first date. A black tweed miniskirt, black silk camisole, and my leather jacket paired with some chunky-heeled ankle boots. Did I know what I was doing when I packed this outfit? I wish I could say no, but I did. I knew exactly what I was doing.

The conversation continues around us, leaving us locked in our own little bubble.

Jordan recovers quickly, maintaining eye contact as he leans over me from behind, placing an ice-cold glass of rosé in front of me. I didn't ask him to order me a drink, and it's silly really, but the fact he remembers my drink order has me smiling up at him. When he pulls his arm back, his fingers brush my almost bare shoulder blades. The reaction to his touch is immediate—my skin tingles, tiny goosebumps spread over the surface, and I'm fairly sure if any of the boys were looking, they'd see my nipples harden beneath the thin fabric.

Luckily, or unluckily depending on what way you look at it, the only person to notice is Jordan himself. A smile plays at the corner of his mouth, but he disguises it well, taking the seat opposite me.

"Cheers, Molly." He points his glass of whisky to me, and I clink my glass against it.

"Cheers."

He may be disguising his smile, but as he raises his glass to his lips, his eyes shine with mirth.

"Thank you," I say, taking a sip.

"You're welcome," he replies, his deep voice doing something utterly magical to my body as the air between us trembles.

"Hey, Molly." Joey approaches the table with a growing smile, unaware of the tension building between me and Jordan. Joey's a sweet guy, a little young for me perhaps, but he's not terrible to look at, not that I've looked at anyone since the man sitting opposite me. "You look unreal."

"Thanks, thought I might as well make an effort since we won." I give him an uncomfortable smile, glancing over at Jordan before turning back to my visitor.

Joey's eyes trail down my body, and unlike when Jordan did the same a moment ago, I want to cover myself up.

"Can I buy you a drink?"

Jordan clears his throat loudly, drawing both of our attention. His face is hard, his jaw clenched as he glares at Joey. "She has a drink, mate."

"Shit, sorry. I didn't mean to…" Joey rambles as his wide eyes bounce between us, his face turning beetroot.. "I don't know why I…"

I laugh, reassured by his bright red cheeks. "It's okay, Joey."

"I'm going to go now," he adds.

Bailey and Aaron do their best to suppress their laughter, but Jordan looks furious.

I nudge him with my foot under the table, and he softens ever so slightly, taking a long sip of his whisky. He wraps his leg around mine beneath the table, and I smile with a small shake of my head at the protective gesture, but I don't pull away.

There's a commotion as a hen party arrives in the hotel bar, the bride wearing a short white dress covered in L-plates and a neon shot glass hanging around her neck, surrounded by a gaggle of already drunk bridesmaids. Aaron, Bailey, and O'Leary clock them immediately, jumping from their seats to join their festivities since Dad isn't here anymore to keep them in check.

Jordan shakes his head with a laugh as the boys insert themselves into the group, lapping up the attention.

"So, today was something," he says, his smile spreading into a grin before adding, "you were amazing; you should be really proud of yourself."

"I felt amazing." My grin spreads from ear to ear to match his.

"I can tell. I don't think I've ever seen you smile so brightly in a long time."

"Today's the first time I've felt a hundred per cent confident in my decisions. Imposter syndrome, am I right?" I give a tiny fake laugh to try to make a joke out of it, but it falls flat. "It helps that I have a great team to support me," I add, looking fondly across the room to our friends, who are showing off for the hens. "And I have the best captain, too, don't forget."

Safe in the knowledge that no one is watching, he takes my hand and squeezes it firmly, entwining our fingers together while he meets my eye.

"We're always going to be here for you. Through the good games and the bad. You're one of us."

"Even after you retire and leave me on my own?" Another failed attempt at light-hearted humour.

"Always, Molly." His thumb traces the back of my hand in a comforting circle, sending a shiver down my spine. "I'll always be here for you."

Chapter Fourteen

Molly

"Four celebrity dinner guests, dead or alive, who are you choosing?"

The others left around one a.m. in search of a dance floor with the hen party, leaving Jordan and me alone. Shortly after the bar cleared out, we tucked ourselves away in the lounge, sitting side by side in a small booth hidden from view. If anyone did wander in at this hour, they wouldn't see us anyway, which is partly why I feel so relaxed leaning into him with my legs resting over his. His fingers trail lazy patterns up and down my knee, soothing the ache caused by standing for far too long today.

"Footballers or general celebrities?"

"Let's go… footballers."

"Okay…" Jordan thinks for a second, and I laugh. "What?"

"I forgot how much I love your thinking face."

"My thinking face?" His smile morphs from curious to amused.

"You do this thing when you're thinking." I mimic his expression, scrunching my nose up and pursing my lips from side to side.

"Okay, I do not look like that," he says, belly laughing.

"You do." I insist on doing the expression again. "Exactly like that."

His laughter trails off, but he still smiles at me. I tuck my hair behind my ears and avert my eyes.

"Four footballers, come on."

"Okay." He resumes thinking, and I suppress my laughter.

This time, he notices he's doing it and chuckles. "I feel it now."

"Don't stop, it's cute. I like it."

His smile is boyish at my compliment.

"I'd invite you, of course. Pelé, Messi, and Jimmy Montgomery because I know you've always wanted to meet him." I smile as he brushes his thumb across the back of my hand and weaves his fingers through mine.

We used to sit like this all the time when we were together, wrapped up in each other as he caressed me. We both craved that tactile affection, and it seems nothing has changed.

"Hey, guys," the barman interrupts us, standing by our table. "We're closing the bar now. Would you like me to bring the bill, or charge to your room?"

I glance at my watch. Four a.m.

Hanging out with Jordan feels so easy and comfortable, and at some point tonight, though I'm not entirely sure when, I let down my guard completely. I let myself look at him, like really look. I let myself laugh and tease him like I would any of the others without worrying about what anyone watching would think because, realistically, the fact I don't act like that with him when I do the others is simply drawing more attention to us.

"Yes, charge to the Montgomery suite, please," Jordan answers before I can give my own suite name. "And can we have a sealed bottle of champagne to take with us, please?"

The barman nods curtly as he leaves us.

Jordan stands and holds out my jacket for me to slip on, then he leads me to the bar with a possessive hand on my lower back. The contact sends thrills coursing through my veins, sparking at my nerve endings. I know he feels it too when he glances at me, his eyes once again swimming with lust. The reasons I have been chanting to myself like a mantra for the past two months, telling myself to stay away, well, they no longer exist in my brain.

"Why the champagne?" I ask as we collect the chilled bottle from the bar on our way out.

"It's for you," he says casually, as if he didn't just buy me a five-hundred-pound bottle of champagne. He presses the button to the lift. "It's your favourite."

"How do you know that?"

"You drank it on our first date, in that dimly lit jazz bar. You told me it was your favourite and you only order it on special occasions because you can't justify the cost any other time. I remember it specifically because when I asked if that night was a special occasion, you told me that it was because you and I were finally in the same room after talking for months and you'd remember it for the rest of your life."

"I still stand by that," I say, walking through the open lift doors and standing with my back pressed against the back wall as I cuddle the bottle to myself. I tell myself it's the chill of the bottle that has my nipples pebbled beneath my thin shirt, not the memories of that weekend flooding back. Jordan presses the button to our floor before leaning next to me. "It was the most magical night of my life."

"The next morning was pretty magical too," he says, bumping his shoulder against mine with a cheeky grin as the lift begins to ascend. "That entire weekend was amazing."

My cheeks heat as we reminisce because, fuck, that was some weekend.

After our first date in the jazz bar, where we listened to live music and chatted all night long, we were both pretty drunk and ended up falling asleep on his hotel bed as we watched reruns of *The Big Bang Theory*. The next morning, after making a rather embarrassing call to the front desk to ask for a spare toothbrush and some make-up remover, we ate a room-service breakfast from a golden trolley, like you'd see in the movies, and then we made love for the first time. I say made love because even though it was hot and filthy, it was way more than sex.

It was the first time I felt I'd found someone I trusted and was so compatible with, who couldn't wait to get to know every inch of my body without remarking on how firm my muscles are after a life playing football or expecting me to be dominant because I'm an athlete. He made me feel sexy and womanly, and when he looked at me, he would get pure lust in his eyes. Kind of like the look he's wearing now as we take a walk down memory lane.

"I wish we still—"

The lift shudders violently, the lights flickering and then turning off completely. I reach out blindly, grasping Jordan's arm as we bounce and jerk to a halt, desperately needing to ground myself. Only seconds pass but it feels like it could be a lifetime that we're consumed by the darkness, the walls feeling impossibly close as I can no longer see them. My heart rate kicks up a notch and my breath comes out harsh, the sound of it filling the air as I begin to lose the ability to fully expand my lungs.

How do I even breathe? Where does the air go?

"Oh fuck," I say, my voice breaking as I teeter on the verge of panicking in the darkness. The only thing stopping me from having a complete meltdown is the comfort of Jordan's arm wrapping around my waist and pulling me in close. "Oh my god. Are we stuck?"

"Just give me a second." I feel him shuffling around, tucking me into the opposite side as he reaches into his pocket. A small light illuminates from his phone. He presses the red button labelled "Help" on the lift keypad.

"How can I help you?" a voice crackles through the radio as the dim emergency lights finally flicker on.

Jordan still has his arm wrapped tightly around me as I do my best to breathe steadily into his firm chest, concentrating on the steady thrumming of his heart instead of my own impending doom.

"We're staying on the fifty-sixth floor of the Grand Harbour West Hylton and we're stuck in the lift," Jordan explains calmly.

"Okay, yes. I can see there has been a power cut in the area. The generator should have kicked in by now, giving you some light, but it won't give enough power to open the doors if you're stuck between floors. I assume the doors haven't opened automatically?"

"That's right, we're still stuck."

"Hold tight, we'll get to you as soon as possible. In the meantime, if the power comes back on, the lift will automatically reboot and take you to your floor."

"Is there any indication of how long it'll take for the power to come back on? Or an ETA for whoever will be coming to rescue us?"

"Let me check." A few beats of silence pass. "Power should be back on between seven and eight a.m., sir. As for the rescue, I have no idea. We've got lifts pinging all over the place now. Looks like it's a widespread power cut, so we're going to have a busy few hours."

Between seven and eight a.m.?

"Excuse me, we have a coach to catch at eight a.m., so I would really appreciate your urgent assistance." I pause. "And also, your discretion."

Jordan raises his eyebrows at me questioningly.

"Of course, we have a good relationship with the Grand Harbour, so their guests are important to us too," the operator tells me, although it's doing nothing to calm my nerves because, truthfully, this guy doesn't sound as though he gives two fucks.

"Not that we're doing anything wrong obviously," I continue. "I'm his boss and we are just friends. We were on our way back to our rooms, our separate rooms actually, which just so happen to be on the same floor. You can check the CCTV."

"Smoooooth," Jordan says, holding back a fit of laughter.

I hit his rock-hard abs with the back of my hand. "Ow," I mouth, shaking my hand.

"We'll be with you as soon as we can," the operator says. "In the meantime, if your situation changes or you'd like an update, press the call button again."

Our call disconnects, and Jordan and I look over at each other.

"This is going to be okay, right?"

"Yeah, of course." He rubs his palms comfortingly down my arms, but I'm still not convinced. "Shall we sit down if we're going to be here a while? It looks like you could do with a rest."

I didn't notice I was bearing my weight on my good side again, keeping my right knee bent with not too much pressure on it. I nod and sit next to him, resting my head on his shoulder, our legs stretched out in front of us.

"Are you scared?" he asks when I loop my trembling arm through his and take his hand, our fingers entwining as I grip him for support.

"I'm not great with enclosed spaces," I admit. "Or the thought of plummeting fifty-six floors to my death."

"Yeah, I didn't think so," he says with a chuckle. "I've got you, Mol. I might not be able to stop the lift from falling, but I can keep you distracted."

"Joking about falling isn't helping."

He traces my knee, massaging it and providing sweet relief.

"If I was going to get stuck in a lift with anyone, I'm glad it's you."

"Me too," he says. "You know, we've got a full bottle of champagne there."

"Are you hinting?" I thrust the bottle at him. "Sounds like a really good plan."

Chapter Fifteen

Jordan

"They say never meet your heroes, but I'm glad I met you," I tell Molly a little while later once the champagne has kicked in and we're both suitably tipsy enough to allow this conversation.

She looks down at her skirt, picking imaginary fluff from the fabric, drawing my attention to it. The skirt pulls in at her waist and flares out around her mid-thigh. It's a perfectly appropriate skirt, but the way it skims over her curves has the same effect on me as if she were wearing something way more revealing. Her long tanned legs are stretched out in front of her and crossed at the ankles. Even though she's drunk and exhausted at whatever time in the morning, she's still the most beautiful woman I've ever seen.

"Talk to me," I encourage her.

"I'm not a hero… I'm a disappointment."

My mouth falls open at her statement. Molly Davison is a legend, not just at our club but in the entire sporting industry. I have no idea where she's got that thought from and I hate that those words even cross her mind.

"Molly—"

"I know, I know. You're going to say I'm being stupid." Her shoulders slump and her eyes drop to the floor as she lets out a heavy breath.

"I was actually going to ask why you feel that way."

She meets my eye again, raising her brow. "Do you really want to know? Because once that bottle is uncorked, there's no stopping it, and I'm a little tipsy, so who knows what emotion is going to fly out of me."

"You can trust me with this, I promise."

"I'm thirty-one years old, living in a granny flat at the bottom of my parents' garden because my career imploded. All those years I gave to football and I have nothing to show for it anymore now I'm on the sidelines. As a team captain and as a Lioness, I had a purpose. I was loved and admired. But now, I don't know, sometimes I feel like I stand out for the wrong reason. I'm not a big fish in a small pond anymore, you know? I'm a tiny fish in a very large pond with a lot of male fish ready to take a bite out of me." She shakes her head at her analogy. "You know what I mean, right?"

"Firstly, you've had a wonderful career over close to two decades. You've spent two years training to be an elite-level football coach at the same time as recovering from a life-changing injury. You could have given up, but you didn't; instead, you worked your arse off, and that takes time and discipline and courage. You're the first woman to coach a professional men's first team in football." I stroke her hair back from her face, resting my palm on her cheek. "Do you know how amazing that is? You're proving that women can and should be involved in all areas of the sport no matter what gender the players are or what league they play. Look at the impact Sian Massey-Ellis has had. You're doing the same. You're building a legacy that will inspire women and girls everywhere to challenge the gender stereotypes in our sport."

"It's hard to overcome my self-doubt when the world doubts me so publicly."

"It might feel like the world doubts you, but believe me, I don't doubt you one bit and no one else on this team or any of our fans doubt you either. Remember little Ella from today?"

She nods softly with tears glistening in her eyes, so I take her hand—a manoeuvre that has come so naturally to us today.

"Here, look at these photographs her mam sent me."

I pull out my phone and bring up the Instagram message, passing her the phone. She swipes through the photos, a single tear streaking down her face as she sees the admiration on little Ella's face.

"I've already sent them to your email," I tell her as she passes my phone back. "I thought you'd want a copy."

"Thank you," she says quietly, her gaze dropping from my eyes to my mouth before she looks back at her skirt.

"I'm always here for you, Mol. When you need a little truth bomb or a little boost of encouragement, all you have to do is ask." I lean over and tilt her face to look me in the eyes again with my hand cupping the silky skin of her jaw.

"I'm here for you too, you know. The past few weeks, you've not been yourself," she says, her voice barely above a whisper.

I drop my hand from her face, leaning back against the wall again as she twists to face me. I'll be the first to admit I've had a low mood lately, but I didn't realise she'd noticed.

"It's my last England match in a few weeks." I look at the ceiling, trying to find the words to this feeling hidden in the wooden panels above us. "It's got me thinking about the end of my time at Wearside too. It's happening all at once and I'm having a bit of an existential crisis. You could say I've been institutionalised. I've been at this club since I was eight years old. I have no idea who I am without Wearside, I've stuck by the club through all the ups and downs, through multiple owners and managers, my loyalty never wavering because this place is my home, everyone here is like family. I'm scared I'll not know who I am anymore when it's all gone."

"Is that why you never moved club?" Molly asks.

"Yeah, I play because I love the game. I've been offered big money to leave countless times in my career, but I don't know, I never felt enough of a pull to any other club."

"How you're feeling is completely normal," she reassures me, drawing me into her with a comforting hug. Her delicate, sweet scent envelops me as her hair cascades around us. If I could bottle it up, I'd keep it with me everywhere I go. "And there is no shame in admitting it. Especially not to me."

She's right—if anyone knows what it's like to give up everything they've ever known, it's Molly. Although in her case, it must have been a hundred times worse, given she had no time to prepare for it.

"I've never been in the position I'm in now, where I don't know what I'll do every day for the rest of my life, and even though I've had close to thirty-five years to think about this, it's knocked me off-kilter." I comb my fingers through her thick shiny hair, loving the way it spills across my skin.

I don't know if it's the champagne or the intimate topics, but when I tug her across my lap, she moves easily, straddling me and pulling me in closer with her arms around my neck. I didn't know how much tension I was holding until she wraps me tighter in her embrace.

"Is this okay?" I ask, glancing at her knee, and she nods.

"There's plenty of time to figure things out. I can help you when you're ready. We can brainstorm and research. Anything I can do to help you, I will," she tells me, slowly dragging her nails through the hair at my nape. "Together, we can achieve anything."

I could stay like this all morning, safe and comfortable, the way it always has been with her.

"How did you know you wanted to coach?" I ask, looking into her rich brown eyes. I brush my fingers up her back beneath her jacket until I reach the soft skin of her shoulder blades. Tiny goosebumps spread over her chest, and she gives an involuntary relaxed shiver.

"I knew I didn't want to commentate and punditry isn't my thing, so Dad signed me up for my next coaching certificate. It was a great distraction from the struggles I was having after my injury, so I followed up those courses until I passed my level five. Truthfully though, I didn't want to coach men, but Dad persuaded me. I was so nervous when I arrived, but when I walked into that dressing room on day one, I knew I was doing the right thing. I knew I was home."

"That's how I feel too—the club is my home. I'm going to miss it and every single person that works there. I'm going to miss you too, Molly."

"That club will always be your home, and just because you're retiring doesn't mean we won't see each other. Things will be different for us when I'm not your superior, maybe..." She pauses to take a steadying breath, igniting a little bit of hope within me that I'm desperate to cling to.

"Maybe what?"

"I've been thinking that maybe… when I'm not your coach, we could revisit us. If that's something you're open to?"

That tiny spark of hope surges throughout my body, building into deep anticipation in the pit of my stomach, the same strong emotion that is mirrored in her eyes as she searches mine. "Molly, when you decide you're ready to take a chance on me again, when you're ready to love me again, I'm right here."

She lowers her forehead, resting it against mine. Her eyes flutter closed as I brush my nose against hers. Shifting her body closer to me, she moves against my lap. Whether it's on purpose, I don't know, but her breathing hitches as she feels my body react to her, my growing erection pressing against her from beneath the rough denim of my jeans.

I look down at my lap and let out a tortured groan when I slide my palms up her smooth thighs as she moves against me once more, this time intentionally. Her skirt rides up with the movement, and I can see her nipples pucker beneath the thin silk of her top.

"Jordan," she pleads with me, her lips brushing against mine when I slowly grind harder against her. She doesn't kiss me though, as if that would be taking things too far.

With my hands on her hips, I answer her plea and pull her even closer to me, drawing her up along my hard length, encouraging her further. She gasps, hanging her head back, exposing the long column of her neck. I don't know how we got into this situation so quickly and I don't question it. I drag my lips across the skin of her exposed throat as her hips begin to pick up a rhythm of their own. I'm so painfully hard that every stroke of her warmth against me pushes me closer and closer to the edge.

"Molly, fuck, this feels…" I say into her neck, not knowing how to finish that sentence.

"Is this a bad idea?" she asks, but she doesn't stop meeting my movements.

"I don't know. I can't think straight. All I can think of is how I wish we weren't stuck in a fucking lift."

With her jacket now discarded somewhere on the floor, I push the thin spaghetti straps of her camisole down her shoulders until I expose her breasts.

"Is this okay?"

"Yes," she whispers.

I pull a perfect pink nipple into my mouth, flicking my tongue over her as she moans.

"I've missed watching you come apart from my touch," I tell her as I urge her upwards with my hand on her inner thigh, just enough to snake it beneath her, finding her lace underwear soaked. "Is this for me?"

She nods as I slide my fingers over the fabric. "Oh god, Jordan, touch me, please."

"Kiss me first."

She lowers her face to mine, her lips parting in an O as I push my finger beneath the fabric of her thong, brushing against her clit ever so slightly. Just as I'm about to tug at her lower lip with my teeth and claim her as mine, the lift bursts to life and the whirring of the generator cuts through the silence.

"Shit," Molly says, jumping off of my lap and putting her outfit back together. She looks at me wide-eyed, as if she's waking from a dream. Fuck, it felt like a dream holding her again and touching her as though she's mine. "What time is it?"

I get to my feet and check my watch. "Seven."

Her glassy eyes drop to my crotch, watching as I adjust myself, before looking up at me. "Oh fuck, that was…" She traces the path of my kiss with her fingertips, across her collarbone and down to her breast before dropping her hand to her side.

"Yeah, it was."

The lift slows to a stop as the display flashes with our floor number, and when the doors open, we're catapulted back to the real world.

Chapter Sixteen

Jordan

"Wakey wakey, sleeping beauties," Aaron says, nudging my arm.

I drag my eyes open, groggily looking around to determine where on Earth I am. The familiar smell of Deep Heat, rows of leather recliner seats, and the sounds of my friends and teammates chatting happily give away my location: the team bus. Next to me, on an identical reclined chair, curled onto her side with her feet on the raised leg rest, head on my shoulder, and her arms wrapped tightly around my bicep, is Molly.

We must have dozed off the second we sat down on the coach because the little TV in the seat in front of me is still on the main menu from where we had planned to watch a movie.

I look around outside for a sign to tell me where we are, but there is nothing but motorway. "Where are we?" I ask Aaron, keeping my voice low so I don't wake Molly or alert any of my other teammates to our position.

"Not far from Scotch Corner, forty-five minutes or so until we're back at the academy."

This time, Molly stirs. With a soft whimper of unconscious protest, she grips me tighter, nuzzling further into me. I smile when I look down at my hand resting possessively between her thighs, my thumb trailing over her jean-clad knee.

"Are you okay, Skip?" Aaron asks. "Lost you for a bit there."

I rub my hand across my jaw. "Yeah, sorry. I'm just trying to wake up properly. I'll wake Molly and get sorted."

"Okay," he says, looking between the two of us. His eyes burn with questions he doesn't dare ask. "Just make sure you wake her before Coach comes down here and spots you like this. I managed to keep the others from seeing you two, but I don't think I could save you from Coach if he came looking."

"Thanks," I say appreciatively.

Without probing for more information, he makes his way back up the bus to where the others are hanging out.

He's right. If Coach saw us like this, what would he say?

Molly's reputation is important to her, everyone knows that. What would he think if I were the one responsible for tarnishing it? Because as much as I hate it, I know if the papers got the tiniest sniff of a romance between us, they'd be turning it against her as yet more ammunition to discredit her.

I can't let that happen to her, but selfishly, I can't stay away from her either.

Molly lets out a soft snore. I really don't want to wake her; we were up over twenty-four hours by the time we got on this bus and the alcohol that had been keeping us going in the lift wore off quickly.

Thankfully, we aren't the only ones who are worse for wear, which is probably why no one thought anything of us sitting down to watch a film together. Bailey, Aaron, and Kieran are in a sorry state after partying with the hens until the early hours. Although, they managed to get back to their rooms by taking the stairs up forty floors when they returned from whatever nightclub they'd found themselves in.

"Molly, hey, Mol," I say softly. "It's time to wake up, beautiful."

Her eyes flutter open like a Disney princess being woken from a spell. That is until she sees she's been clinging on to my arm and jumps back as if she's been burned. Surprise and worry are etched on her face as she looks around, realising that anyone could have seen us together. When she's satisfied that no one is watching us or is even remotely close to us, I expect her to relax, but she doesn't.

"Where are we?" she asks, looking out the window as if she knows every stretch of the motorway by sight, much like I did when I woke up.

"Just past Scotch Corner."

"I need to go to the loo," she says, her voice shaking as she fumbles in her seat. She tries to stand but is quickly pulled back to her seat, forgetting she fastened her seatbelt earlier.

I hold back my grin as she quickly unclips it with a dismissive laugh. I know she's making an excuse to put some distance between us—she's said on numerous occasions that she'd rather stick pins in her eye than use the tiny toilet after a coach full of blokes. I let her think I'm oblivious and shift slightly so she can pass. She doesn't wait for me to move or to lower my leg rest completely before she tosses a leg over me, tangling us both together.

I wrap my arm around her waist, pulling her closer until she loses her footing completely and straddles me again. She looks at me wide-eyed as her breath hitches. This time, I can't hold back a grin, which spreads over my face. After the progress we've made in the past twelve hours, I don't want our bubble to burst, and that's exactly what will happen if I let her brain spiral alone.

"Molly, that was the best five-hour nap I've ever had on this bus," I whisper so no one else can hear me. "And I meant what I said earlier. I'm officially waiting for you. Whenever you're ready, I'm ready to go all in. I thought you understood that."

There is a war raging inside those brown eyes of hers. She wants to believe me. "We got carried away in that lift. We should never have let it get that far. And besides, eight months is a long time. You might meet the woman of your dreams in that time."

"I've already met you."

She rolls her eyes at me, doing her best to hold back a smile. "Come on, you moved on from me once, you'll move on again."

It kills me that she believes it.

"I never moved on, Molly."

"Jordan, I've seen photos of you out on loads of dates in the past three years. Dates with women who are more in your league than me." Her jaw tightens and her shoulders slouch as she looks away from me, making it harder to read her emotions. "There are so many other women out there that are perfect for you."

I take her face in my hand, forcing her to look at me. Vulnerability is reflected in her eyes, maybe a little jealousy too. "What's that supposed to mean?"

"You know… blonde, big boobs, supermodel types. Actresses. Popstars. Women that are nothing like me." She flicks her hair and points to her boobs as though that proves her point. She's not wrong; I did date after her. I dated a lot in the hopes that spending a night with another woman would help me move on. It didn't, I just developed a sense of self-loathing.

She is wrong if she thinks she's not exactly my type though.

"I'll be really honest with you, Mol. I dated casually after we broke up. Because I was hurt, I went after women that looked nothing like you in the hopes it'd help me forget you. Maybe it was a shitty way to go about it, but I was willing to try anything to take away the heartbreak I felt when I lost you. I wish I could go back and change it. I'd do everything differently. I'd fight for us for a start." I look deep into her eyes, praying she sees the sincerity in mine. "I don't ever want to hear you say you're anything less than perfect for me."

"I'm sorry," she whispers, combing her fingers through the hair along the side of my head.

"Let's just take this one day at a time," I tell her, mirroring her gesture. "I'll wait as long as I have to if it means I'll get to keep you for the rest of my life."

Her features soften into a touched smile as I finally break through those walls she attempted to build.

"Why do you have to be such a smooth bastard?" She finally releases that sweet laugh of hers, and relief washes over me.

"Do you still want me to let you out?" I ask, grinning up at her.

"Absolutely not." She flops back into her seat next to me. "I'd rather stick pins in my eyes than use that toilet."

Chapter Seventeen

Molly

"Press *X*…" I hear Luke's commanding voice as soon as I let myself into Natasha's Riverside flat.

"Which one is that?" Jordan asks, sounding overwhelmed, to say the least.

"The one with the *X* on it. *Quickly.*"

"You're going down," Bailey shouts, followed by joyful cheering from Aaron.

Although I can't see them from where I shrug off my jacket and hang it on a coat hook by the door, the tension in the air is thick as they bicker.

"I can't see the *X*," Jordan panics.

"*That one.* It has a giant fucking *X* on it. Oh, for fuck's sake." A clatter follows, and as I turn the corner, I realise it was Luke throwing his controller onto the floor like a toddler throwing a strop.

"Oh." Jordan winces in realisation just as the sounds of zombie slaughter fill the room.

"That's how it's done, bitches." Aaron leaps up onto the armchair, jumping around like Tom Cruise on *Oprah*.

"See why we kicked him out of our team?" Bailey chuckles at a sulking Luke.

"You're so shit, Jordan, even Luke loses when he plays with you, and he designed the thing." Aaron laughs, the pair of them taking their seats.

My heart swells as I watch them, so far going unnoticed. That is until Natasha walks out of her kitchen and spots me across the room.

"Molly," she says, excitement in her voice. Luke, Aaron and Bailey don't bother turning to me, instead, they wave absent-mindedly over their shoulders as they reload the game. Jordan on the other hand, it's like he can't keep his gaze away, his eyes meeting mine with a smoulder only breaking eye contact when Natasha pulls me in for a hug. "Finally, someone I can talk to. I've been listening to this lot for an hour already, and my head is battered."

"Are the girls not here yet?"

"Not yet, they should be here soon. There are beers in the kitchen, come on."

I follow her to the kitchen, leaning on the kitchen island to take some of the weight off my troubled knee. Usually, the pain would be enough to put me off going out, but tonight is a big night. Natasha and Luke are celebrating reaching the next stage of Luke's video game based on the Women's Super League, so before our monthly quiz night at The Eighteen—a local bar and community hub owned by ex-Wearside footballer Jamie Carter—we're meeting at Natasha's to raise a toast.

It's taken a lot of hard work and healing from Luke's past traumas to get to this point, and although he usually hates attention, Natasha couldn't let the achievement pass without making a fuss.

"Molly, sort him out, will you?" Luke groans as he stalks past me to the fridge to fetch some beers for the lads, handing one to Jordan, who trails in behind him. Standing close beside me, he reaches an arm around my shoulders and pulls me in for a sideways hug, supporting my weight effortlessly as if he knows I need it today.

"I'm only his boss on the pitch; what he does off it has nothing to do with me."

Jordan raises an eyebrow as he looks down at me. I nudge him gently with my shoulder, plucking his fresh beer from his hand and taking a long pull from the bottle with a smirk.

"Believe me, what I do off the pitch has everything to do with you," he murmurs. The seductive tone of his voice intensifies the ache I always feel when he's around. An ache I fear only he can soothe.

When he drops his arm from my shoulder and rocks back onto his heels, there's a feeling of emptiness left behind.

Two weeks have passed since the West Hylton match, and it feels as if we're stuck in limbo.

We've laid all our cards out on the table and we both very much want the same thing. If circumstances were different, there would be no problem. But here we are, trapped in the friend zone. How long will it be before being friends isn't enough, though? Because, right now, I'm teetering on the edge of giving in and there's still half the season to go.

I bat his stomach with the back of my hand, and he lets out a low chuckle.

"Easy, Jordan." I match his flirty tone as he slides a stool along for me to sit on, placing his palm at the base of my spine, steadying me as I take the seat.

"Sorry, sorry. I know, we're late. We're terrible," Brooke calls out before sweeping into the room with Bridget and Luke's sister, Hannah. She kisses Natasha and then Luke on the cheek before making her way around the room.

"Congratulations, Luke," Bridget says, taking her turn to greet the couple. "I saw the preview the other day, and it looks incredible."

"It's okay, the lads have just finished up a game. You look…" Natasha trails off, looking Brooke up and down. Bridget is always dolled up to the nines, even on quiz night. But Brooke… well, this is new for her.

"Unreal," I finish for her, my eyes glued to my baby cousin's boobs contained in a tightly fitted corset. Who knew they were hidden under her baggy T-shirts and football tops?

"Ah, this little thing." She smooths down her short baby-blue dress that fits her like a second skin. "It's a special night, so we thought we'd make an effort."

"She's on the pull tonight." Bridget claps excitedly.

"So is Bridget," Brooke adds. "We're wingwomaning each other."

"It's about bloody time." Natasha chuckles. "Let's see the back."

Brooke does a half-turn, giving us a view of the back of her dress when Aaron walks into the kitchen in search of his beer.

"Oh fuck," he says, his voice breaking as he takes her in from head to toe, his jaw slack and his usual bad-boy exterior melting away the way it always does when she's in the room. "What are you wearing?"

A crease forms between Brooke's eyebrows as she turns to face him, her blonde hair styled in bouncy waves swishes around almost hitting him in the face. "What's wrong with my outfit?" She crosses her arms tightly across her chest, getting the completely wrong end of the stick. We all see the way Aaron looks at Brooke; we all suspect his feelings for her go a little deeper than best friends. Not that he'd ever admit that, not even to himself apparently.

"Nothing, you look… nice." I'm pretty sure he wants to say something else by the way his eyes drop to her boobs. "Pretty."

A slight blush stains her cheeks at the compliment. "Thank you."

There's a long silence as everyone is watching their interaction with rapt attention.

"Can I have that beer?" He clears his throat, finally tearing his eyes away from Brooke. He doesn't wait for a reply before taking a bottle from Luke's hand, then he swiftly turns away and out of the kitchen.

"Wait, come back," Luke calls. "I'd like to say a few words."

Once everyone is standing together in a huddle, Luke passes out drinks to those who stand empty-handed and returns to Natasha's side. He takes a deep breath as he looks at Natasha, steadying himself before he speaks.

"I just wanted to say thank you. I couldn't have done any of this without you all, especially you, Nat. I owe everything to you. I love you so much and can't wait until I get to call you my wife."

There's silence in the room as we all look at one another, checking we all heard him correctly. Wife.

Nat holds up her left hand, showing the sparkling diamond that rests on her fourth finger.

How on earth did I not notice that when I walked in?

My shock quickly morphs into excitement, my best friend is engaged.

"Oh my god," I step closer, taking her hand in mine to get a better look at the huge teardrop emerald set in a thin diamond band. It's absolutely beautiful and a ring I recognise. This was Lauren Ramshaw's ring, Luke's mam. "Congratulations." I pull her in for a hug.

"When did this happen?" Brooke asks.

"Last night. He'd been acting off all week and I was getting a bit annoyed, to be honest. We'd been for a run at Herrington Country Park and then he got down on one knee on the roof of Penshaw Monument at sunset," Nat tells the room, tucking herself under Luke's arm as they stand wrapped around each other, gazing at each other.

"In my defence, I was so nervous I didn't know how to act around you all week." Luke laughs. "Thankfully, she said yes."

"Of course I did, I love you."

"I love you too." Luke leans down and kisses her softly in a gesture so intimate it feels as if we're intruding.

I'm happy for my friend, though I can't help the feeling of longing. Longing for the same love and happiness for myself that is just out of reach.

Chapter Eighteen

Jordan

"Anyone fancy a quick game? Two on two," Bailey asks as Aaron, O'Leary, and I gather around on the pitch, enjoying the unseasonably warm weather after our training session.

"There's no way I'm going up against you lot," O'Leary says. "I'll go in goal; someone else can make up the pair."

"I'll play," Molly says, looking up from her spot on the ground where she sits cross-legged, writing in her notebook.

I can't help but watch her as she walks to the nearby bench and takes off her hoody, placing her books down carefully and bending over to tie her laces, giving me a perfect view of her arse. Keeping my distance gets harder and harder every day. I didn't anticipate how hard waiting for her would be. It's barely been a week, and all I can think of is having her again.

O'Leary thumps me in the stomach with the back of his fist, drawing my attention. A grunt escapes me as I clutch the area that's now a little tender.

"You want Coach to see you looking at his little girl like that?"

"I bagsie Molly on my team." My hand shoots in the air, ignoring O'Leary's warning, to lay claim on her before anyone else can pick her for their team.

The guys exchange a look, doing their best to hide their smirking. They all clearly know I have a thing for her, but I doubt they know the depths of our feelings.

"She's a better footballer than all of you put together."

"You don't need to defend yourself to us." Aaron grins as he holds his hands up in surrender.

"Are we going to play or gossip like schoolgirls?" she asks, eyeing Aaron, then plucks the ball from his arms, tossing it to O'Leary. "Ladies first," she adds, moving aside to let him onto the pitch first.

"You're going down, Davison," he threatens her, narrowing his eyes as he walks past her.

"We've got this, right?" she asks me quietly once the others are out of earshot.

"We're in our thirties, playing against two twenty-five-year-olds in peak physical fitness. The only thing going for us is your peak confidence."

"I'm not above playing dirty if it means we win."

"I'm well aware how dirty you can be, Mol." I wink at her before striding away to join the others, pleased at the hitch in her breath.

She quickly catches up with me. "If you want to win this game, try not to get me all flustered and turned on," she murmurs as she passes me, standing facing off with Aaron and Bailey so I can't fire back.

She bends forward, touching her toes as if she's stretching. I know she's getting her own back by giving me a view of her perfect arse. This is going to be interesting.

"Right, we'll play on one half of the pitch. Molly, heads or tails who gets to kick off," O'Leary says.

"Heads," she calls.

Although Bailey wins the coin toss, he doesn't have the ball long before Molly effortlessly tackles him, taking the ball from his feet with ease. She sprints up the pitch, keeping it close to her feet as she leads Aaron on a chase.

Calling my name, she crosses it to me before Aaron even has time to think about tackling her. Catching it on the volley, I send it straight past O'Leary, into the back of the net.

Molly comes bounding over to me, throwing her arms around my neck in celebration. "That was amazing," she tells me before turning to the others and sticking out her tongue.

O'Leary laughs at her reaction and takes the goal kick, sending the four of us hurtling back to the halfway line in a race to catch it first. This time when Bailey gets the ball, he anticipates Molly's next move, dodges her expertly, and sends the ball straight to Aaron, who scores their first goal, not even giving me a chance to catch him.

Each play, we continue to outsmart each other until we're sitting at four-four.

"The next goal wins," Bailey says, doubling over with his hands on his thighs. "I'm knackered."

"You're knackered?" O'Leary pants. "Fucking hell, I'm exhausted." I'm not surprised; he's saved way more goals than we've scored in the past hour we've been playing. I'm actually surprised I'm still standing, especially since we've been training all morning too.

"I can't wait to get your data off those vests," Molly says, grinning in anticipation.

None of us removed our GPS vests before we started playing, so I'm sure she'll see some interesting results, like the spikes in my heart rate when she bends over in front of me, whips her hair over her shoulder, or just generally looks in my direction.

"Right, ha'way, let's do this, Brooke's mam is making chilli for tea and I'm starved," Aaron says, clapping his hands together loudly.

O'Leary kicks off for the final time from the eighteen-yard box, and we all take off running. This time, I win the ball and sprint up the right, dodging Bailey's tackle and sending it directly to Molly's feet. As Aaron quickly closes in on her, she passes to me to get a better position with more space. When I cross the ball back, I overshoot my target, causing Molly to slide, her right leg extending as she tries to reach the ball.

"Argh, fuck."

My stomach bottoms out at the sound of Molly's scream as she slides to a stop on the ground across the pitch. Time slows as I gasp, the sudden intake of air burning my lungs.

Her leg.

The four of us spring into action, running at full speed towards her. Aaron is closest since he was marking her just a moment ago, so he reaches her first where she lies on her side, one hand clutching her knee and her forearm covering her eyes so that we don't see the true level of pain she's in.

I can feel it though through the trembling air between us.

My mind jumps to the worst-case scenario. It could be her ligaments have torn or a break in her leg or her artificial kneecap detaching. Can that even happen? I don't know. I should know, I should have asked her more about her surgery so I knew how to protect her.

"Shit, Molly," I say as I skid on my knees beside her. She groans in pain, as she turns her head further towards the grass.

I don't dare touch her body, instead I stroke the rogue wisps of hair out of her clammy face as I try to calm my trembling hands. I look at her leg, wishing I had X-ray vision so I could see the problem, but I can't.

"I'll get help," Bailey says before sprinting towards the main building.

She attempts to sit. A sob escapes her and tears roll down her cheeks.

"Molly, don't move." I wince at my trembling voice, hoping she didn't notice, not wanting to add my fear to an already awful situation.

"No, no, I'm fine," she lies, her jaw clenched. She presses her temple to the grass again, gritting her teeth so hard I worry they might crack. "I just need to stand. Help me up, please?"

I shoot a worried glance at Kieran and Aaron, which Molly is oblivious to.

She groans as she rolls to a sitting position. "Please," she begs again.

Against our own judgement, Aaron and I carefully lift her so she's upright again, bearing her weight on her left side with her arms strewn around our shoulders.

"Can you put weight on it?" Kieran asks, bending down to check for obvious signs of damage. He's no medic, but we've all seen our fair share of ACL injuries over the years.

Molly extends her leg and tries to bear weight on it, but a whimper comes out as soon as her toe grazes the ground.

"Can you flex it?" he asks.

This time, she bends her knee ever so slightly without wincing.

"Please help me inside. I don't want anyone seeing me like this." She takes a deep breath before trying to bear weight on her leg again. With a whimper that slices through my composure, she manages to limp once.

"Fuck this, I'm not letting you walk." I don't give her a chance to flatten her foot for a second time before I'm scooping her into my arms. She looks up at me with starry eyes as I carry her towards the medical entrance, leaving our friends trailing behind us.

"Are you okay?" I ask.

Her breathing is heavy as she tries to talk through the pain. "That would have been the hottest thing that's ever happened to me if I wasn't in excruciating pain," she says so only I can hear her, and I can't help but laugh.

"Good to know for the future."

I'm rewarded with a tiny smile and a soft giggle as she winds her arms around me tighter. She moves her leg and winces, burying her face into my chest with a hiss.

As the four of us approach the main academy building, Coach emerges with Bailey by his side. His eyes widen and his skin pales when he sees me carrying his injured daughter.

"It's just a sprain," she says.

I won't be convinced until we see a medic, but I keep that information to myself.

"What happened?" Coach's voice is dangerously low as he narrows his eyes at me, ignoring Molly's explanation. He's in protective-dad mode, and frankly, he's fucking terrifying. I gently lower her so she can stand, but I keep my arm around her, supporting her weight. At least Coach isn't glaring at me anymore. For now.

"We were just playing, Dad," Molly says, drawing the attention back to her.

"It was my fault," I confess. Guilt engulfs me even more than it already has when he whips his head back to me again. "I overshot my pass and… she slipped. I'm really sorry."

"Molly." He scrubs his hand across his face. "This isn't just a kick about with a couple of kids in the park like you used to do when you were little."

"I was in the moment; I let it take over. And… I just forgot." Her eyes fill with tears again that have nothing to do with the pain. I could see how she smiled as she was playing, she was enjoying herself and this accident does nothing more than remind her of what she's lost.

"We all forgot, Molly," Aaron says, clutching her forgotten possessions like a security blanket. "We should have been more careful. I'm sorry."

Coach's eyes soften as he processes the anguish beneath her words and the guilt emanating from all of us. Aaron's right—as professional athletes, we should have known better than to put her at risk.

"Go and see Phil," he tells her, sighing. "You can't drive like this, so I'll get your mam to pick you up in a few hours once she finishes work. I've got a meeting with the board tonight, so I'll be late home too."

"I can take care of her."

Everyone's eyes, including Coach's, burn into me.

"I'll drive her home in her car and Aaron can drive mine."

Coach narrows his eyes at me for the second time. Fuck, am I that obvious?

I stand firm, holding my hand out for her hoody and phone, which Aaron hands over.

"Mam has that show tonight she's been looking forward to all year. It could be huge for her business, and I don't want her panicking and leaving early because she thinks I need looking after," Molly reminds him.

Coach nods reluctantly, rubbing his hand harshly across his brow. "Fine. Ring me when you're home safe. Robinson, take her inside, please."

Chapter Nineteen

Jordan

The blue vinyl physio bed squeaks as I put Molly down onto it, placing her things next to her. The office is empty apart from the two of us.

"Ow," Molly whispers as she pulls herself up the bed, getting comfy. Well, as comfortable as she can be.

I pick up the radio from the bench and hold down the button on the side. "Phil?" I say down it, shrugging at Molly when she laughs. "What am I supposed to say?" I ask, frowning. "I'm not important enough to have a radio."

"You're supposed to say, 'Come in, Phil, over,' and wait for him to respond."

"Come in, Phil, over," I repeat down the radio.

A second later, his voice crackles back. "Aye, mate, what's up?"

Molly's shoulders vibrate as her giggles turn into hysterics.

"I didn't need to say it like that at all, did I?"

"Nope, I just wanted to see if you'd copy me."

I'd laugh myself if I weren't so stressed about her leg.

I turn away from her so she can't distract me further. "It's Robinson. I've got Molly in physio room three. She's hurt. We think it might be a sprained knee, but can you come check her out?"

"Her existing injury, or a new one?"

"Existing."

"I'll be fifteen minutes. I'm on my way from the far pitch—there are injuries left, right, and centre today. Get a cold compress out of the fridge and place it on her knee in the meantime to try and reduce the swelling."

"Gotcha."

I place the radio back on the bench before getting a blue gel pack from the fridge and sitting on the bed next to Molly, placing it gently on her knee. She winces—a combination of cold and pain.

"If I don't move it, it doesn't hurt."

"I'm sorry, Molly. I should have been more careful."

"Don't be sorry, I should have let the ball go. There was no need for me to slide like that, especially since I always have something to say when you slide unnecessarily," she tells me with a teasing smile.

"I forgot how incredible it is to watch you play," I say, reassured that she's feeling a little better now the tears have stopped. "A few times, I forgot I was supposed to be playing too."

She blushes, that dusky pink I love so much staining her cheeks.

"What are you talking about? Did you miss the part where I did this?" She waves her hands dramatically around herself.

"Bailey and Aaron are elite athletes and they were both knackered trying to keep up with you."

"Yeah, suppose so." She looks down at her knee, where I'm still holding the cold compress in place.

I cup her face in my hand, tilting her chin so she's looking at me again. A final rogue tear streaks down her cheek, so I wipe it away with my thumb. I hate seeing this look in her eyes, that soft vulnerable look of self-doubt.

"You're an incredible player, Molly. I hate that you got injured and I hate that it haunts you after all this time. If I could, I'd swap places with you in a heartbeat if it meant taking away that pain."

"Jordan," she whispers as she winds her arms around my neck, pulling me closer to her, grazing her fingers through my hair. My body yearns for her as she holds me tightly. I want her… no, I need her, more than I need air in my lungs.

Her eyes meet mine as the air thickens around us. She leans into me slowly until our faces are millimetres apart. I could close the distance now and claim her with my kiss, but is that what she truly wants, or is it just the heat of the moment?

I breathe her in, terrified this moment is going to end before it even begins.

"Molly?" My voice is thick with lust, and my eyes drop to her chest, which is rising and falling in rapid movements.

"Kiss me, Jordan," she pleads, and my name falling from her lips sounds like heaven.

She pulls me over her on the bed, and who the fuck am I to tell her no when we both want this so badly? Finally, I'm kissing her again, tasting her as I sweep my tongue inside her mouth. Using my hand on the backrest over her shoulder to support my weight, I adjust our position so I'm lying over her good side. She moans softly as my tongue dances with hers, each lick bringing back a rush of memories.

I brush my hand up her stomach, cup her breast, and run the pad of my thumb across her hard nipple. Her hands grapple at the waistband of my shorts as she pulls me closer, and my already solid dick stiffens as she grinds her firm thigh against me.

"I'm done with pretending we're just friends. I want to be happy again. I want to be happy with you."

"I can't tell you how much I've wanted to hear you say that, Mol." I groan when her hand brushes against the skin of my stomach.

A noise coming from the hallway acts like a bucket of ice water being poured over us. We freeze as a voice gets closer.

Molly pulls back first. "Shit," she whispers.

Her fingers feather over her swollen lips as I jump off the bed, not wanting to get caught dry humping my coach on club property. I don't know what's worse—the fact that she's my coach or the head coach's daughter. Either way, getting caught like this wouldn't be good.

Hurriedly, I take a seat in the chair furthest from Molly, putting some distance between us as Physio Phil continues his conversation on the other side of the door. In my thin training shorts, my erection is on full display. She tosses her hoody to me as a cover as she tries to conceal her smirk before breaking completely, her laughter echoing around the room.

"Really? You did this to me and you're laughing?" I whisper loudly, breaking into laughter myself.

"You're in a good mood for a knee injury, Molly," Physio Phil says, closing the door behind him.

He stops just inside the room, leans down, and picks the cool pack from the floor where it must have fallen away as we were on the bed. With suspicion in his eyes, he continues into the room without questioning us and pulls on his medical gloves. Thankfully, he doesn't ask why the pack was on the floor or why I didn't pick it up for her, because with all the blood rushing south, I doubt I'd be able to form a coherent excuse.

She winces when he touches her swollen knee and lets out a further cry when he applies more pressure, examining the joint. The sounds of her pain are enough to have me balling my fists in my lap. I should have been more careful with her. I should have looked out for her on that pitch, just like she does for the rest of us.

"It's likely just a minor sprain," Phil tells Molly as he wraps a compression bandage around her swollen knee. "But to be safe, I'll get you booked in for a private MRI and X-ray in a few days once the swelling reduces to check your plates and screws haven't dislodged."

I blow air into my cheeks as the words sink in. I wish I could find complete relief in Phil's words, but I know I won't settle until I see those MRI and X-ray results.

"Sounds good. Can we go home now?"

"Remember painkillers and RICE," he tells her.

"Rest, ice, compression, and elevation. Got it," she recounts perfectly, smiling sweetly at him like a teacher's pet.

Chapter Twenty

Molly

How on Earth did I get so lucky to end up with Jordan Robinson cooking me a delicious-smelling meal in my own kitchen while I watch from my couch with my knee propped up on cushions? Did I die out on the pitch today and this is heaven? Because it definitely feels like it. The man has no business looking this good.

"While the pasta bake is in the oven, do you mind if I take a shower? I didn't manage to get one back at the training ground, since I was busy being your knight in shining armour," he teases, a smile tugging at his lips.

"You'd be naked? In my shower?" My eyes involuntarily drop to his dick, which only an hour or so ago was pressed into my thigh.

He chuckles. "That's usually how showers work, Mol."

"Sure, yeah, that's totally fine, I mean… showers. We all do them," I ramble. The thought of him being naked in my home has my brain turning to mush and my heart racing erratically.

"'We all do them'? Molly, are you okay? Did you hit your head as well as your knee? You sound like you're short-circuiting."

"I just…" I do my best to swallow, but my mouth is so bloody dry at the sight of him being so domesticated, caring, and relaxed in my home as if he belongs here. Fidgeting in my seat, I try my best to ignore the throbbing need between my legs that has been aching constantly for about an hour.

I track his movements as he advances towards me with a confident swagger.

"Molly Davison," he says, drawing out my name in a way that penetrates any barrier between us. "Are you turned on?"

I think turned on might be an understatement, to be honest.

"Yes," I whisper. "That kiss ruined me. It was perfect, but at the same time, nowhere near enough. I meant what I said, I'm done pretending I'm fine without you. I need you."

"You can have me, Mol. We can figure it as we go."

"I want it. I want everything."

My heart pounds as he leans over me again, caging me in where I rest against the arm of the chair.

"I'll not let you go this time. I won't lose you again," he promises, bringing his mouth to mine.

I surrender to him, giving him total control. It's just the two of us, like it was all those years ago.

The hand he has pressed tightly against my waist slowly travels higher beneath my T-shirt until his thumbs graze the underside of my sports bra. When he rubs my sensitive nipple through the fabric, I gasp. It's as though he remembers every sensitive part of my body and plays me like an instrument until I'm a whimpering mess, begging for more.

"I've missed those sounds, Molly," he tells me, groaning as I rub my palm over his erection that bulges through his shorts. "Oh, fuck." He moans as I tighten my grip.

"I want you so much right now." My voice is breathy, which only fuels the burning fire between us.

I kiss him harder, urging him closer, desperate for contact as I spread my legs, inviting him in. A white-hot pain shoots up through my knee. I gasp and grab my leg.

Jordan leaps up from the couch so fast he almost topples backwards into the low coffee table.

"Shit, Molly, are you okay?" He looks terrified, as though it's him who's hurt me.

"I'm sorry." I readjust my position again, propping myself up on my elbows. "I got a little too enthusiastic."

He groans, rubbing his hand over his face, then through his hair as he battles with his own restraint.

"As much as it kills me to say this"—he looks down at the bulge in his shorts—"Molly, I think we need to wait until your knee feels better before we go any further."

"No, I don't want to wait."

He kneels on the floor next to me and gently strokes my bandaged knee. "I don't want to hurt you. Now, I'm going to go shower and then we'll have some food. There's plenty of time to get properly reacquainted. I'm in this for the long haul; there's no need to rush."

I don't have time to protest because he kisses me in a much more chaste fashion and leaves the room to shower.

I collapse onto my back, wincing in pain again.

Just my fucking luck.

***

When Jordan steps out of my bathroom, his dark hair is still damp and he's wearing nothing but clean football shorts. I can't help the way my eyes roam across his body. Each ridge of firm muscle is exactly how I remember.

I don't bother trying to hide the fact I'm staring, and he doesn't seem to mind.

"Are you comfortable?" he asks, kneeling beside me and checking my cushions haven't shifted since he left the room.

"Extremely comfortable. I think the painkillers have kicked in." I lift my eyebrows suggestively.

He laughs, shaking his head, then leans down to brush his soft lips leisurely against mine, and my heart feels as if it's about to take off. The smell of mango shampoo and cocoa butter body wash envelopes me. It satisfies a possessive side of me I didn't know I had, knowing Jordan will leave here smelling of me.

Drifting my palms from his shoulders to his pecs, I run my nails through the dark sprinkling of chest hair and lower so I can trace the firm lines of his obliques and abs.

Ding.

"Just as things were getting interesting." He presses his forehead against mine before reluctantly stepping away.

From my spot on the couch, I watch as he gathers cutlery and plates, easily making himself at home. Of course, I never pictured this happening in the granny flat in my parents' back garden, but this is always how I imagined our life would turn out.

"I could get used to being waited on by the shirtless man of my dreams," I say as he carries my food over to me on a lap tray. He places it on the coffee table before carefully helping me upright again. Once I'm settled with the tray on my lap, he returns with his own food as well as a bottle of wine he had delivered with the shopping earlier.

"This is non-alcoholic, so it probably tastes like shit," he says, pouring me a generous glass. "But I wanted this to be romantic and you can't drink alcohol on those painkillers."

"I'm sure it's fine."

He hands me a glass, and I take a big swig that I immediately regret. I swallow it quickly, trying to hide my wince.

"It's not that bad." I stare at the glass, wondering how I'm going to drink the rest, wondering if I can put it on the table and "forget" about it. Will my knee hold up to get to the sink and back when he goes for a pee? My eyes move to the Monstera plant at the side of my chair. *You look as though you could do with being watered...*

"Urgh."

My eyes snap back to Jordan.

He frowns at his glass, screwing his face up. "That is not good at all."

Before I can respond, he plucks the glass from my hand and takes both back to the kitchen, returning with two glasses of orange squash instead.

"Cheers," he says as we clink our glasses together.

"Cheers." I smile, having never been so happy to see orange squash in my life.

I put the glass down onto my tray and pick up my fork, taking a bite of the deliciously creamy pasta bake he's made for us. "Mmmm."

Jordan glances at me, heat dancing behind his eyes as he groans again, readjusting himself in his shorts.

"What?" I laugh.

He grins, and I pop another piece of pasta into my mouth, rolling my eyes back at the burst of flavour.

We eat in relative silence, enjoying each other's company and the gorgeous food, and when we're done, I watch from the couch as Jordan puts the dishes neatly in the dishwasher and cleans the kitchen as though he's in an intro to a porno. He bends over, still shirtless as he wipes down the breakfast bar separating my living room and kitchen, and all I can think of is how amazing it would be to have him bend me over it.

He tosses the cloth in the washing machine and returns to me on the couch.

"You're going to chew that lip off if you're not careful," he says, resting his arm along the backrest as he faces me.

I release my lower lip from my teeth, my breath hitching as he runs his thumb across the tender flesh. "Kiss it better?"

"I do like the sound of that."

I smile as he slowly leans in.

Buzzzzzzz.

I pull back and groan.

"Sorry."

"Mhmmm." I sigh, literally swimming in sexual desperation.

Jordan picks his phone up off the coffee table and turns it to face me. Aaron's picture peers back at me.

"You should answer it."

"Are you sure?" His finger hovers over the answer button, but he hesitates. I assume he either doesn't want to break the once again building suspense or wants no interruption now we're finally spending time alone together.

I nod.

He presses the accept button and puts it straight on speakerphone. "Alright, mate." He leans back again, wrapping his arm around me, and I take the opportunity to burrow into his chest.

"Alright, just checking in on Molly. I've not seen you come home yet, so I was a bit worried."

I run my finger along the waistband of his shorts again.

"Ummm." Jordan looks down, struggling to put words together. "Phil said it's likely a mild sprain, but she needs an MRI and X-ray done just to be on the safe side."

"That's a relief." Aaron lets out a breath, and my heart pulls at the genuine worry from my friend. "Where are you anyway? I thought you'd be back by now. I was going to head down to The Eighteen with O'Leary and Bailey if you fancy a pint? Luke and the girls are going to be there too. Brooke messaged Molly to see if she wanted to come but didn't get a reply."

I shrug as I grab my phone from the arm of the couch, turning and showing him the unread message from my cousin. In the entire time we've been here, I haven't checked my phone once.

"I'm with Molly. Her mam isn't home yet and I don't want to leave her alone, you know? We're just watching a movie. I don't think she's up to moving much right now."

"Okay, well, give her our love, and I'll catch you in the morning."

Aaron accepts the excuse much easier than I thought he would. Does Jordan and me hanging out alone not surprise him?

"Will do, mate. Catch you later." He hangs up, placing the phone back on the coffee table along with mine.

"How are we going to make this work?" I ask nervously. The thought of this ending before we can begin again has my stomach roiling. "Keep it between us for now?"

He nods. "It'll be hard, I know, especially when I can't tear my eyes away from you whenever you're around," he says, combing his fingers through my hair and relaxing me. "And I hate that I can't shout from the rooftops that I finally have you back in my arms. But if it means we have the best chance in our relationship, then… it'll be worth it."

"We've kept our relationship secret once before with no issues and we won't have to hide anymore when the season is over," I tell him, clinging to that one sliver of light at the end of the tunnel.

"Until then, we can be careful," he agrees. "And we can get reacquainted properly without the media or anyone else watching us."

Chapter Twenty-One

Molly

The morning sun peeks through a crack in the blinds and the birds nesting in trees outside my bedroom window chirp happily. Propping myself up onto my elbow, I turn to find the source of the ringing that woke me up. As I reach for my phone on my bedside table, my knee protests with a bolt of pain up my thigh that has me hissing out a breath. I swipe to answer with a groggy, "Hello".

"Morning, beautiful," Jordan's husky morning voice floats down the phone, and the smile that is now permanently attached to my face widens even further as I remember him tucking me into bed last night and his lingering kiss that has left behind so much promise for the future.

"Good morning." I clear my throat and wipe my eyes, the bright room coming back into focus. I look at the red glow of my alarm clock blinking back at me. Eleven a.m. I can't remember the last time I slept this late. Even after my accident, I'd wake up early to work out.

"Did I wake you up?"

"Yeah, but that's okay." I burrow back into my quilt, inhaling the pillow he used last night as we lay together. It smells exactly like him.

"Have you seen my note?" I can hear his lips quirk up in a smile as he asks.

"Note? What note?"

Jordan's only response is a laugh.

Sitting up again, I look around the room until my eyes land on a folded-up piece of paper resting on the opposite bedside table. I can't help but wonder what Jordan made of this room. Other than a new deep-forest-green bedspread, matching curtains, and a few photos scattered around, I haven't changed a thing since I moved in. I guess fully redecorating would be a commitment to living in my parents' back garden I don't want to make.

I reach out and pick up the note, running my fingers over my name. "I've just found it."

"Open it. It's a very important question."

Anticipation builds further, my chest rising and falling in shallow breaths as I unfold the note and read the words written in Jordan's messy handwriting.

Molly Davison, will you be my girlfriend?

Oh my god. I inhale sharply, caught completely off guard, as my heart skips and my brain takes a second to register. Girlfriend? It doesn't feel real even though the words are right there in front of me. How did my future feel so uncertain not even that long ago? Only once has it ever felt certain, and that was the first time round with Jordan.

"Yes," I say, giggling. If I could kick my feet, I would. I feel like a teenager being asked out by her first crush. Saying that,

I don't think anyone has ever asked me to be their girlfriend so officially before. "Jordan Robinson, I'll be your girlfriend."

He chuckles, his own happiness weaving its way down the phone and into my heart. "I'm so relieved. I wanted to do it right this time."

"You old romantic." I clutch the note to my heart as I fall back onto the bed. "God, I wish you were here."

"Me too, but I couldn't risk staying and being caught by your dad. As much as I would have loved to see your reaction in person."

I hold up the note, grinning as I re-read the words.

"How is your knee doing today?"

I lift the blanket to look at it. The pain is under control for the most part, but I'm yet to try walking. "It's sore, but nowhere near as bad as yesterday. The swelling has gone down too."

"That's a good sign. Still, take it easy today."

"I will. I think Brooke is going to swing by later, but other than that, I'm planning to stay in bed."

"I'm sorry I can't be there today—I've got Zoom interviews all afternoon ahead of England camp in the morning; otherwise, I'd be sneaking in the back gate just to come snuggle with you."

"Wait, what?" I frantically pull up the calendar on my phone to check the date, then lean back with a heavy sigh. Why now? Why today? I just need some time with him. Even a couple of days will do. Most of the lads on the England team won't arrive at camp until next week, but as England captain, Jordan is there early to put in some extra time with the England coaching team and to record some promotional material. It was approved weeks ago, I know this, but it slipped my mind completely.

He is predicted to break records in the next few weeks for England in number of matches played and goals scored. It's also his final game, so I know the club has a lot planned. Dad and I have even recorded footage for a TV programme paying tribute to him that will be shown before the game.

"Molly?" His voice falters when I don't respond.

"I'm sorry… I forgot it was so soon. I wanted to be there for you, but... this stupid knee. I won't be able to fly."

"It's okay, Mol. I know you'll be cheering me on at home with the rest of Wearside. Just make sure you get plenty of rest. We can video call while I'm away, then when I come back and your knee is better, we can have our own celebration." He lets out an audible sigh. "I'm really going to miss you."

"I'm going to miss you too." I give a sorry smile even though he can't see me. "I'll be thinking of you every second of the day."

Chapter Twenty-Two

Molly

I fidget in my chair as I look around at the white walls covered in medical posters and the small table in the corner with a stack of magazines on. I can't remember the last time I held a magazine in my hands, much preferring to just read articles online. Although, I mostly stay away from them now, not wanting to read anything about myself. I thought being trapped in an MRI machine would be the worst part, but I was wrong, waiting for the results is. I'm pretty sure they'll come back clear—the swelling has gone, I've had no pain for a couple of days, and I can walk normally again. But that doesn't mean I don't have that all-too-familiar anxious ball in my stomach.

"You okay?" Brooke asks, handing me a coffee cup from a vending machine in the hallway before taking a seat next to me. When Jordan found out I had planned to go to my appointments alone, he insisted I ask Brooke. Peace of mind for him that I won't be going through this alone apparently, but really, I think he knows I need my little cousin to hold my hand.

"Just a little nervous. I hate these places."

I jump as my phone vibrates in my hand, the sound echoing throughout the empty waiting room, Jordan's name flashing on the screen.

"Go on, answer it," she says, grinning when she notices who is calling.

I roll my eyes and bring my phone to my ear. "Hey," I say, looking away from my cousin.

"Hey, I'm sorry, I don't have long between sessions today, only a few minutes, but I couldn't concentrate without making sure you're feeling okay."

Although we've spoken every day in the week since he's been gone, I don't generally hear from him during the day, since his training and media schedules are so packed.

"I am. Brooke is with me, so I'm not alone."

His voice drops to a hushed whisper on the other end of the line. "Shit. I'm sorry, I didn't think."

"Don't worry about it, she's cool." Brooke obviously doesn't know about us, or at least she didn't prior to now, judging by the way she dances happily in her seat.

"Hi, Jordan," she says, leaning towards the phone.

"Tell her I said hi back." He laughs. "I'm sure you'll have some explaining to do when we hang up."

"Is that okay?"

"If you're happy with that, then so am I."

Glancing at my cousin, I laugh too. "She was bound to find out sooner or later."

She claps her hands together like an excited kid at Christmas. "I knew it."

I shake my head, returning my attention to Jordan's call.

"Robinson, time to get back to it," a voice commands in the background.

"I'm sorry, babe, I've got to head back out there. I'll call you tonight so we can talk properly, but can you please text me and let me know when you've heard about the results?"

"Of course. I should get back too before Brooke combusts."

"I miss you."

"I miss you too. I'll speak to you soon."

When I press the end call button, Brooke grips my arm and gently shakes me with excitement.

"I'm so happy for you, Molly. You both deserve to be happy again. I know how tough the past three years have been for both of you. I assume it's a secret?"

"Just until the end of the season. I can't risk the press getting wind of it—they'll do anything to discredit me, and for a while, they've left me alone. It's been calm."

"I honestly don't think most people would care, but I understand why you're doing it."

A nurse appears in the doorway. "Molly Davison, room four."

My stomach flips as nerves take over.

"Come on, it's going to be fine."

Brooke links my arm as we walk towards the office, my hands trembling as I take in the stark white corridor. I've always wondered why hospitals aren't colourfully decorated; I'd feel much calmer walking down a corridor that's sunshine yellow or has a mural of David Attenborough or someone equally as precious.

White just seems so clinical, like I'm about to receive bad news.

The doctor is waiting for us as we reach the door. She's a young woman, probably around the same age as me, dressed in a white coat over a burgundy dress. Her bright expression is instantly reassuring despite meeting her for the first time today. Until now, all my care has been in London.

"Miss Davison, take a seat," she says, leading us into her room, still smiling at me. Her smile has to be a good sign, right? We take our seats next to her desk as she takes hers in front of her computer.

"Full name and date of birth, please."

I relay my information to her as she checks the screen. I try to read as she opens my file on the screen, but the writing is far too small.

"Your images have come back fine. Thankfully, it's just a mild sprain, as your physio suggested. There is no serious damage to the ligaments and your artificial knee is in very good shape. There's nothing to worry about, just remember to be careful in the future and avoid too much strenuous exercise."

"I'm fine?" Relief oozes from every pore. "Really?"

"You are indeed. I suspect you hurt yourself because you've not been keeping up with your physical therapy exercises." She raises an all-knowing eyebrow.

"I mean…" I start to formulate a lie about how often I do my exercises. *I've only missed a day or two here and there. I slacked the week before my sprain, but that's all.* I let out a sigh of reservation. She's the expert here; she can tell I haven't been doing them with just one look. "I'll do better with my exercises. I promise."

I give my cousin an apologetic look. Between Brooke and Jordan, I doubt I'll be able to get away with skipping them again.

"That's all we ask of you," she says, smiling. "You can go now. I'll send these results to your club physio and recommend he follows up with you soon. I'll be satisfied to return to yearly check-ups going forward."

"Thank you," I say as she turns back to her computer screen to type up my notes.

This time, I practically skip along the corridor to the waiting area, where I thank the receptionist with a perky wave before breezing out of the private clinic. Everything seems brighter after getting good news. The sun is shining, the air is warm, and even the concrete feels softer beneath my feet.

"I can't tell you how much of a relief that is," I say to Brooke once we reach her car in the car park.

I had been telling myself all week it was going to be fine. I used all the manifestation techniques I could find on the internet. But deep down, I was convinced I'd faced a major setback and would need more surgeries. Not that I voiced any of that to Brooke or Jordan.

"You don't need to, I can see." She hugs me tightly, her shoulders relaxing. "I'm so happy everything's fine. But you need to keep on top of those exercises."

When she pulls back, I can see the stress in her eyes. Stress that I caused by not being careful. I imagine Jordan and my parents will react the same when I tell them.

Oh god, I haven't even thought about what Physio Phil will say. I'm going to be in so much trouble.

"I will, I promise."

We break apart as we climb into the front seats of Brooke's car. I do as I promised and pull out my phone, typing a quick text to Jordan to tell him the good news.

"Are we going to celebrate? We could do a bottomless brunch," she suggests as she turns the ignition, the car purring to life.

"I have a better idea. How would you like to go book some flights to Portugal?"

Her eyes light up at the prospect of watching Jordan, Aaron, and Bailey play for England.

"I'll ring Bridget and Natasha and get them to meet at your place with their bank cards and a few bottles of fizz. Either way, a celebration is called for."

Chapter Twenty-Three

Molly

The Estádio da Luz is the home stadium for the national team of Portugal. As expected, the sold-out 65,000-seat stadium is packed full of England fans who have journeyed to watch the men play for their country. Me, well, I'm here for one reason: to be here while Jordan plays his final game as England captain.

The boys make their way out of the tunnel to warm up on the pitch. We're so close to the pitch that if they knew we were here, they'd probably be able to spot us.

"Excuse me," Bridget asks a passer-by. "Can you take our photo, please?"

The stranger obliges, and Bridget hands over her phone before she, Brooke, Natasha, and I stand with our arms around each other. Jordan, Aaron, and Sam Henderson are caught in the background of the photo.

As more and more people join the crowd, the singing and chanting intensifies, and the atmosphere is pulsing with nervous excitement. Before long, I don't even care that I paid over the odds for a beer from one of the vendors inside the stadium. I'm acting like a superfan of Jordan, taking countless photos of him warming up to show him later.

Pointing at a tiny Jordan in the distance, I take one final selfie and send it to him as he walks off the pitch back down the tunnel to the dressing room. It's not long before my phone vibrates in my hand. A smile stretches across my whole face as I imagine his happiness that I've made it. The only thing that could make this situation better right now is if I were able to see his face.

Jordan: You're here? In Portugal? How long for?

Molly: We landed two hours ago and came straight here. We fly home at one a.m. We have the fundraiser tomorrow night and Bridget and I have a lot of work to do for it, but I couldn't miss your last England match. I'm so proud of you!

Jordan: You're amazing, you know that, right? Will you have time to see me before you fly home?

Molly: An hour or so depending if
the game goes to extra time or
penalties.

Jordan: Send me your seat number
and I'll get someone to bring
passes.

I quickly send him our seat numbers before turning to Brooke.

"Brooke, can you take a picture of me in my shirt?" I ask, handing her my phone. I turn my back to her, moving my hair out of the way so that *Robinson 13* is on full display. I give the sexiest smile I can as I gaze seductively down the camera lens.

"Hot," she says, then hands it back to me, and I quickly send it. I'm cutting it fine here; they're due to kick off soon.

Jordan: Fuck, Mol. When we get
home, I want you in nothing but
that shirt.

He doesn't need to ask me twice. And if I have my way, maybe we won't need to wait until he gets home.

Molly: It's a deal.

Jordan: All jokes aside, we're getting ready to come back out. I'm really happy you're here. I was dreading doing this without you.

Molly: You're going to be great. Believe me.

I put my phone in my pocket, unable to hide the smile plastered across my face. The girls glance at each other before looking at me.

"What?" I ask defensively as they smirk.

"We're just waiting patiently for you to tell us about you and JR," Natasha says discreetly, noticing how busy it is around us. It's hard to take her seriously when she has little England flags painted on her cheeks and is wearing a St George's bucket hat.

"I have no idea what you're talking about."

"Come on, Molly, you're grinning at your phone like a lovesick teenager," Bridget says, nudging me with her hip. "We just want to know you're happy, that's all."

"No, we want filthy details too," Natasha adds.

"Molly Davison?" a woman asks from the end of the row, and the four of us jump in surprise.

"That's me," I confirm, regaining some composure.

"Jordan Robinson sent up some security passes." She smiles and hands over lanyards to each of us. "Would you like to come up to the family and friends' box, or would you prefer to stay here?"

"I think we'll stay here if that's okay and come up to the lounge after?" Bridget already offered to get us seats in a private box, but we agreed that watching it from the stands with the fans would be a better experience.

"Of course. I'll come back after the game and escort you to the players' lounge." And with a swish of her long blonde ponytail, she disappears up the steps and out of sight.

"Okay," I say when we return to our huddle. "What do you want to know?"

"*Everything*," Natasha says.

"How and when did it start?" Bridget asks.

"This time around, about two weeks ago, but it's been building since I came home."

She gasps. "What do you mean this time around?"

"We were together before I had the accident, and I ended things." I glance at Brooke, remembering the disagreement we had when I told her to break up with him for me. "It's a long story," I add, not wanting to get into too many details. I still haven't forgiven myself for what I did even if Jordan has. Thankfully, the girls don't probe me on my decision to break up with Jordan the first time around.

"Is he a good kisser?" Natasha asks instead, lightening the mood.

"The best."

"And the other stuff?" Brooke asks.

"Even better," I say, and the three of them swoon collectively. "Although, this time around, we've not yet—"

The interrogation ends abruptly when the music blasts around the stadium. I clap as the players come out onto the pitch, lining up to sing the national anthems. I see a lot of familiar faces in the England squad, but I'm most interested in Jordan, and, further down the line, Aaron.

They're both lucky to be here, after back-to-back relegations for Wearside, any other international manager would have probably dropped the pair of them from the squad, but it seems like they've been given one last chance to prove themselves worthy of playing at an international level. Not that it matters to Jordan, he just wants to end his career on a high, but I know Aaron has a lot riding on this game and the rest of his season at Wearside too.

Once the anthems have been sung, the players and officials shake hands and get into position, awaiting the first whistle that signifies kick-off.

Just like the others, I'm nervous. I want nothing more than for tonight's game to be a success, but Portugal is a brilliant team, one we're going to have to constantly keep on top of if we have any hope of winning.

It's clear from the start both teams are equally matched. England and Portugal have a few shots on target, and when Aaron takes a shot that flies over the crossbar, he throws his head back in frustration.

"Oh for…" I trail off when I notice kids seated near me and put my head in my hands instead. He should have scored, and yet I can't help but criticise the manager. I know it's easy to criticise when I'm not the coach of this team, but come on.

Jordan is a striker, so his position is up front, but for this game, he's been put on the right with Sam Henderson taking the centre-forward position. Aaron is usually on the right for Wearside, yet here he is playing on the left. His left foot is his biggest weakness, everyone knows that. And it's obvious the changes have confused the whole team.

Brooke lets out a groan at my side, justifying my frustrations. "This is ridiculous," Brooke complains, turning to me as we go into extra time for the first half.

"What's wrong with 4-4-2 these days? Jordan and Sam would be brilliant up front together. Then bring in Aaron on the right wing and Kershaw on the left."

"Are you trying to revive the good old days of Wearside?" Bridget asks me, not taking her eyes off Sam, who thunders down the pitch. The problem is that when he runs with the ball, their defence is so tight he can't get through on his own. He needs help in the attack. "You know it's going to take more than nostalgia to bring Sam back now."

She's not wrong. Back when Sam played for Wearside, that was the usual formation but adding in Bailey on the left. But it didn't last more than a few years, as he was young and talented and had a promising career ahead of him. Everyone wanted a piece of him. They still do.

It's common knowledge that Sam has hundreds of offers flying in from all over the world including Wearside. But not one to break a contract or to leave his team in the lurch, he's determined to win the Premier League trophy before he moves on.

It's admirable really because the last I heard, there were some big-money offers floating around.

"Come on, ref, blow your whistle and let them re-group," Natasha mutters to herself.

Thirty seconds later, the half-time whistle blows and the team walk off the pitch looking tired and deflated. They're going to need a good pep talk before they come back out here if they stand a chance of winning.

"Can we go to the bar?" Brooke asks and is met with unanimous agreement from the rest of us.

We file out of the stands, swept away with the crowd throughout the concrete labyrinth. Thankfully, it doesn't take long before we have a fresh drink in our hands despite the crowd.

Resting my fresh beer on a bin lid as we gather next to a cool-to-the-touch wall, I can't help but feel lucky. This is the real football experience; we wouldn't get this in a box or the players' lounge.

Guys cheer at me as they pass while they shout things like, "What a game, eh?" or "Go down to the dugout and show them how it's done." I tip my drink to them in a salute, unable to suppress my grin. Seems we have some Wearside fans in the house.

"Can't take you anywhere." Bridget laughs.

I can't lie, it feels good to be recognised for my coaching ability and not for the tragic accident I'm mainly asked about.

"It's not a bad shout though," Natasha says thoughtfully. "You could always text him."

"Unless he's managed to sneak his phone out of his locker without anyone seeing, he won't have his phone on—Coach Bell runs a tight ship. The only reason he let Jordan have his phone at training the other day is because he told him he had a family emergency," I say, but when I pull out my phone as we make our way back to our seats, his name flashes up at me again with an unread text from five minutes ago. A swelling feeling builds in my chest as I read the risky text message he sent.

Jordan: We're doing our best, but their defence is tight as fuck.

Molly: You're doing great, you've been on them all night. You just need to push the boundaries of your position and finish. Sousa is tired. If he's not subbed off at half-time, squeeze past him on the right, it's his weak side and you're faster when you go flat out. You'll have a clear shot at the goal or at the very least, a clear path to cross to Sam. Use him.

If Coach Bell finds out I'm coaching Jordan via secret text messages, we'll both be in trouble. I've seen a manager fine a player for way less than this. But I can't help it when a possessiveness washes over me. He's my player too, and I want him to do his best on an international stage.

Jordan: Look at you, coaching from the crowd. I love it.

Molly: I can't help it; you deserve an amazing final game. Good luck.

I put my phone back in my pocket and lean back in my seat, waiting for the second half to start. The team is re-energised as they jog from the tunnel back to their positions, and I'm happy to see Sousa is still playing. It won't take much to get around him now that he's exhausted, so they need to take advantage before he is subbed out for someone full of energy.

The second Jordan has the chance, he flies up the right. As I predicted, Sousa isn't quick enough to catch up, and before long, Jordan crosses to Sam, who shoots at the goal. I grip the seat of my plastic chair as I watch the ball fly towards the goal.

"*Nooooo,*" I shout as a Portuguese defender jumps in and blocks the shot with a high kick, sending the ball careening into the air.

The ball begins to drop just in front of Aaron. Everything moves in slow motion and my breath catches in my lungs. One of Aaron's feet is in the air and the second quickly follows in a scissor kick. I hear his boot connecting with the synthetic leather and watch as the ball hits the back of the net.

I'm on my feet going wild with the rest of the England fans, screaming so loud my voice cracks, but no one is as loud as Brooke, who is jumping up and down, screaming at the top of her voice in celebration with her best friend.

He slides on his knees, coming to a stop at the touchline facing us with his arms spread wide. He punches the air before he jumps to his feet again, performing the little shuffle dance he and Brooke have been using as a celebration since they were kids. He might have the façade of a tattooed bad boy, but deep inside, he's a big softie when it comes to Brooke.

"That was amazing," Brooke yells on the verge of tears as she wraps her arms around my neck, giving me a big sloppy kiss on the cheek.

Thankfully, Aaron's goal is just the beginning of a fantastic second half. England dominates, keeping majority possession and defending their one–nil lead.

"What if Jordan doesn't break the record?" My nails are non-existent by the eighty-eighth minute.

He has broken the record for most England caps by playing today, but he is one goal shy of taking the record for most goals scored for England, and I know it's a record he's desperate for.

"There's still time," Natasha says, keeping her eye on the pitch.

An official holds up an electronic board that reads four minutes just as Aaron is subbed off for a midfielder and Sam is subbed in favour of a fifth defender in the hopes they can defend this lead the whole way. Jordan moves over to centre-forward.

This is what I'm talking about. He is finally where he belongs, and although I know he's got to be pissed off that he's spent the better part of ninety minutes in the wrong position, I know he's capable of converting that anger to power on the pitch.

"Come on, you can do it, Jordan," I mutter under my breath.

The scoreboard counts down the seconds, and less than two minutes remain when the ball goes out. It's an England corner, so Kershaw steps up to the mark. He takes a deep, steadying breath as he looks towards the goal, where Jordan waits unmarked.

My lungs have completely stopped working; I couldn't take a breath even if I wanted to.

Kershaw steps back, giving himself a run-in before his foot connects hard with the ball. Every eye in the stadium watches as it sails through the air towards the box. Three players jump into the air, but aside from Jordan, I couldn't tell you who the other two are.

With a flick of his head, he connects with the ball.

My heart races in my chest like a rapid drum beat as I leap to my feet in time to see the ball crash against the back of the net. The four of us pull in close, wrapping each other up in a tight embrace as we jump up and down.

A smile spreads across my face as I watch him through my tears of happiness, drenched in mud and streaked with grass stains, pure euphoria radiating from him as his team smothers him to the ground.

He's done it.

He's broken the record.

Chapter Twenty-Four

Jordan

Faces blur past me as I scan the crowd for Molly. I know roughly where she should be from her picture, but I can't spot her anywhere in the sea of fans.

Did she move? Did she leave already?

"There," Aaron says, leaning over me with one arm around my shoulder, pointing at one of the staircases. She runs down them far too quickly for someone who has been instructed by her doctor to take things easy.

Brooke, Natasha, and Bridget quickly follow her.

"Let her through, please," I call out to the fans who now gather as close to the railings as possible, and thankfully, they part like the Red Sea as Molly squeezes through, leaving the others at the back of the growing crowd, fighting their way through.

"Thank you. Thank you so much," she says to those who help her.

I leap over the advertising boards and meet her with only a metal railing between us. She throws her arms around me, hugging me tightly as the crowd gathered around us join the embrace. I want to pull her over the railing, but for the most part, I don't think this crowd is a threat.

Sam and Aaron are the next to climb over the boards, and they reach over to join our hug. Molly places a soft kiss on my cheek, and butterflies erupt in my stomach at the contact. I've missed her so much the past few weeks. Not one to leave the others out or to single me out too obviously, Aaron gets a shoulder squeeze and Sam gets his hair ruffled.

"I'm so fucking proud of you," she says, pulling back to look at us all, her eyes shining in the floodlights. "You all did fantastic. But, Jordan…" She looks at me, glowing with pride, and I laugh, embarrassed by her praise.

"*You did it,*" Molly screams and flings herself into my arms again. This time, she clings only to me. I wrap both arms around her waist and lift her off her feet. "You broke the record, Jordan. You're England's top scorer. I knew you would do it. I'm so proud of you."

Her words echo back at me.

I did it.

I actually did it.

All that doubt I've felt since the end of last season has been weighing heavily on my mind in recent months, but Molly's belief never once waivered. Every time we talked about this game together, she was always so sure I was going to do it. She believed in me even when I stopped believing in myself.

My mind overflows with all the things I want to say to her, all the things I need to thank her for. But all of that will have to wait until I have her alone.

I plant her back on her feet. My hands tremble as I run my fingers through my sweaty hair. Her brows knit together in concern as she takes in my expression.

It's all too much. The noise of the crowd, the praise, the weight of my insecurities lifting. Having my girlfriend fly 1200 miles just to watch me play for a couple of hours.

"Oh, Jordan." This time when she hugs me, tears spring to my eyes and don't stop. As I cry, I bury my face into her hair, taking a deep inhale of mango shampoo. God, I've missed this smell.

"I'm so fucking happy you're here, Mol."

"I would have found a way here even with a knee injury."

As I lift my face from her neck, she wipes the tears from my cheeks with the sleeve of her cardigan.

"You should go in there; you've got interviews to give." She nods her head towards the tunnel.

I look around, noticing for the first time that there are more empty seats than people remaining in the stadium. I nod and pull my shirt off over my head. "I want you to have this."

She looks at the sweat-stained shirt clenched in my hand and shakes her head in disbelief. I reach for her hand and wrap it around the fabric before she's even had chance to process it.

"Seriously?" Her eyes light up. "This is a lot; you can't just give me a match worn shirt. Especially not your last one. Don't you want to keep it?"

"It's only right considering I own yours." Her eyes go wide at my confession and I hold my hands up as I back away from her, grinning when she pulls it close to her chest, hugging it tightly. I know I'll have to explain that one later but this isn't the place.

She turns away to follow a group of stewards up the stairs. When she reaches the top step of the lower block, reuniting with the rest of the girls, she turns and smiles over her shoulder. It's all the encouragement I need to complete my final interview as England captain.

Catching up with Aaron and Sam as they wait at the mouth of the tunnel, they throw their arms around my shoulders as we walk down it together for the last time.

"Robinson and Milburn, you're needed for interviews." Liv, the PR manager for England football, waves us over to a press board where Coach is just finishing up his interview. She looks down at her clipboard as she holds out a fresh England shirt for me to pull on for the camera. "Milburn, you're first."

Watching Aaron being interviewed gives me a chance to pause and compose myself. Familiar faces congratulate me as they pass on their way into the stadium, and others clap me on the back, or in Sam's case, ruffle my hair. Each interaction has my cheeks aching.

"Can I add one final thing? And, I'm sorry because I know you want to interview Jordan, but I need to say this on the record and then I'll leave." Without warning, Aaron tosses his arm around my neck and pulls me, laughing as I stumble into the frame. "I know I'm lucky enough to play with Jordan at Wearside for the rest of the season, but playing alongside him tonight, and every other time I've played for England, has been a real privilege." He turns, this time talking directly to me. "I'm so proud of the player and the captain you've become, Jordan. I love you, Skip." It's hard to process how far we've come. Aaron was sixteen the first time we met. I was twenty-three at the time and he came along to train with the first team having played in the youth teams most of his life. The other lads had a lot on at the time so when coach asked for one of us to mentor him, I took him under my wing. He was a cocky teenager who in all honesty, did my head in. But as time went on, I started to think of him more like a little brother, and looking at him now, it's really starting to hit home how much I'll miss being his teammate.

My voice breaks as I say, "Love you too, mate." I pat his chest.

He smiles at me before adding, "Right, I'm off." And with that, he disappears down the corridor like a whirlwind.

I shake my head, grinning as I look down at my feet, checking I'm on the right mark. With a flip of his notepad, the reporter begins.

"Well, that was a bit emotional." He laughs.

"Yeah, it's going to be a miracle if I get through this without bawling," I joke, trying to make light of my emotions. Or am I joking? They feel pretty close to the surface.

"What a game for you tonight, Jordan. Tell us a bit about it."

"Mate, I don't even know how to put it into words," I say, looking past the camera that is focused on my face to the reporter. "Today was a tough game, you know? Portugal is an incredible team and their defence was solid, so it took some out-of-the-box thinking in the end. I could see Sousa getting tired and his right side is always the weakest. That's something I've learned from Molly Davison, my coach at Wearside. She's taught me to look for the weak spots, and it paid off tonight."

It's true; even if she didn't text me at half-time, I would've heard her voice clear as day reminding me and the Wearside lads to "think outside of the box".

"Congratulations are also in order. Not only have you broken the record for England caps, but you're England's top goal scorer. Did you expect it tonight of all nights?"

"Uh, I hoped." I laugh. The sound is alien to me, as though I'm listening in from afar. "I'm so happy I got there, especially in my final game, but I hope I'm not the record holder for long. All the lads out there on the pitch are incredible players. They all deserve that too."

"Coach Bell was a bit emotional earlier when I asked him about you. It seems like it's going to be an emotional reunion in the dressing room."

I rub my jaw, grazing my nails along my stubble. "Oh for sure, I've already cried once tonight, it won't be the last time."

"You mentioned Molly Davison before?"

"Yeah." Anxiety prickles at my skin as I wonder where he's going with this. Our behaviour out there, although spontaneous and natural, was also risky considering the number of cameras pointed at us. I didn't plan on pouring fuel onto the already smouldering fire, but it seems I might have done just that.

Great, I can already picture the headlines.

"We saw her here tonight, in the stands. Did you plan on giving her your match shirt?" he asks, a lilt of genuine curiosity in his tone. I don't blame him—if I were in his shoes, I'd be curious too.

"No, I didn't know she was coming. It was a nice surprise to see her here. She's my best friend." Anticipation balls in my stomach as the image of her running down the steps to meet me replays in my mind. I don't think I'll ever forget the feeling of her holding me, telling me how proud she is of me, accepting me as the emotional mess I am.

"She's done a fantastic job at Wearside so far this season. Any thoughts on that?"

I'm grateful for his line of questioning. He could have taken the juicer route, probed me further about my sudden close friendship with my coach, but instead he chose to highlight her success and it has me beaming with pride. "Honestly, I owe much of my success this season to her. She's a fantastic coach. She sees the bigger picture as well as the minute details. Her way of thinking has helped me adapt my techniques and skill to this new way of playing. After last season, I couldn't have done any of this without Molly."

"Thanks very much," the reporter says. "It's been a pleasure interviewing you all these years and I wish you the best of luck." He moves his notepad into the hand with his mic, then reaches for my mic.

"Thank you," I say. "It means a lot." I nod, waving at the boom and camera operators.

"Well done," Liv says as she escorts me down the corridor, her phone in hand. "It's the end of an era."

I blow out a long breath. "You can say that again. Thanks for everything, Liv."

"You ever need anything or you just want to catch a game, just let me know. You'll always be welcome," she says as we reach the dressing room door. "Now, go in there and enjoy yourself." With that, she turns and walks in the opposite direction, where I assume her office is set up. I take in a deep breath as I plant two palms on the door.

This is it.

Pushing against the door, I walk into a wall of sound.

Aaron, and Sam are the first to pounce on me, cheering and singing along to the music in the dressing room. One plants an inflatable crown on my head, and my money is on Sam.

Everywhere I turn, arms pull me into hugs. Familiar faces from the current squad and coaching staff embrace me, as well as players and coaches I've known for as long as I can remember. Many are retired or have moved to different areas of the sport.

They've all come here to wave me off.

Their words blur together as they speak over one another, voices overlapping in a rush. Overwhelmed and overstimulated, I can hardly process it all. But I'll remember their faces, all plastered with bright smiles and laughter lines, for the rest of my life.

"Alright, settle down," Coach Bell calls out through a megaphone that's seen better days. It screeches loudly as he speaks, causing some of the lads closest to him to wince. "Everyone, take a seat. Jordan, up here with me."

Everyone disperses around the room, grabbing space where they can, and it's the first time I can properly take it all in. The current squad are all in some state of undress in front of their lockers. Some sit in their boxers and others in towels, having bagged early showers. Some, like Sam and Aaron, are still wearing their match-worn kits and are in desperate need of a shower.

Pressed against the walls are people from every stage of my past. There isn't a person in this room who hasn't had a direct impact on my journey as an international footballer, and it's humbling.

I rake two hands through my hair as I blow out a long breath. My nose tingles. I blink at the ceiling, but it's no use, my eyes go misty and my lower lip trembles.

"Congratulations, Jordan, from all of us," Coach says.

Laughter bubbles out of me mixed with a sob when he presents me with a framed photo.

A baby-faced, fifteen-year-old version of me stares back at me from behind the glass.

I remember that day as though it were yesterday. Mam drove me to meet with the club after months of trials. She took the day off work since it was such a long drive, and Tony, my stepdad, paid for her to get her hair done especially. I was convinced I would throw up and that would be the final nail in the coffin. Why on Earth would England want a kid who can't handle his nerves?

I sat at the tiny desk, as Andy Hall, the youth coach at the time, presented me with a contract.

"I cried that day too. I've come full circle," I say with a laugh as I turn the picture to the room before standing it up on the foldable table at my side.

"We also got you this to celebrate breaking the record for highest number of England caps in history…" Coach presents me with what looks like a deep-burgundy velvet jewellery box. "Open it, son," he says with a nod.

I reach over as he holds the box, running my hands over the soft material as the room falls into complete silence again. My thumbs brush against the lid before I lift it. The front of the display box drops forward, revealing a special-edition red England cap.

I choke back another sob as I read the embroidered peak.

Jordan Robinson. 126th cap for England Senior Men.

And that's not all, the gifts keep on coming as I'm presented with another, much larger frame, this time by my long-time friend and new England captain, Sam Henderson. In the frame is a brand-new England shirt with the St George's Cross embroidered on the collar. Below this is my name and the number 70 representing the number of goals I've scored wearing an England shirt.

"How did you—"

"Oh, come on, we all knew you'd do anything to get that final goal," Sam says with a smile.

I grin and shake my head. He's not wrong. I can't deny I doubted myself, but that didn't mean I didn't have an eagle eye and eager feet on the ball. "I'll swap you, mate?" I say, handing over my black armband with the word "CAPTAIN" written on it in bold white writing as I take the frame from him.

"You've left big shoes to fill," he says, squeezing my shoulders.

"You've got big feet."

He laughs, turning to take a seat on the bench, holding the armband in two hands.

"*Speech*," Aaron calls out across the room.

The whole room erupts with, "*Speech, speech, speech*" as they stomp their feet and clap their hands on their thighs.

"I don't know what to say." I laugh, looking around the room. I'm rarely lost for words, yet here I am, looking into the eyes of my England family, and I can't find a single word that would do my feelings justice.

I take a steadying breath and attempt to swallow the lump in my throat. If this is the last time I'll address this team, I want it to be meaningful. "This has been one of the greatest days of my life. It was a hard match to play, but we pushed on as a team and overcame the hurdles that Portugal threw at us. I couldn't have done this"—I hold up my framed shirt—"without each and every one of you. A lot of you in this room met me as that gangly fifteen-year-old who couldn't control his left foot for love or money, but you had faith in me, and that means more to me than anything else. I've known a lot of you in this room since you were gangly fifteen-year-olds too, and now you're all grown men leading the new generation of England players. Without a shadow of a doubt, I know you're all going to go on to do great things for this team, and even though I'll not be playing alongside you, I'll always be supporting you. Thank you for the best nineteen years of my life.

Everyone stands to applaud me one last time as I make my way to my usual spot between Sam and Aaron, collapsing onto the wooden bench. I lean back against my locker with my head tilted to the ceiling, soaking up the atmosphere and committing it all to memory as "Sweet Caroline" blasts through the room once again.

Chapter Twenty-Five

Jordan

Despite being the last to arrive at the dressing room, I'm the first to finish getting showered and ready into my post-game suit and tie. I don't normally wear a suit; most of the time I wear my England tracksuit and sneak out of the stadium. But this is no normal game and this isn't a normal post-win celebration.

As the lads continue to get ready leisurely, knowing they have all night to celebrate, I don't bother drying my hair or checking my reflection in the mirror before I'm out of there without a backwards glance. The celebration with my teammates will likely be a late one—we've got the suite booked all night—but my time with Molly dwindles by the minute.

I take the three flights of stairs down two steps at a time from the hallway outside of the dressing room down to the players' lounge, using the chrome banister and the adrenaline coursing through me to propel me faster. When I reach the suite, I pause at the door to catch my breath, then grasp the metal handle and easily pull the door open.

It's obvious why this room is called the Grand Suite—it's ginormous. Crystal chandeliers hang in rows from the ceiling, the bar to my left is fully stocked with all kinds of expensive alcohol, there is a dedicated whiskey snug in the back corner, and the cream and gold carpet is so lush and soft it feels as though I'm walking on clouds as I step over the threshold in my expensive designer loafers that Aaron insisted I buy for the occasion.

It's moments like this I realise how lucky I am to live this life.

My eyes scan the room full of friends and families of the players celebrating our win with waiters circulating with glasses of wine and bottles of Portuguese beer on small trays held in their hands. It's hard to spot Molly through the dense crowd, and with the music and the chatter around me, I can't even try to listen out for her.

As I venture deeper into the room, weaving my way through clusters of people, I try to use my height advantage to look above the crowd, and that's when I spot her. My breath catches as I look at the woman I love standing with her back to me at a high cocktail table with the girls, wearing my name proudly on the back of her shirt. She talks animatedly to her friends and someone else I can't quite see behind Brooke. Jesus Christ, she looks like my wildest dream come true.

It awakens something feral inside of me. Like my name on her back is proof that she's mine and all I can think of as my eyes drift south to take in the curves of her ass in her tight jeans is claiming her right here, right now.

Over the past few weeks since we've been apart, things have gotten hot and heavy with us over the phone, but I stopped it before it went too far. I don't want the first time I make her come to be over video call. And yes, I know that's stupid because it's not the first time—we tried absolutely everything last time around, and I mean *everything*—but I see this as our fresh start. We can have all those firsts again and I want to do it all right.

Even if I have been living with a constant semi.

I linger for a moment, watching her, taking her in. That's when I spot another familiar face crossing the room from the bar with two glasses of whiskey in his hands making his way to where Molly is. Tony spots me and raises one of the glasses, greeting me proudly. That must mean…

Mam peeks out from around Brooke, clumsily putting down her wine glass before racing over to hug me. I open my arms wide for her, tightly embracing her as she wraps her arms around me, loving every second of being held by my mam.

Mam's been my biggest supporter, ever since my first class at Toddling Kickers when I was two. And now we're here, thirty-two years later and she's still my biggest fan.

Another lump forms in my throat as I hold onto her, not ready to let go of this moment just yet. Even when it was just the two of us and she was working multiple jobs just to make ends meet, she always made sure she was there and now it's the last time we'll ever get to experience this on an international level. It's bittersweet and probably why Tony has hung back at the table, not wanting to intrude.

"Jordan, you were brilliant." She pulls back, holding me by my shoulders. This is her 126th game too, yet she still looks at me with as much love, excitement, and support as she looked at that lanky kid making his debut. "I could burst."

"Thanks, Mam." I hold out my arm for her to link, and we walk to the table where our group wait. Molly has her hand placed over her heart as if she's trying to hold back her tears and Tony looks at Mam with a deep love in his eyes. "I see you found some friends?"

"She still looks as beautiful as ever," Mam says.

I frown and look at Mam, then follow her eyes to Molly and smile. She was always fond of her. Even after we broke up, she never had a bad word to say about her.

"It's nice she came all this way to support you boys."

"Yeah, it is," I say, not ready to reveal too much to her just yet. Not until Molly and I have had a real chance to discuss all of this, anyway.

When we reach the table, Tony pulls me into a hug, slapping my back. "Congratulations, son." He hands me a glass of whiskey I assume he was saving for me. I know he shares the same love and support for me as my mam and is just as excited to see me as her, but he always does and always will hold back to allow my mam those initial private moments with me.

Natasha, Bridget, and Brooke all take their turn to congratulate me until, eventually, I make my way around the table to where Molly stands. We silently face each other, tension hovering between us that grows as the girls watch us eagerly. Now that the adrenaline has settled, it's hard to know how to act with her in public. I close the final few steps between us, then wait for her to make the first move.

She awkwardly holds her hands up for a double high five.

"Seriously, Mol?" I smirk as I return her gesture, linking my fingers with hers and pulling her closer so I can wrap her arms around my neck, lifting her off the floor with my arms around her waist.

"I thought that was how we do things now," she jokes.

Even though I know there is a strict no-pictures rule in here, it doesn't mean we're safe from the gossip, so I don't linger with my embrace and reluctantly put her down and step away.

"I think Tony and I will go and grab a bite to eat from the buffet," Mam announces.

"We've just eaten," Tony replies, to which Mam gives him a stern look. "Oh, yeah. Good idea. I didn't try one of those dessert things."

The pair whisper as they walk away, turning to look over their shoulder at Molly and me.

"You look good in that suit," Molly says, her thick black eyelashes fluttering as she looks up at me.

"You look good in that shirt."

My gaze drops to her lips before continuing down. Her nipples are pebbled beneath the nylon. I wonder what bra she's wearing today. Fuck, it must be non-existent.

"Fucking hell." If it weren't for Natasha breaking the silence, I would have been convinced Molly and I were alone in here. "I thought she was bad, but look at him."

I shoot a questioning glance at Molly, and she laughs with a shrug.

"We aren't being as discreet as we thought," she explains.

"Ah, young love," Brooke swoons, placing a hand across her heart.

"I have to ask… this isn't going to turn into a PR nightmare, is it?" Bridget watches us intently, reading our reactions, torn between being our friend and the club publicist. She knows as well as we do that this has the potential to go tits up with the media.

"We're keeping it under wraps until the end of the season. Until then, as far as the public know, Molly is my coach and I'm her captain."

"And you're best friends, according to your interview," Bridget adds.

"Exactly."

"Well, well, well, if it isn't Molly Davison," Sam Henderson says, coming up behind us, the first of my England teammates to make it to the party. There's a fondness in his voice as the two friends reunite.

Molly gasps excitedly. "*Sam.*" She greets him with a brief hug, then grins at him. "I'm so sorry about West Hylton."

"No, you're not."

"No, I'm really not." She laughs as Sam rests his arm casually around her shoulder, looking at the group. "How are you liking your new gig? Are these idiots behaving themselves?" he asks as Aaron finally joins us at the table, completing our group.

"Of course we are. She cracks a mean whip, man. You can tell she's a Davison; she's a natural at busting my balls." Aaron winks at Brooke, who punches him square in the stomach.

"Ugh, I was talking about the gaffer," he whines.

"What a load of bollocks, Aaron Milburn." Brooke rolls her eyes and links her arm through his. "Come on, let's get a drink. You've got forty-five minutes to tell me everything."

The pair wander off to find the bar, followed closely by Natasha.

"What do I have to do to get you to come home, Sam?" Molly asks, cutting to the chase. She's talked about poaching Sam a few times lately, but he keeps his cards so close to his chest that there's no predicting what he might choose to do when his contract comes to an end next year.

"I've told Bridget if the offer was right, I'd consider it." He and Bridget exchange a loaded look. It makes zero sense; Bridget has nothing to do with contracts or offers at the club. Pretty sure if his agent found out he was discussing things like that with her—and cutting him out—he'd have some choice words to say about it too.

"Really?" Molly looks just as confused as I am as her head bounces between the pair.

"And I've told Sam, it's not my place," Bridget responds.

"I think we both know that's not—"

"Can I talk to you in private?" Bridget doesn't wait for him to answer before she turns and walks off towards the nearest corridor, swishing her hair over her shoulder.

He lets out a resigned sigh as he watches her wistfully. "It was good to see you, Molly. I'm sure we'll speak soon," he says with a smile, raking his hand through his dirty blonde hair.

We tilt our heads dumbfounded as we watch him walk off, following the direction Bridget took.

"Do you know what that was about?" I ask Molly.

"Absolutely no idea."

"Speaking of privacy, though." Molly holds up a shiny black key card. "I called in a favour."

"How do you have favours here?"

"Bridget owed me and Liv owed Bridget, so we cashed in and got us forty-five undisturbed minutes in a box down the corridor."

I immediately look around for a clear exit. "Why didn't you mention this the second I walked in?"

She brushes her hand against mine as she slips past me, leading the way through the crowded room. My teammates are far too preoccupied celebrating with their families to notice us slip out of the ballroom together.

"Do you know where we're going?" I ask her as we hurry down the corridor.

"Of course," she says as though she's walked this route a thousand times. We come to a long line of doors, each with a number written on it. "We're looking for number thirteen."

"Coincidence?" My number for England and Wearside is thirteen.

She looks at me with a smile and shakes her head. "It's your lucky number, right?"

"Yeah."

"Well, let's see how lucky we get in here." She swipes the card against the keypad, leaning on the handle to open it, then holds her hand out for me, her eyes clouded with lust.

"Fuck." With my hand in her hand, I push her inside the dark room, letting the door slam closed behind us. I crush my lips to hers exactly as I wanted to down on the side of the pitch. Our kiss is hard, it's desperate, it's unrelenting, and fuck do I need more.

With my hands on her arse, I lift her so her legs wrap around my waist. We line up perfectly, so perfect I can feel her warmth through her jeans. I bet when I undo them, I'll find her soaked too.

I'm already hard as a rock, so when I slam her back against the door, she gasps.

"Table," she murmurs against my mouth as I pull her lower lip between my teeth.

I look over my shoulder and see the banquet table in question. Perfect. Crossing the room in long determined strides, I place her onto the table, spreading her thighs apart so I can step between them. "I've missed you, Molly," I say, keeping my voice low in her ear.

Hanging her head back, she arches her back and pushes her breasts into my chest as I tower over her. I kiss her neck, loving the way her goosebumps pucker against the sensitive skin.

"How much?" she asks, wiggling her hips and rubbing herself against my erection straining behind my pants.

I pull her sharply towards me with one hand in her hair and the other on her hip, grinding my cock harder against her. Whimpers of pleasure escape her swollen lips.

"You've consumed every waking thought I've had. And every night, I've pictured your face because it's the only thing that would soothe me enough to sleep. I'd wake up having dreamed of being with you only to be left unsatisfied and alone."

"Jordan," she whispers against my lips, urging me back to her mouth, but I make her wait for it, desperate for her to understand.

"Can you feel how hard I am for you?" I moan as I grind into her again and again, a sheen of sweat gathering on the back of my neck as I restrain myself. "Every fibre of my being hurt without you. Only you can give me relief. Does that explain how much I've missed you?"

"We're together now."

With a hand on my chest, she forces me to stand upright so she can reach between us. Her hands move to my suit pants, unbuttoning them and reaching inside. I let out a tortured groan as she wraps her delicate fist around me, part relief and part desperation for her.

"Stand up and turn around," I order through gritted teeth as I take a step back.

Her eyes stick to mine as she slides off the table and turns slowly, swiping her hair away so I can see the back of my shirt.

Mine.

The word repeats in my head like a chant as I let my eyes roam over her body.

"My name looks like it belongs there," I whisper in her ear as I press against her. "I mean it when I said I want you in nothing but this shirt when I get home."

Taking her hands in mine, I lift them above her head and wrap them around my neck as she rests her head back on my shoulder. Her breathing intensifies when I stroke my hands down her front, across her breasts, over her stomach, and settle at the waistband of her jeans.

"Jordan... please fuck me."

Slowly, I unbutton her jeans, pull down the zip, and slide my hand inside, stroking her over the lace of her underwear.

Fuck.

"You're so wet, Mol," I say as I brush my fingertips across her clit. She squirms against me in an attempt to increase the pressure. "I'm not going to fuck you here because once I feel you around my cock, I won't want to let you go." I pause, bringing my free hand up and around her throat, tilting her head to the side so I can nip at her neck with my teeth. She places her hand over the top of mine, tightening my grip on her, making sure I don't move. She always did like sex on the firmer side.

"But I am going to make you come. Do you think you can be quiet?"

"Yes." Her answer comes out on a sharp inhale of air as I press three fingers against her harder, rubbing her above her underwear.

"Good." I kick her feet apart so her legs spread wider, then dip my fingers beneath her underwear, fluttering my fingers across her, spreading her wetness and toying with her swollen clit, giving her some relief. And keeping her begging for more.

Her hips move involuntarily, increasing speed as I roll her clit in my fingers.

She moans quietly as I tease her entrance, and I drink in all her little sounds.

"I want your jeans off and you back on the table."

She nods. In the darkness of the room, her eyes appear black as she obediently kicks off her shoes and her jeans and climbs onto the table, resting her feet on the arms of two chairs as she lets her thighs drop open.

With the moonlight streaming through the slits in the blinds, she looks completely edible.

We watch as I move aside her poor excuse for a thong and push two fingers into her slowly, feeling her stretching around them. What I would give to feel her gripping my dick like this right now. She lets out a moan before covering her mouth with her hand as I withdraw my fingers and push into her over and over again, adding a third when I know she can take it and pressing my palm against her clit. Her body tightens and clenches against me as I push her closer to the edge with each thrust of my hand. I'm so painfully hard now, my cock throbbing against my pants, the open zip providing friction. I wouldn't be surprised if I came just from watching her come apart.

She whispers obscenities as she struggles to keep quiet the closer she gets to her release.

"I'm so close. Oh fuck."

With my free hand on the back of her neck, I bring her face to mine, kissing her hard and swallowing her moans until I feel her climax hit in tight waves. She spasms against my hand and around my fingers as I continue to draw out her pleasure.

"Jordan, fuck," she whispers, hanging her head back as she continues to clench around me.

Withdrawing my fingers, I drop to my knees in front of her and lap up every drop of her cum until her legs quiver and she can't take it anymore.

"That was… shit… I can't think straight."

I chuckle, moving her underwear back into place before leaning down to pick up her jeans. She takes them from my hand, then rests them on the table next to her and kicks out one of the chairs she was resting her feet on.

"I didn't get to tell you how sexy you look in this suit." She pushes my chest until a chair hits the back of my knees and I fall into it. With a hand on either armrest, she cages me in and leans down to kiss me. "Do you think you can be quiet now?" she asks, nipping at my lip with her teeth the same way I did to her moments ago.

My dick stiffens in my pants setting off a chain reaction of heat across my skin and anticipation deep in my stomach. Holy fuck, I've waited years for this moment, dreamed of it even, so no, I probably won't be able to keep quiet.

"I'm not making any promises."

Her lips pull up into a cheeky smirk as she drops to her knees.

My breath catches in my throat. "*Shit,*" I say, unable to think of any other words or anything other than my need for her. I lift my hips, and she pulls my trousers down to my ankles, my bulging dick straining beneath my black boxer briefs.

Palming at my cock, she looks up at me, fluttering her thick black lashes again, watching my reaction as she grabs the waistband with her fingers and pulls them down, freeing my erection.

"I've spent so many nights dreaming of having you on your knees in front of me, Molly. But I didn't think I'd be lucky enough to have it here."

"You didn't think I'd let you go back in there like this, did you?"

I don't get a chance to answer her before she wraps her fist around me and strokes, watching as a droplet of moisture seeps out onto the tip. She licks the head with the tip of her tongue before following a trail with her tongue down my shaft.

"Fuck," I groan. "You look so fucking good."

I gather her dark hair in my hands, holding it back from her face as she licks her lips so I can watch the moment she takes me into her mouth. Maintaining eye contact, she closes her warm, wet lips around me. Slowly, she takes me into her mouth, her tongue applying pressure down my shaft before coming back up and sucking the head, letting go with a satisfying pop.

I watch her repeat the process as I raise my hips to meet her, unable to stop the carnal grunts coming from me. It's sensory overload, every nerve ending in my body charged and ready to blow as my head falls back and I surrender to her.

My thighs tense as she sucks and licks me, stroking the part of me she can't fit in her mouth. When she moans against me, sending vibrations straight to my core, my toes curl painfully as my breathing stutters.

Fuck, I'm close. I can already feel my release building in my balls, which is only heightened as she cups them in her free hand. I spread my legs wider, giving her the green light for more, something I've only every experienced with her. Lifting my head, I watch as she takes her hand off my balls and dips between her legs, moaning as she makes sure her fingers are nice and wet.

She returns her hand to my balls as she continues to suck me, her cheeks hollowing out. This time, she squeezes my balls tighter as she slides her middle finger against me, massaging my tight hole until I relax enough to take her inside of me.

The sensations hit me all at once. The way her mouth feels sucking me in, the sound of her enthusiastic moans, the way her delicate hand grips the base of me…the added pressure. The fact that it's Molly, *my* Molly, kneeling in front of me as though no time has passed.

"Molly, fuck, I'm going to come."

I feel the tip of my cock hit the warm back of her throat and then she swallows, taking me impossibly deeper as her throat contracts around the head of my cock. My mouth opens and my eyes widen. *Oh God.* This… this is new. I grip her hair tighter as her hand is relentless around the rest of my shaft and her finger slides deeper inside me, triggering a chain reaction along my nervous system.

"*Fuck, Molly,*" I growl, looking down and meeting her eyes, her hair overflowing from my fists. My body tenses, my thighs going rigid as I lift my hips, and I burst into her with no further warning. My moans are loud as I praise her over and over again, thrusting my hips as she bobs her head against me. I don't even think my words make sense, but I couldn't give a fuck.

Her name falls from me in a curse as I let the world know what she does to me, let everyone know that I fucking belong to Molly Davison. My orgasm is so intense I don't think I've felt anything quite like it before in my life. White-hot bolts of electricity continue to surge through my body as I pour everything I have into her. She amazes me as she devours every last drop, not letting up until I'm completely spent, my vision blurred, and I melt into the chair. My arms feel like lead and my thighs protest as I tuck myself away and tug a dazed Molly onto my lap, stroking her face tenderly as she kisses me.

Time means nothing anymore as we float in our post-orgasm bliss sharing lazy kisses and tender touches. The spell only broken when we're illuminated by the artificial light coming from Molly's smart watch.

We both look at the text from Bridget at the same time as a feeling of disappointment washes over us.

Bridget: Car will be here in five minutes.

I let out a sigh as her sad eyes mirror mine in the dim light. It's too soon. "I'm not ready for you to leave."

"I'm not ready either, but in a few more days, you'll be home, and I'll have you all to myself in nothing but this shirt," she promises.

Chapter Twenty-Six

Molly

It's a mild autumn evening and the sun has recently set in the distance as I stand alone on the balcony of the main ballroom at Wearside Stadium. I'm relieved for the light breeze that cools me down from the hectic scenes inside. It's the first moment I've had to reflect on the past twenty-four hours, and standing here, watching the changing trees along the riverside sway in a vast expanse of deep reds, oranges, and greens, I feel as though I can finally organise my thoughts.

These sorts of charity events always drain me. As well as being rewarding in the sense we have raised a lot of money for charities supporting children and young adults across Wearside, there's also a lot of smiling and sucking up to investors, sponsors, and general people of influence. Hence why I've escaped onto the balcony to have a breather.

Although I am very much back in Wearside, my mind is still in Portugal with Jordan, remembering all those little moments we had that built into one explosive finale. I wanted much more with him than we had the chance to have.

And now, due to his media commitments at St George's Park (England's training ground), it'll be another few days until I see him again.

Tonight is particularly hard without him. Every new step I've taken in my coaching journey at Wearside, he's been there supporting me. Even when things were really difficult between us.

The sound of the balcony door opening behind me draws my attention, and for a moment, I think it's Jordan until I meet a set of cold eyes, blurred and unfocused.

"I don't believe we've met." Club chairman, Mike Rodgers, closes the door to the suite behind him and swaggers across to where I stand. The curtains are closed inside and a cold sensation washes over me. No one knows I'm out here other than Bridget, and she's far too busy making sure the communications team are all in the right place to notice Mike's exit.

He grins when he sees my confused look. We might not have met in person yet, but I'm sure he knows who I am. Right?

Mike is in his forties, a newly divorced billionaire, the kind who was born into money and is so far out of touch with not only the fans but the majority of club employees too, so then again, it wouldn't surprise me if he's oblivious to me.

"Molly Davison," I introduce myself politely, not wanting to ruffle my boss's feathers with my attitude.

"Are you here with one of the players, babe?" He sidles up to me far too closely, the smell of alcohol on his breath strong enough I can almost taste it in the air between us.

"I'm sorry?" I ask, taking a step back. My body prickles uncomfortably as his eyes roam across what I would consider a conservative dress. It has a respectable neckline and a hem that ends just above my knees. With him looking at me this way though, I feel far too exposed.

He steps closer to me again, and I take another step back followed by another and another until I can feel the cool railing of the balcony pressing into my lower back. I try not to panic as his smile turns into a sinister smirk. He licks his lips as he focuses on my mouth. Bile fills my throat as he scrutinises me.

He sways, and I realise he really does have no idea who I am.

"I know your type; if you're not here with a player, you must have come looking for one. But why settle for one of the boys when you can have me, the main man." He reaches out to me, but I can't move away. I beg my body for fight or flight, but instead, I'm frozen as a million terrifying things race through my mind at once, and not one of them will help me escape right now.

"Molly Davison is a footballing legend in her own right and we're lucky enough to have her as our assistant coach," a low voice growls from the doorway. My breath rushes out of me and tears spring to my eyes as, finally, Mike steps aside, turning towards our visitor.

"I'm sure she is, but she's also a good–looking woman. I'm surprised one of you hasn't tried to snap her up by now." He speaks to Jordan as though I'm not here, as though he wasn't seconds away from trying to...

Jordan's eyes narrow and his jaw clenches so hard I can hear his teeth grinding.

I slide out of the corner Mike forced me into, hurrying to stand by Jordan's side. He holds out his arm for me, tucking me in so I'm safe.

"Don't do something you'll regret." I place a hand on his chest, firm but gentle.

Mike lets out another sinister laugh. "The coach and the captain. Should have guessed. She's your type—desperate for attention."

"I'm looking out for my coach. She's a part of our team, and make no mistake, we protect each other."

"Jordan, we should go back inside," I say firmly, aware of his anger bubbling in sharp breaths beneath my hand.

He looks down at me tucked under his arm, torment raging behind his eyes.

"Please?" I add in a whisper.

"Don't forget who signs your pay cheque, Robinson." Mike swirls his whisky, the tiny ice cubes clinking against the glass the only sound out here as the weight of his words hit me.

"You might sign my pay cheque, but mark my words, when I'm out on that pitch, I'm not playing for you," Jordan says, keeping his voice low and threatening. He takes my hand firmly in his, keeping a tight hold until we disappear back through the door to the ballroom, where we're faced with a crowd of people, none of whom can know about us.

He reluctantly drops my hand but hovers protectively close as we weave through dining tables full of people enjoying the food and drink on offer. Guests greet him as he passes, and I can see the strain in his expression as he keeps up appearances.

With every step I take deeper into the room and away from the balcony, a small piece of me uncoils until I'm not looking over my shoulder anymore.

"Has that happened before?" Jordan asks once we reach a gap in the crowd on our route back to the table reserved for players, his voice low and harsh as his jaw remains tight, trying not to be overheard.

"It was the first time at Wearside."

The way he grabs my elbow and ushers me to a quiet spot along one of the walls tells me that was the wrong thing to say when he's already feeling so on edge.

"Jordan, calm down. People are watching us." I glance to the side as a group of women I don't recognise quickly turn away.

"You need to do something about it, Molly. Tell someone."

"It's nothing new. Me saying something will only make people look at me differently. Just drop it, please."

We engage in a silent stand-off.

"Molly—"

"Just drop it. *Please.*"

"I don't want you alone with him again, please promise me that."

"I promise, I'll be careful."

He nods reluctantly and continues our walk across the room, but his body is still too tense.

"Are you going to explain what you're doing here when you have a full weekend of press appearances in Staffordshire?" I ask, trying to change the subject.

"I asked them to squeeze it all in so I could come home. I needed to see you. I would have been here earlier, but Aaron forgot his phone charger at the training ground and we missed our original train." His jaw clenches again. "I should have been here earlier, then that wouldn't have happened."

Looking at him, I take in his stiff posture and gently place my hand on his back in an attempt to calm him lingering a little longer that would be deemed appropriate between player and coach. "This protective alpha stuff you've got going on right now is really working for me."

"I'll bear that in mind when we leave."

Once we make it through the thick of the crowd, our table, placed closest to the stage, is now full. Sam and Aaron have joined Bailey, Keiran, Brooke, Bridget, Natasha, and Luke. They've pulled chairs together and squashed them around the too-small table to make sure we all fit.

"You're all here?" I ask, once we reach them, grinning at them in disbelief. Brooke moves along to sit on Aaron's lap to make room for me and Jordan to take the two spare seats.

"We missed you," Aaron says. "Some more than others apparently," he adds, nodding at Jordan. Clearly, he's figured it out. I can't remember keeping our relationship secret being as hard as this last time.

Bailey looks between us, his eyes wide with shock as he pieces it together. "Are you two fucking?"

Jordan thumps him on the arm harder than he would normally, his anger still seemingly just below the surface. "Shit, I'm—"

"Sorry, that was disrespectful," Bailey cuts in, apparently not even noticing the extra strength to the thump.

"I mean, it's a valid question," O'Leary adds.

Jordan looks at me, handing me the reins of this conversation, and I shrug in response. They've already figured it out anyway. He nods, concluding our silent conversation.

"Listen," I say, lowering my voice and leaning in closer. "If we tell you what's going on, we need you to promise it won't go further than this table."

A chorus of promises echo back at us.

"This isn't a new thing. Well, it sort of is but isn't at the same time," Jordan begins.

"We were involved a few years back. We had a long-distance relationship while I was playing in London, but it didn't work out…"

"We got back together a couple of weeks ago, and this time, it is working out," Jordan finishes for me, unable to stop the smile from lifting his lips.

"So, it's serious, then?" Bailey asks, clearly feeling bad about the "fucking" comment.

"Yeah, it is," Jordan says without taking his eyes off me. "She's my one."

Chapter Twenty-Seven

Molly

I carefully slip off my heels, letting the cool tiles of the hallway soothe my aching feet as Jordan locks his front door behind us. The drive from the stadium to here only took half an hour along the quiet streets. Not long after we came clean to our friends, the ballroom lights dimmed and the dance floor opened, where Aaron and Brooke took it upon themselves to teach the rest of us their "moves". It started with the shopping trolley and the sprinkler, but when Aaron busted out the worm and almost shattered both his knees, we decided it was probably time to call it a night.

"I bet the ladies loved this place," I say, looking around, taking in the hallway's warm, welcoming, and homely feel for the second time. As soon as the words are out of my mouth, I regret them. I really don't want to picture him bringing those girls back here and taking them to his bedroom.

He turns to me, his eyebrows knitting together. "I've never brought anyone back here."

I snort out a laugh. "Yeah, okay, then." I mean, that would be nice and all, but realistically, what are the chances?

"No, really." He takes both of my hands in his and looks deep into my eyes. "I bought this house for us, Molly."

"What do you mean you bought this for us? You've lived here…"

I remember when Brooke helped them all move in. It was entertaining to hear how she stepped in to take charge of Aaron and Bailey. She didn't mention Jordan much, aside from telling me he moved in, too. I guess she knew I couldn't handle it.

You've lived here for three years.

"Oh."

"Sam came to us all about two months before your accident. He told us that his uncle had developed this old patch of farmland into five houses and that we had first dibs if we wanted to buy them. Me, Bailey, Aaron, Kieran, and Sam all bought a house each. I didn't tell you at the time because we hadn't really talked about what our future looked like together even though I knew I saw you in mine."

"I can't believe you did that, and then I messed every—"

He stops me abruptly with a soft kiss. "It felt wrong bringing someone here that wasn't you. I mean, I would have eventually, of course, but only once I found someone I considered an actual future with. But… that didn't happen. No one compared. This was where we were supposed to come home after a long day of work to sit together in a hot tub in the back garden and make love under the stars. This house was where I pictured us raising our children, where I imagined we'd teach them to ride their bikes in the paved courtyard out front and play football on the grass in the back garden. It's where I saw us growing old together."

"Do you still want that?" I ask hopefully. "The hot tub? The family? The growing old together?"

"I'll always want that with you." There's a genuine sincerity in his voice, as though he's opening up all of his vulnerabilities and spreading them out on a table for me to see. I don't have a doubt in my mind that I love this man beyond anything else in my life, and I want that too, with him.

"I love you, Jordan." My heart pounds in my chest as I say the words out loud. I loved him back then and I love him impossibly more now.

He grins as the words register, then he kisses me again, long and slow, pouring his heart into it.

"I've been in love with you since the moment we met," he says against my lips as we break apart for air.

"Take me to bed."

He lifts and carries me effortlessly up the grand staircase and to his bedroom, stopping only when we reach the foot of the super-king-sized bed. The streetlamp in the courtyard outside his home illuminates us in an orange glow.

He sits me gently on the edge before dropping to his knees in front of me.

That's when I see it over his shoulder almost hidden in the shadows. My match worn shirt, complete with grass stains and mud from that horrific day, expertly framed and hanging on his bedroom wall.

My mouth hangs open and he follows my gaze.

"You really do own it," I say. "Four hundred thousand that went for at auction. And you bought it?"

"Yeah," is all he says, his hands resting on my hips as he sits on his heels.

"Why?"

"I heard a rumour it was going up for auction after you officially announced you wouldn't be returning to football. I understand why you gave it up in the moment, but I couldn't bear the thought of someone else owning it other than you so I tracked it down at the auction house and refused to back down. I told myself that one day, if you wanted it, I'd make sure I got it back to you." He mistakes my shock for something different. "I'm sorry if I over stepped."

"There wasn't a day that went by that I didn't regret giving up that shirt." My voice is barely above a whisper as I meet his eyes. "And all along it was here, safe with you, exactly where I belong."

"Maybe we can hang mine up next to it one day." And I nod, emotion clogging my throat, because that sounds perfect. I take his face in my hands kissing him in the hopes it will convey my appreciation when words fail me.

Pulling back, I watch him as he carefully lifts my right foot to rest on his shoulder. He places a gentle kiss on my inner ankle followed by a line of kisses up my calf and across the scar that stretches down over my knee. He lingers a little as he brushes his fingers over the purple and silver mark before continuing up my inner thigh where my dress has ridden up.

"Lie back, Molly." In the bedroom, Jordan has been known to be commanding, but right now, his words are spoken softly. Tonight is about us coming together again in a connection of mind, body, and soul.

I do as he asks, propping myself up on my elbows as I continue to watch as he takes his time, paying attention to the sensitive skin leading to where I want him most.

With his palm, he rubs the inside of my opposite thigh, and as he does, he spreads my legs wider, opening me up to him with an appreciative moan from deep in his chest. His sensual kisses down the seam of my underwear heighten my arousal that has been building all night. It's intensified when he flattens his tongue right above my clit, his breath spreading warmth throughout me.

There is no need for words as he works off my underwear, planting a kiss against the sensitive flesh between my legs. When I spread my legs further, he grins at me wickedly as he strokes his finger slowly over every sensitive nerve ending I possess, sending sparks flying across my body.

Resting my head back on the soft duvet, I revel in his breathless appreciation.

"Oh, God," I say on a whispered sigh as he returns his mouth to me in leisurely licks, alternating between twirling his tongue around my clit and long soft licks from my arse all the way back to my clit and back again. He gradually increases in pressure each time.

"Oh, fuck. Yes," I cry out in pleasure, writhing against his face, the sounds of my wetness mixing with his grunts of satisfaction.

Jordan has always had a way with my body, knowing exactly what I need in order to feel pleasure. He licks me, sucks me and toys with me so expertly I can barely see straight and he hasn't even been inside me yet.

Reaching up, he palms my breast before dragging the pad of his thumb over my nipple, tweaking and tugging along with the rhythm his mouth provides before swapping sides. It's more than enough to have me hurtling towards my release. When I think I can't take any more stimulation than this, he brings a finger to my opening, testing my readiness, finding me super ready for him. He pushes his middle two fingers into me with ease, curling them inside of me as I grip onto anything within reach, the bed quilt, his hair. I tug hard.

"*Jordan*," I moan louder as my back arches from the bed.

He holds them there against my most sensitive spot as he sucks my clit into his mouth, rolling it between his lips before letting go again.

"Jordan, I need you. I can't wait any longer. Please."

His eyes are dark as he looks up at me, his pupils dilated with his own tortured arousal. It's apparent in his dress pants as he stands too, straining against his zip.

Holding out his hand for me, he helps me to my feet. Every brush of his hand leaves a trail of fire across my skin as he unzips my dress, letting it fall to the floor at my feet. His eyes take me in greedily—I guess he didn't realise I wasn't wearing a bra. He's patient as he waits for me to undo his shirt button by button, pushing it off his shoulders as I take in his firm chest, feeling each ridge of muscle with my fingers as I move south to his belt buckle, undoing it with a clink so I can push his pants down, where he sweeps our clothes to the side with his foot.

He watches me carefully before he brings his hands to my shoulders, running his thumbs down the column of my throat before following a path down my arms, grazing his thumbs over my breasts.

I know my body is different since we last had sex—my muscles aren't as defined and my stomach is softer—but he looks at me as if I'm the most beautiful woman he's ever seen.

"You're so beautiful, Molly," he says as if he can read my mind, sliding his palms down my waist and over my hips, picking me up again and lying me on his bed on my back. "I can't believe you're mine," he adds as he crawls over me, caging me in with his arms on either side of my head.

We kiss as our bodies brush against each other, his taut muscles flexing beneath my hands, the thick head of his dick rubbing against my clit as we seek that connection. We barely break apart as he leans over to the bedside table to pull out a condom. He lets me take it from him, and I rip the foil packet before taking the condom out and sliding it over his straining erection as he moans my name, anticipation hanging in the air as our heartbeats thrum in a steady rhythm.

Our tongues dance as he enters me, stretching me inch by inch as my body remembers how to accommodate him. It's an intimate kind of pleasure, one that we draw out as we get reacquainted, in no rush to finish. His movements are slow and purposeful, because he knows I need the roll of his hips to ease him all the way in.

He caresses my body, moving from my hips to my breasts until he reaches my jaw, angling my face and kissing me deeper.

We had a lot of sex the first time around, hard and wild at times and we made love too. But this is something more, something deeper. It's the beginning of our second chance.

"Molly, fuck. I've missed this," he tells me as he stills inside of me, taking a shaky breath and dropping his forehead to mine. I revel in the familiar feeling of having him bury himself deep inside of me. "You feel so good."

My fingers dig into his back muscles so hard I know I'll leave crescent shapes from my nails as I urge him closer. He pulls out slowly and thrusts back in with a curl of his hips, moving a little faster each time until he finds a rhythm that drives us both wild. Sounds of our bodies crashing together and carnal moans fill the room as instinct takes over and our bodies act on impulse and desire, leaving a thin sheen of sweat across our skin.

"Yes, Mol. Fuck," he encourages me as I draw my nails harder down his back. "Mark me."

I cry as he takes a nipple between his thumb and forefinger, toying with it before his lips seal around it, adding to the inferno spreading through my body.

"Are you close, babe?"

"*Yes*," I cry breathlessly, arching my back, urging him deeper.

He switches position so he's sitting on his heels, angling my hips upwards so his dick reaches impossibly deep inside of me. His fingers bite into my flesh as he holds me in place, driving into me and pushing me over the edge. I may have physically marked him tonight, but this will leave a mark on my soul forever.

"*Jordan*," flies from my lips like an expletive when my orgasm slams into me.

Stars burst behind my closed lids as I combust, clenching and spasming around him until he stills deep inside of me and roars with his own climax. With heavy grunts, he continues to empty himself until we're both completely spent, collapsing onto his bed next to me. He looks so perfect, the light from outside reflecting in the sheen of sweat across his body.

"I love you, Molly." His voice is thick with satisfaction as we turn on our sides to face each other.

"I love you too." My voice is thick with emotion as tears prick my eyes. I do my best to keep them in, but the waves keep coming, washing over me as I realise exactly what I let go of for so long.

"What's wrong?" He strokes my damp hair from my face, tossing the long strands over my shoulder so he can see me.

"I'm so sorry I took this away from us," I tell him, giving in to the tears. "If I regret one thing in my life, it's that I broke us."

"Molly, please don't get upset." He gently wipes the side of my face with his thumb just before the tears hit the quilt. "Shit."

He envelops me in his strong arms. In the safety of his presence, the floodgates open.

"What if I mess it up again?" I ask with a sniffle.

"We're stronger now. We won't mess it up this time, I promise."

Chapter Twenty-Eight

Molly

"Hey," I say as Jordan walks into the media room. His eyes light up when they meet mine, and I get a little flutter in my chest at the sight of him. It's sickening how far gone I am for him already.

The two weeks since the fundraiser have been a whirlwind for us. It's not easy sneaking around to spend time with each other, and I'm pretty sure we aren't as discreet as we think we are, but when we are together, it's worth the hard work.

"Hey, Mol." He flashes me a charming smile as he looks around the area, confirming we're alone before kissing me until my brain melts.

The media room at Wearside is one of the most high-tech media rooms in English football. Built in an auditorium style, there are rows and rows of seats that face a long stage—where we set up our press conference tables—and a large split-screen OLED TV monitor. That's what makes this place ideal for pre- and post-match analysis.

It's crazy that there's no CCTV in here considering all this high-tech equipment, but lucky for us because I get to have a hot make-out session with my boyfriend in the middle of my work day.

When he slides his hand down over my bum, pulling me closer, I let out a soft satisfied moan, only pulling back from our kiss when I hear footsteps approaching.

"Be careful; I can hear the others coming down the corridor." I place a hand softly on his chest, but I'm not ready to step out of his embrace even though the boisterous sounds of the team draw in closer. He must feel the same, as he continues to stroke my sides.

"I can't help myself."

I tear myself away just in time for the first players to cross the threshold and appear at the top stair of the auditorium. Although Aaron, Bailey, and Kieran know about us, the others don't, and we need to keep it that way.

"No, yeah, that's a really good point. Thanks," he says as our friends reach the bottom step.

"Smooth cover," Aaron says under his breath, squeezing through the small gap between Jordan and me.

Jordan casually slides into a seat in the front row after Kieran, Bailey, and Aaron as if nothing was going on. My heart is still beating a mile a minute.

Chatter continues as the entire squad files in one by one, finding their usual seats. Footballers are creatures of habit, and at this point in the season, I generally know what seat they're going to be sitting in.

"Are you ready to start?" I address the lads from the front of the auditorium when everyone has taken their seats.

"Go for it, Coach," Jordan says with a smile I know is about to be wiped off his face. I press the button on the projector remote, bringing the screen to life.

Jordan recognises the footage immediately, and his face hardens in annoyance.

"Pottsbark United, last season," I confirm to the mumblings around the room.

"Jonny Stephenson, what a fucking prick," Bailey says, mirroring Jordan's anger. "Might as well have been Pottsbark's twelfth man."

"Yeah, but even having him onside couldn't save them from relegation, and we get to face them again," Aaron says.

"I've got some news for you all. Jonny Stephenson is the referee on Saturday too."

The room, as expected, erupts into protests and groans.

"Okay," I say loudly to be heard over the grumbling. "Settle down, please."

"I don't like it, Molly." Jordan shakes his head. "I don't fucking like it one bit. He's a sexist pig; he's going to take one look at you and go in for the kill."

"We'll cross that bridge if we come to it. What we need to focus on is making sure you give him no reason to turn against you." I press play. "Watch closely." A few seconds into the play, I pause again.

"This here," I say, pointing at a section of the frame where Jordan stands close to another player. "This definitely wasn't a yellow card. He should have given a verbal warning at the most. Yes, your hand was in the wrong position, but you didn't intentionally hit the player and that's obvious. I want everyone to make sure your physical awareness is on point, okay?"

I press play once more, and Aaron slinks down in his chair, as he knows what's coming next.

"Aaron, this was just fucking stupid, don't do it," I say, referring to a risky tackle that resulted in the second yellow card awarded that game. "Just because you won the ball doesn't make it acceptable."

I don't give them chance to grumble too much before pressing play again.

"Now, watch this." I point to a play. "That footwork was incredible, Ash, but can anyone tell me what was wrong with the play?"

"No one was there for me to pass to," Ash says from the back row of the group.

"Exactly. Guys, you need to pick a player and stick to him like glue, okay? Ash had three players on him; there was no way he was getting out of that challenge with a ball. He needed someone to pass to, but no one was waiting in that big open space. That can't happen."

We continue analysing the game longer than we usually would, but it's important we cover everything; this referee is unpredictable, and as much as I don't want to admit it, this is the first time this season I've felt uneasy in our own ground.

"Tomorrow, we need to go out there and show Jonny Twatting Stephenson that we are worthy of a win, and we won't need to play dirty to get it," I say, doing my best to seem confident. "Anyone got any questions?"

"Can we talk about the stuff he's said about you lately?" Kieran asks. "Are you okay facing him?"

I look around the room and see the same concerned look etched onto all their faces, most of all Jordan's.

Jonny Stephenson is another one who hasn't held back in the media when it comes to me coaching. Although, as a referee, he should be unbiased, and yet, he's out there shouting his mouth off. It wouldn't surprise me if he and Mike founded a hate club against me.

"Don't worry about me; I can handle Jonny Stephenson."

Chapter Twenty-Nine

Molly

Ron Michaels, Pottsbark's largest defender, charges straight into Jordan with deliberate force, sending him crashing to the ground and skidding across the grass. I'm on my feet and at the touchline within seconds, ready for war. It's not the first time this game Pottsbark players have gotten physical with my players.

"What the fuck was that, ref?" I shout, throwing my arms in the air, but Jonny Stephenson signals the game to play on as Jordan clambers onto all fours, inhaling deeply and trying to catch his breath.

"That should have been a red card," I yell, but Jonny keeps his back to me and ignores despite the fact I know he can hear me.

I'm not the only one who reacts, everyone in the dugout is on their feet.

"What on earth was that?" Joey shouts.

"We fucking knew this would happen," Tom, one of the junior physios throws his arms up before gathering his supplies, preparing to go on if Jordan doesn't get up in the next few seconds.

The unintelligible roar of noise from the stands is deafening as obscenities rain down on the ref and only then does he blow his whistle, stomping over to check on Jordan.

"Coach, he needs a medic," I say impatiently, my eyes glued to Jordan as I will him to get up and be okay.

"Go on," Dad confirms, and the medics make their way onto the pitch. Dad is stressed—he's made his way through an entire packet of chewing gum on the touchline and it's not even half-time.

I pace the sideline, anger building in my chest as I watch Jonny stand above Jordan, arms folded and constantly huffing impatiently, clearly not bothered that he's hurt or bothered about how he ended up hurt.

"Why isn't he doing anything? *Are you fucking blind?*" I yell my second question louder and aim it at Jonny Stephenson, whose behaviour all game has been questionable. "You can't ignore that foul."

I should be relieved when Jordan finally rises to his feet and joins the medics at the touchline as he attempts to walk off the impact of the foul, massaging his sternum as he looks to the sky, but the relief is second to my anger.

"I *said,* are you fucking blind?" I shout louder, gaining Jonny's attention.

"*Molly,*" Dad warns me, but I'm blinded by rage.

Jonny steps closer until he's looming over me, his face twisted in annoyance. "What's your problem?"

I meet his challenge willingly, refusing to let him intimidate me with his size. "That was clearly a red card, and you let him play on without allowing us to check on the welfare of our player." I square my shoulders and stand taller.

"Your player did nothing more than dive. Now, pipe down," he snarls.

Dad pulls me back by my arm and steps between us, sensing I'm about to lose it.

"He was winded because that moron body-checked him with so much force I felt it from all the way over here. He needs a red card. Do your fucking job."

"Calm down and take a seat, sweetheart," he says, turning away and dismissing me. "Let me do my job. I actually know what I'm talking about."

"What did you call her?" Jordan says, his voice dangerously low as he comes out of nowhere and squares up to Jonny.

"Back off, Robinson. That's your last warning. I should have given you a yellow for the dive, but I let you off."

"He didn't dive, you fucking prick," I yell.

"Walk away, Molly. We'll deal with it later." Dad dismisses me with a flick of his head towards my seat in the dugout.

"For fuck's sake." I throw my hands in the air again as I turn my back on Dad, Jonny, and Jordan.

The sharp blast of a whistle cuts through the air. I spin around just in time to see Jonny Twatting Stephenson pull a red card out of his pocket, but instead of showing it to the defender, he points it at me.

He has got to be kidding me.

"No fucking way," Jordan shouts.

"You absolute prick." I try to take a few deep breaths to control myself, but the red is too consuming. My hands turn into fists and I start storming towards Jonny. "Bellend. Arsehole. Scum—"

"*Molly.*" Dad grabs my arms and holds me in place as I try to thrash out of his grasp.

"*Get off me,*" I scream, pulling forward with my entire body weight.

Jordan steps even closer to Jonny, their foreheads nearly touching. I can't hear what he's saying, but he's literally spitting venom.

Aaron grabs Bailey by the wrist and quickly pulls him to Jordan, where they each flank him with a strong hand on his chest, holding him back.

"Can we talk about this?" Bailey's voice is calm, and I can't work out whether he's talking to Jordan or Jonny.

"There is nothing to talk about; my decision is final." Not making eye contact with any of us, Jonny focuses on writing in his little black notepad before sliding it into his top pocket.

"Burn in fucking hell, you arsehole," I scream.

"You can't do that," Jordan argues.

"I'm warning you one last time, Robinson. You'll walk away if you know what's good for you. And you"—he points to me—"get to the stands so the big boys can play on."

I turn to Dad, seeing if he's going to let him speak to me like this or if he'll loosen his grip to at least let me stand up for myself, but his grip remains strong, although he clenches his jaw tightly, biting back his words as he stares down his nose at the referee.

Jordan shakes his head and laughs with disbelief. "You're a joke."

"You think so?" Jonny laughs and pulls out a yellow card, presenting it to Jordan. "Now you're on your last chance," he snarls.

Aaron steps between Jordan and Jonny, facing Jordan. "She'll be fine." His voice is commanding, forcing Jordan to look at him. "Get your head straight and let's get this game over with. You'll only regret it."

Jordan's chest is heaving as he backs onto the pitch, torn between finishing the game and defending me further, but in the end, he lets out a huff of frustration and jogs back into position.

I'm seething as I walk down the tunnel and through the concrete warren of corridors until I find the closest exit to the stands, hoping there will be a spare seat for me.

Another wall of sound hits me as I walk out, freezing me in my place. I glance around stunned.

"Davo, Davo, Davo," the crowd chants for me.

"There are some seats down the bottom." I turn to see a steward dressed in a yellow high-vis jacket with a radio on his hip. "I can watch you from here."

"Thanks," I say, following the path he sends me on.

With every step I take, encouraging hands reach out for me. Some pat me on the back and others grip mine in firm handshakes.

"Are those seats free?" I ask a man at the end of a row. Despite it being mid-December, he wears a black hoody and no coat, as though the cold doesn't touch him. "Would you mind if I sit with you?"

"Of course, love. Take a seat. I'm Alan, and this is my wife, Lisa."

"Thank you, I'm Molly. It's lovely to meet you."

I slip past the couple to the empty seat and sit down, greeting the fans nearby. That's when the entire stand begins to sing in unison.

"And she's Molly Davo, Molly Davison, she's by far the greatest coach the world has ever seen… The referee's a wanker…"

I look around, my eyes wide in amazement as laughter bursts out of me.

"They're not wrong, pet," Lisa tells me, noting my wide-eyed gaze. "Don't let Jonny Stephenson make you feel otherwise."

Chapter Thirty

Molly

My head hangs low as I walk into the dressing room at half-time, refusing to make eye contact with the team sitting on the benches as I take my spot next to Dad. The silence is deafening and disappointment hangs heavy in the air. I can feel all eyes on me. Now that the adrenaline has worn off, I've never felt more ashamed in all my life, and the sinking feeling in my gut is a reminder of everyone I've let down today.

Ignoring the massive elephant in the room, Dad begins his half-time analysis by scribbling on the whiteboard and moving magnetic markers to explain potential plays. I nod along, but I don't pay attention to a single word that leaves his mouth.

"Before we go back out there," he says, and my ears prick up, "I wanted to tell you I've already instructed our lawyers to file an official complaint against Jonny Stephenson. I need you all to play clean going forward."

"You're filing a complaint?" I ask.

"Yeah, we are," Jordan says before Dad can answer. "He's made some biased decisions against us today, letting some disgusting behaviour slide and making bigoted comments about our assistant coach. You're a big part of our team, Molly, and he disrespected you."

There's anger in his voice, but also a protective determination echoed by the team when they murmur their agreement.

Tears prick my eyes and a lump forms in my throat as I finally look around the room at my dysfunctional, sometimes crazy, but always loving family. Having not had this kind of support for three years, their camaraderie takes me by surprise. I've missed being part of a team.

"Thank you," I say quietly to the room, hoping the emotion in my voice gets the message across.

"Molly and Jordan, I need to speak to you both in private. The rest of you can go wait in the tunnel," Dad says, cutting through the thick atmosphere.

Jordan and I exchange worried glances as we wait for the room to clear out until the three of us remain. Are we busted? Was our behaviour out there too obvious? Has he heard rumours?

"Chin up, Molly," Aaron says as he passes me before leaving the room.

Kieran pats my shoulder with his gloved hand, and Bailey gives me one of his famous dad hugs.

Dad stands there silently until all the players have left the room, then turns to me and Jordan.

"Listen, what happened on that pitch was completely out of order, and initially, that was no red card for you. A yellow? Absolutely. But, Molly, your reaction to getting a red card was disappointing, and yes, you deserved to be sent to the stands for that." He scrubs a hand over his face. "What on Earth has gotten into you both?"

I can feel Jordan watching me carefully, ready to take my lead as soon as I give him direction, but Dad continues.

"It won't help our case if you're mouthing off, giving him a reason to punish you, Molly."

I feel like a kid again being told off. "Jordan could have been seriously hurt with that tackle. He has half a season left, and I wasn't going to let that slide, Dad. Not after..." I let my words trail off, not wanting to bring up my accident.

If I'm truly honest with myself, I know I wouldn't have had the same reaction if it was anyone else on the receiving end of that tackle. Sure, I would have been concerned and mad, but no way would I have gone off like that. I would have approached the situation calmly, just like Dad did, and if that didn't work, I would have filed the appropriate complaint with the club and the FA.

"The guy needed to hear it, Coach. He's a dick and Molly put him in his place."

"We all know he's a nasty piece of work, but today isn't the day to put him in his place. You both need to lead by example." He rakes his hand through his salt-and-pepper hair. "Robinson, don't give him another excuse this match, please. I can't afford to lose you for two games if you get another yellow today."

Sensing this isn't an argument we're going to win today, Jordan rolls his lips through his teeth, biting back whatever it is he wants to say and nods in defeat. "For what it's worth, we're sorry."

"Sorry, Coach," I echo.

"Let's just get this half over with, okay?" Dad sighs, running both hands down his tired face as he groans and walks to the door. "We can sort the rest out later."

I watch as he leaves us behind, his disappointment lingering.

"Babe, it's okay." Jordan's calming voice does little to extinguish the gut-wrenching disappointment I feel in myself, but regardless, I lean into his embrace as he presses a soft kiss to my forehead.

"He's right." I keep my voice low. "This was completely out of character for us; neither of us would have reacted like that before we got together."

There's nothing for him to say—he knows it's true—so instead, he holds me for a long minute, brushing his hand through my hair and kissing my forehead softly.

"You should go. They're waiting for you."

Chapter Thirty-One

Jordan

"Is our girl okay?" Aaron asks as I step in front of him, taking my position in the line.

I shake my head once, not wanting to draw attention to our conversation while the other team is so close. Leaving Molly behind in the dressing room while she's clearly upset felt unnatural, but she's right… we have no other choice.

Aaron lets out a frustrated growl. "What's the plan?"

"We go out there and play every single second for her."

"Got that right," O'Leary agrees from his position ahead of me. The music begins to play, and we jog back out onto the pitch to continue the game. I can feel Jonny's eyes on me as we get into formation, but I ignore him, not giving him the satisfaction of knowing he's bothering me. Instead, I jump on the spot, pulling my knees up to my chest before stretching out my neck and tilting my head side to side. Every muscle in my body is coiled up tight, and that's how players end up hurt.

And I can't afford to get hurt, because I need to do this for Molly.

The whistle blows and we start the second half strong, working hard to keep possession. Our passion and determination to win have been reinvigorated. Each of us in this team wants to prove we can still win even when the match officials are actively working against us.

Aaron, Bailey, and I work hard, pushing forward towards the goal, and it's not long until Bailey delivers a perfect cross. I strike the ball hard, hitting it with the inside of my foot, not giving the goalkeeper time to react. It hits the back of the net with a familiar *swoosh*.

The stadium erupts into cheers as I take off running across the pitch to the nearest corner. My heart is pounding so hard I can hear it in my ears as I slide on my knees, my arms spread wide and almost taking out the corner flag. I've scored some amazing goals in my career, and although technically this wasn't the best, it was by far one of the top goals I've ever scored in my book.

It's not hard to spot Molly—she's right in front of me, grinning wildly, jumping up and down with her hands in the air as she cheers. Seconds later, the crowd disappears, replaced by darkness as my teammates pull me to my feet and envelop me in a group huddle. We've equalised at least, putting us in a better position than we were at half-time, but we're nowhere near clear from danger.

Keen to get another goal in quickly, play continues and we take possession. We take off, Aaron on my right as we push forward. Defenders converge on Bailey so he passes the ball back to Ash who quickly passes to Aaron. The ball lands perfectly at his feet and he takes off, sprinting with the ball up the line. I follow his lead, getting into position in the box even if he is faster than me.

"Yes," I call out to Aaron, holding my right arm out indicating where I want the ball.

Without looking, he swings his leg back to kick the ball, but instead of connecting with the ball at the right angle and sending it my way, a defender's boot connects with his ankle and the ball rolls off being intercepted by another of their players.

"Ow, fuck." Aaron takes a tumble clutching at his ankle.

Like earlier, the ref ignores the blatant foul, and continues play despite Aaron appearing badly hurt on the ground.

"What the fuck?" I yell towards Jonny as I jog over to Aaron to help him up. He sits with his arms crossed over his propped-up knees, his head bowed for a second before taking my outstretched hand and hauling himself to his feet. He limps as he tries to walk it off.

On the sidelines, our team medics are poised to run on yet again, medical bags in hand.

"Play on," Jonny says, although we all know it's the wrong call.

"You're fucking insane," I say, gesturing in disbelief to Aaron.

Jonny turns and approaches me. "Wanna try that again, Robinson?"

"That was a foul at the very least. A second earlier or a few millimetres either side, he would have snapped Milburn's legs."

"What is it with you lot thinking you know this game better than me?"

"I clearly do; you're useless, mate."

"Skip, drop it," Aaron warns.

"One more chance and then you'll be up with your girlfriend in the stands." His voice is venomous. Heat creeps up my neck and all I can think of is how good it would feel to smash my balled-up fist into his face.

"Leave Molly out of this," I snarl through gritted teeth.

Stay calm. Whatever you do, stay fucking calm.

"They let a woman in here and the entire team turns into little girls."

I close the distance between us quickly, my movements fuelled by the burning fire rushing through my veins, my ragged breathing nothing to do with exertion. I'm taller than he is by a good few inches, and broader too. If I could be certain there would be no consequences, I know it would feel so fucking good to teach him a lesson.

"She has more right to be here than you do."

"We all know she only got the job because of her daddy. Spoiled fucking princess needs to stick to what she's good at—wrapping you around her little finger. Jesus, she must give good head."

His statement makes me feel sick to my stomach. Everyone at Wearside knows Molly's story, they know she got her job based on merit and hard work. The fans know this, other clubs know this. So why is this such a problem for him?

Because she's a woman? He'd never say that do a man.

He has no fucking excuse for his sexist remarks and I won't stand back and let him tarnish her name like that.

Both of my hands connect hard with Jonny's chest, my entire weight behind them, sending him flying backwards onto the grass. I stand over him, breathing heavily, the shove somehow feeling not enough in comparison to what I want to do to him. He pushes himself into a sitting position on the grass and looks up at me.

Why is he smiling?

Slowly, he stands from the ground and brushes himself off.

And then it dawns on me, and all the blood drains from my face. He was playing a game and I took the fucking bait.

"You're done, lad." He smirks as he pulls out a red card. "*Off.*"

Fuck.

"You…" But there's no point. Shaking out my clenched fists, I stalk back towards the sidelines.

"What the fuck?" Bailey reaches for my arm, but I shrug him off. I don't need to hear it. I don't want to hear it. I should have known that prick was goading me; I should have known better than to react.

"What the fuck was that, Robinson?" Coach snaps at me.

I ignore him, passing my captain's armband to Aaron and letting him tell Coach what was said out there because there's no way I'm repeating it. Without stopping to acknowledge the fans, I reach the mouth of the tunnel.

"*Fuck,*" I scream, taking my rage out on anything that stands in my way—the double doors leading into the stadium that I send careening into a wall, a plastic bottle abandoned on a random side table that is swiped to the side.

And then I see her standing in front of the dressing room, waiting for me, and everything goes numb.

"Let's go inside." She holds the door open for me, and I slide past her, my head hanging low in shame. "No one, and I mean no one, comes in here until I say so," she adds to the security guards who wait outside the door. "Not even my dad."

"Got it," a guard says, and she follows me inside the dressing room, allowing the door to close behind her.

I pick up another water bottle from a table, drain it, close the lid, and launch it into the closest wall as hard as I can.

Tentatively, Molly approaches me, her eyebrows knitted together. I can't blame her for being cautious—I just attacked a match official in front of thousands of people and put a dent in a wall with a water bottle.

Her warm hand takes mine, and she inspects my red knuckles.

"I'm sorry, Molly."

"Sit down and tell me what happened."

I sit on the bench at my locker as she kneels in front of me, placing her hands on my knees comfortingly. I tell her play-by-play exactly what was said, refusing to meet her gaze, instead concentrating on removing my boots and shin pads until I'm barefoot and have no other distractions.

"I couldn't let him talk about you like that, Mol. I hate that the thought entered his mind. I hate that he said it in front of everyone on the pitch."

I stand and pace the room, all the nervous energy I've been suppressing bubbling over the surface. I follow the motions, stripping off and tossing my kit into the laundry cart. Molly doesn't speak as she watches me.

When I walk into the showers, she follows me, sitting on a low wall as I attempt to wash away the match, replaying everything he said to me out there and wishing I could have done more. As the hot water soothes my muscles, I start to feel the tension leaving my shoulders until I can finally look at her.

Leaning past me, she shuts off the water and hands me a towel that I tie around my waist.

"Are you mad at me?"

"Tell me to take off my jacket," she says, ignoring my question.

My brow furrows. "Take off your jacket?" I say, but it comes out more like a question than an instruction.

She steps back as she unzips her training jacket and turns to hang it on a peg.

My eyes linger on her shirt. A Wearside shirt with my name on it. It was one thing for her to wear my England shirt, but here, it would be obvious that there's something more going on between us.

She turns back to face me, smiling as she watches the thoughts flit through my mind.

It kills me that we have to keep us a secret; I hate that I can't walk out of here holding her hand, that I can't take her on a date that isn't a clandestine meeting in one of our homes.

But she's proudly wearing that shirt here today despite everything.

"You're wearing my shirt?" It's all I can manage to say, because just like her gesture, I can't replicate the feeling of wholeness, of warmth, of love into words.

She nods. "This is the shirt you wore when we played away at Wessington AFC. It was the first time I coached you in a match. I took it when no one was looking, and I've worn it every single game since beneath my jacket. I'm your biggest supporter, Jordan. I'd fight for you just as you did for me today and back in Wessington if I had to. So, no, I'm not mad. I'm just sad it got to this point."

I take a step closer to her, reaching out for her hand.

She's worn that jacket every single home game. Even back in the summer when we had a heatwave. I thought maybe the jacket was her lucky charm. But all this time, it was my shirt.

"That day," she says, running her fingertips through the beads of water that run down my neck and over my collarbones, "you told me you care for me, that you still have feelings for me."

"I meant it."

"I wanted you so bad, Jordan," she says in a whisper against my lips. "Every night after that, before I fell asleep, I'd imagine what would have happened if I had given in that day. I'd fantasise about what you would have done to me in that little office." She bites her lower lip and lets it go as I stroke my hands down her waist, walking her back until she hits the wall.

"Is that all you did? Fantasise?"

Her eyes shine with building arousal as she remembers. "No," she breathes. "I'd close my eyes and imagine it was you touching me. In my mind, I would remember all the filthy things you used to say to me, I'd remember the way you made my body feel, how you fit every part of me just right. I'd remember how you sounded and the marks you'd leave behind. It was the only way I could find a sliver of relief from the ache that consumed me."

The towel wrapped around my waist is doing nothing to hide my straining erection, and her eyes drop to it hungrily. "I was close to losing my mind in that little office with you. I was desperate. I wanted to fuck you over that desk until you relented and told me you care about me too."

Molly brings her lips to mine in a soft whisper of a kiss. Her eyes glance at the clock on the wall, and mine follow. There are twenty-five minutes left of the game. "Show me what you wanted to do to me. Fuck me here."

The last thread of control I was clinging on to snaps, and I kiss her hard, crushing my mouth to hers as though she holds the air I need to breathe. She gasps at the sudden contact, and I lift her into my arms.

"There are over 46,000 people in this stadium. Odds are one of them will catch us."

"Then be quick," she says, returning her mouth to mine.

Chapter Thirty-Two

Jordan

"The physio room?" she asks as I place her on the bed, lying her back and crawling over her.

"It's kind of poetic, isn't it?" I ask. "At least, I hope it is." As much as I want to fuck her in the showers, it's too much of a risk. At least there's a lock on the door here.

I lean back on my heels, pulling her tracksuit bottoms off, leaving her in nothing but my shirt and her black lace thong.

Fuck, she looks incredible.

She runs her hands down my stomach to the towel knotted around my waist. She bites her lip again as she undoes the knot, letting the towel fall. "Fuck, you're so hot." She's needy and breathless as she wraps her fist around my aching cock, spreading my pre-cum over my tip.

Letting out a soft moan, my chin drops forwards to watch as she starts to slide her hand up and down, slowly, teasing me, the movement stirring up something deep inside my stomach.

"Mol, you're torturing me." I run my knuckle down the centre seam of her underwear, brushing over her clit loving the way a soft gasp falls from her lips.

"Then fuck me."

I lean back on my heels, tilting her hips up and holding her knees over my arms. I need a taste of her before I sink into her.

A groan stirs from deep inside me as realisation hits. "Shit, I don't have any condoms with me."

Her chest heaves as she looks down at our clasped hands and back to me again. "I'm okay with that if you are?"

She isn't on the pill, so her question hits me hard. I know we're both clean, we had the conversation after our first night at her place, but am I okay with the prospect of getting her pregnant?

"I fucking love you, Molly," I tell her as I pull down her thong and toss it on the floor with the rest of our things before spreading her thighs apart.

"I love you too." There's a sharp intake of air as I bring my hands up her thighs, spreading her arousal across her with my thumbs.

My hands keep exploring, caressing her hips, her waist up to her breasts, and finally, I take her wrists and pin them above her head, where they grip the top of the physio bed. I kiss down her body, wasting no time before I take my first taste. When we're at either of our homes, I prefer to savour this moment, using slow, languid licks, but now, we don't have time.

She arches her back as I suck her clit into my mouth, rolling it between my lips and letting go again, loving the way she writhes against my face to meet my movements. She cries out as I push a finger into her followed by a second, taking me easily.

"I need to fuck you," I groan as I wrap my hand around my dick, desperate to take away some of the tension.

"Where do you want me?" she asks, her eyes dark with desire.

"Bend over the bed. I want to see my name on your back as I make you scream it."

I pull her off the bed, and she turns, propping a knee up as she bends forward, opening herself up to me. I stroke my hand down her backside, letting my fingers explore every inch of her as she moans loudly.

It's hot as fuck that someone might hear us. That if they did, there would be no mistaking that this woman belongs to me and I belong to her.

She pushes her hair over her shoulder, letting it fall forwards to reveal my name, worn like a brand on her back.

"Are you ready for me, Mol?"

"Yes, fuck me, Jordan," she begs.

I line myself up to her entrance, pushing in the tip ever so slightly. I've never gone bare with anyone before and she's so tight and wet that I worry it'll be over for me before I get her there. I still, taking a deep breath.

I moan as I push into her, stretching her with every inch until I'm buried deep inside her, our bases connected. "You feel so good." I put my thumb into my mouth, making sure it's wet before I bring it down to her, rubbing her tight hole.

"Oh, shit," she cries as I pull out and thrust back in again hard and unrelenting, gathering speed with every stroke. "Fuck, Jordan. Yes." I bring my other hand around, nudging her clit with my middle finger, spreading her wetness around the sensitive bud. "*Jordan*," she screams in response, all other words failing her as she pushes her hips back to meet each hard thrust I give her.

"That's it, Molly. Fuck, I love the way you take me."

"God, yes. Don't stop. I'm so close."

My own release is imminent as my balls start to tighten and my body tenses. "Come for me. I'm ready," I grunt.

"Jordan," falls from Molly's mouth with a steady stream of expletives as she lets go, the intensity of her climax squeezing me so hard my toes curl against the cold tile floor. I pull her knee down from the bed and back to the floor, making her feel even tighter around my cock, slamming into her from behind as she continues to convulse around me.

"*Ah, fuck,*" I roar, pushing into her as hard as I possibly can when my orgasm hits. I spill everything I have inside her in long, deep strokes.

In the distance, I hear the stadium come to life, reminding me where we are, but I couldn't care less. All that matters right now is Molly and me and the knowledge that no matter what happens next, we've got each other.

With our breathing heavy and sweat pouring from our bodies, I pull out of her slowly, turning her to face me and lifting her onto the bed so I can prolong her orgasm. Her moans soften when I use the tip of my middle finger to slowly rub the length of her, coaxing every last drop of her orgasm until she can't take any more.

Sitting on my usual bench in the dressing room, I hold Molly in my arms as we recover, stroking back the loose wisps of hair that don't quite fit into her plait. She looks beautiful, with her hazy eyes and post-sex glow that not even a quick shower to clean up could wash away. "I can't wait until I can shout from the rooftops that you're mine, Mol. Every man and his dog is going to know how much I love you."

"That means you'll be retired. Is that not bittersweet?"

"You know, for the first time, I'm not worried about what comes next. I've actually thought about what I want to do after I retire."

"Really?"

"When I was a kid, my mam put me through football lessons. I always had the newest Wearside kit and the best boots money could buy, and honestly, I thought that was normal. It wasn't until I was older that I found out she would often skip meals and sacrifice things she needed so she could afford that stuff for me. And then there was my coach. Tony was like a dad to me, and he taught me all the man things because, as you know, my biological dad wasn't around. Like what happens during puberty and how to shave my beard. I also found out he paid my subs when Mam couldn't afford to. He paid them on the day the Wearside scout came to watch. If he hadn't, I would have missed that practice, I would have missed out on all of this. Without them, I don't know who I'd be."

"And then Tony became your stepdad."

I nod. "I want to pay that love and support forward while I have the money and resources to do so. I want to coach grassroots football. I want to offer free coaching to people who might have to choose between their kid's dream and feeding their family, you know? I have the money to start it up. Long-term, I might have to look at alternative streams of income, but at the moment, that's the idea I've got."

Molly's eyes meet mine, pride evident in the shine of them. She smiles and wraps her arms tightly around my neck. I smile back although she can't see. Her reaction confirms that my mind is on the right track.

"That sounds amazing, I'm so proud of you. Have you told your mam and Tony?"

"Not yet. I'd like you to be there when I tell them. I was hoping you'd get involved too, you know, when you can."

She's grinning at me proudly. From anyone else the reaction would probably embarrass me, but from her, the excited sparkle in her eyes makes me want to do more of this. To do more to make her proud. "Of course. I'll support you through anything, especially something so incredibly selfless."

I laugh, feeling weightless as she peppers kisses all over me.

"I think I've just fallen in love with you all over again."

"I fall in love with you a little more every day," I tell her, placing a soft kiss on her lips. "You really have made me the happiest man in the world."

Chapter Thirty-Three

Molly

Bridget bursts into my office, a blur of long slender limbs and dark hair, waving a letter in the air excitedly. Over the years, she's perfected her usual calm and collected persona, keeping it together when no one else can. It's what makes her so good in a PR crisis. But now, her emotionless mask is nowhere to be seen, revealing the Bridget I met all those years ago. The Bridget who has been slowly coming back to life after breaking up with her toxic ex last year.

"Molly, Molly, look." She does a double take as she spots Jordan leaning against my desk watching me work. "Oh shit, sorry. Didn't know you were here."

"It's fine, you didn't interrupt anything," I say, laughing at her alarmed expression. "What's up?"

"Oh, thank god… This arrived for you this morning." She blows a misplaced strand of hair out of her face and hands me the letter. "It was addressed to the club so I opened it. But it's for you."

The first thing I notice on the loose piece of paper is the scripted logo for the North East Sports Awards, a prestigious awards ceremony recognising notable sports personalities in the North East. Every sports person in the North East has dreamed of winning one day, but I've never been lucky enough to be nominated even when I captained the Lionesses.

The paper crinkles slightly as I hold it, my hands trembling.

"Read it," Jordan urges, but I don't think I can. I feel sick with anticipation. What if it's not what I think it is? What if it's just junk mail?

Oh, come on, grow up.

"Molly Davison," I start, my voice rushed as I read the letter out loud, "please find enclosed an invitation for you and a table of nine further guests to attend the North East Sports Awards at Ramside Hall. I'm thrilled to inform you that you have been nominated for"—I let out a scream, leaping out of my chair and sending it spinning out of control behind me—"the best up-and-coming coach award, which will be voted for by our carefully selected board of trustees and announced live at the event..."

Months of hard work. Months of long days and late nights analysing performance data and match reports. Months of constantly trying to prove myself worthy of this job. All come down to this piece of paper in my hand. Well maybe that's a little dramatic, my success has been demonstrated in the results of our games but to have it acknowledged by a panel of influential sporting officials, well that's vindication at its best.

"Molly this is incredible."

"I can't believe it." This is... it's everything. Hysteria takes over as I dive into Jordan's waiting embrace. I wrap my arms around his neck with an excited squeal as he spins me around. I couldn't care less that Bridget is in the room when I crush my mouth to his in a butterfly-inducing kiss.

He chuckles lightly, putting me back on my feet but keeping his arm around my waist. "I'm so proud of you."

"It is real, isn't it?" I double-check with my friend, reading the letter again just to make sure. "It's not a prank?"

Bridget nods. "It's definitely real."

"I… I'll be right back," I say, stepping out of Jordan's hold. "I need to tell Dad."

I run out of my open office door and sprint down the corridor to his office, holding the letter to my chest. Luckily, the corridor is empty.

"*Dad*," I call as I skid to a stop. I'm out of breath as I brace myself in his doorway. "*Dad.*"

"What's wrong?" he calls out from behind the closed door.

I burst into the office, and he stands at his desk, his eyebrows knitting together in concern.

"Nothing's wrong, Dad. Look."

I thrust the letter towards him, and he reads it at an agonisingly slow pace. I pace his office and try to focus on calming my breathing as I wait for him to finish. Eventually, he puts the paper on his desk and shakes his head as he chuckles, his eyes widening with pride as he looks up at me.

"Molly, this is… this is amazing. I'm so proud of you."

I dive into his waiting arms, hugging my dad tight as I try to process the news. My nose tingles, and I swallow down a lump in my throat before I'm able to speak. "Thank you, Dad. Thank you for convincing me to do this."

Chapter Thirty-Four

Jordan

Molly quietly chews on her lip as we pull up outside my mam's house.

"Are you nervous?" In the entire time I've known her, I've never seen her as nervous as she seems to be right now.

"Yeah, a little." Her hands fidget with the cream cake box on her lap as her knee bounces. "I'm meeting your parents."

"You've met my mam and Tony loads of times." I place my hand on her knee and hold her steady. "You saw them in Portugal."

"I've only met them as your coach," she says, spiralling in her panic. "Never as your girlfriend. What if they don't approve of me? What if they don't approve of our relationship?"

"They will, Molly. Trust me."

"But they know we dated last time, they know why we broke up—"

"Stop," I interrupt her before she can argue. "I love you, Molly. You make me incredibly happy, and they see that. That's all that matters now." I take her hand and brush kisses across her knuckles.

"I love you too," she says, calmness washing over her.

We climb out of the car, meeting at the front of the bonnet, and I kiss her softly on the cheek, taking the cake box from her before we walk down the garden path knowing Mam won't be able to hold back. When I asked Molly to come with me today, we decided we wouldn't hide here. There's no need.

"Molly," Mam says, flinging open the front door and jogging down the few steps to greet us. I say us, but what I mean is Molly. Her eyes light up as she ignores me completely, pulling my girlfriend into a warm embrace as I predicted. "I'm so happy to see you, sweetheart."

"I'm happy to be here." Molly mirrors my mam's elated smile when they pull apart.

Watching the two most important women in my life come together with a natural and genuine fondness for each other fills me with a sense of pure undeniable joy.

"I need all the details." Mam links her arm through Molly's and pats her hand. "I knew something was going on when I saw you both in Portugal."

I groan. Knowing my mam, I know exactly where she's going with this. "Mam, please don't."

"Fine, you can leave out the dirty bits."

Molly's cheeks flush as she glances back at me.

"Let's get inside before you interrogate us."

"Oh fine." Mam sounds exasperated, but I know it's an act when she turns and grins cheekily at Molly.

"You have a beautiful home," Molly says, looking around the wide-open foyer. From the outside, the place looks like a small double-fronted bungalow with dormer windows built into the roof. In reality, the place is huge, with two staircases, one leading up to the bedrooms and another down into the main living area.

"Thank you. We have Jordan to thank for this place. He bought this home for us when he was first signed at Wearside."

Molly beams up at me as I take her jacket and hang it on the coat rack by the front door along with my own.

"Where's Tony?" I ask.

"Out the back," he calls up the stairs.

Taking Molly's hand in mine, I follow Mam down the stairs into the living area, where we find Tony reading the sports pages of *The Echo* in the adjoining room.

"Wow," Molly says, looking out the glass wall of the sunroom over the vast fields that stretch as far as the eye can see.

"Son," Tony says, standing and pulling me into a fatherly hug. Although I've never called Tony Dad, he's as good as a dad to me. "Molly, good to see you, love."

His eyes warm when he sees me wrap an arm around her, pulling her to my side. "Ah, finally." He lets out a hearty belly laugh. "Callum didn't think you had the balls to go after this one again, but I knew you would."

Molly laughs along with him as I roll my eyes.

"Oh great, you've been talking to Callum."

"Speaking of your brother, he's on his way too," Mam says. "I'll stick the kettle on."

"I'll help you. We brought a cream cake." Molly takes the cake from my other hand and follows her to the kitchen.

"So, you're happy, son?" Tony asks, his demeanour serious this time.

"Yeah, we are," I say, my smile spreading into a grin as he nods.

In the distance, the front door opens and closes, signalling my stepbrother's arrival. I haven't seen him since the night we played golf due to our conflicting schedules. I can't imagine how he's going to react to seeing Molly here. As per usual, his feet are heavy as he practically stomps down the stairs.

"Alright, mate," Callum says, breezing into the sunroom. He wraps me in a bear hug as we thump each other's backs a little harder than necessary before taking our usual seats, him on the arm chair that matches the one his dad sits in and me on the sofa.

"Callum, pet," Mam shouts from the kitchen, "tea or coffee?"

"Coffee, please," he calls back. "I need a serious caffeine hit. I had a date last night," he adds for our benefit only.

"Anyone we know?" Tony asks his son.

"She's just someone I know," he says dismissively.

"From the village?" I ask.

"*Never* from the village."

We always joke that Callum retired from professional sports to become a PE teacher because, for some reason, women love them. There is always a gaggle of mams at the school fawning over him.

"How's working with Miss McKenzie?" I ask him with a smirk.

"It's Miss Maguire, and she's still busting my balls." Callum shrugs, trying to act nonchalant.

"He has the hots for the new head of year."

"Everyone has the hots for Riley," he says, his cheeks turning a vivid shade of red. "At least I'm not the one head over heels in love with my—"

"Jordan's in love with who now?"

Callum turns, his jaw dropping as he stares at Molly, who is holding a tray with the cake and a stack of plates balanced on it.

"Uh…" He looks at me, panic in his eyes, before turning back to Molly.

She places the tray on the coffee table, and I pull her into my lap, kissing her.

His laughter booms. "I knew you'd get her back," he says, finally finding his voice. "It was the voice message, wasn't it?"

"It definitely helped," Molly confirms, sliding off my knee and into the empty spot next to me on the couch.

"You are welcome," he adds, shooting me a pointed look.

Mam walks in and places down another tray, this one filled with cups of tea and coffee that she hands out to each of us before picking up her own and taking a sip.

"So, Molly, how are you finding the new job?" she asks, sitting in her usual armchair, crossing her legs and getting comfortable.

"I love it." Molly's eyes light up. "Of course, there have been some challenges, mainly the media and online trolls, but I've come to expect that now. Working with the lads though is one of my favourite things."

"I have to say, Jordan's gotten a second wind since you've been coaching. You must be doing something right," Callum says.

"It helps having someone to play for," I tell him, kissing Molly's cheek.

"Take notes, Callum," Tony says. "This fucker's got some smooth moves."

"Well, it's only taken him thirty-four years to get there," Mam teases. "And how are you, Son?"

"I'm great. Everything is finally falling into place," I say, leading into my speech. "Actually, on that note"—I place my cup on the coffee table—"I've decided what I'm going to do when I'm not playing anymore."

"Oh, good." Mam turns in her seat so her full attention is on me. "What is it?"

"I plan to open an inclusive football academy for kids that don't have the money or resources to join teams and train regularly. I want to do what you did for me, Tony. You changed my life." I pause, taking a steadying breath to gather myself.

Tony nods, emotion passing over his expression as though he's trying just as hard as I am to keep it together.

"There's no way I would have gotten to where I am now without you. I'm under no illusion that I got lucky, there are many others who didn't get the chance I did, so I want to pay my gratitude forward to as many kids as possible."

"Wow," Tony says, tears brimming in his eyes.

We've been through a lot as a family. Raising two teenage boys together through their professional sports careers wasn't easy for my parents, but they never complained about the sacrifices they had to make.

Mam and Molly dab at their tears and even Callum has gone all misty-eyed.

"I've already set up the charity and have a grant from the council as well as using my own money for the build. To start, it'll be me and Molly on occasion until I get more coaches involved and maybe some mental health professionals and nutritionists. We've found a venue—an old youth centre that has a playing field already. We went to view it this morning. It needs a little revamp, but it'll be ready for the summer if we get stuck in. It has a lot of potential."

"I've not seen you this passionate about something in a long time." Tony grins proudly at me. "I can't wait to see what you come up with."

Chapter Thirty-Five

Molly

"I feel like I might throw up." My eyes water, making me thankful my eyeliner and mascara are waterproof as I look at myself in the mirror. All four cubicle doors are open and empty behind me, meaning no one is listening in, and therefore, I don't have to put up a front.

Bridget pauses with a blusher brush in her hand and gently takes hold of my chin, turning my head back to face her as she touches up my make-up ahead of this week's press conference. It's no surprise the club wants to release a joint statement from me, Jordan, and of course, Dad after the incident with Jonny Stephenson.

"You can do this," she says firmly, rifling through her make-up bag that's sitting too close to some splashes of water for my liking on the vanity sink. "You have to take control of the narrative; otherwise, that prick will continue to spread misinformation about the incident."

"The reporters at these things are always so mean to me." My hands tremble as I wipe them on my trousers. The action is futile—my palms remain clammy as my chest tightens. "And we've all seen the rumours that have begun to circulate about me and Jordan. They're all true, and I don't think I can outright lie about it. It's only a matter of time before we're asked directly." I step away and start to pace, slowly unravelling. "And I definitely won't ask you or the others to lie for me."

"Molly—"

"What if they ask Dad what's going on between me and Jordan? Oh my god, he isn't prepared either..."

"Molly—"

"Oh my god, what if—"

"*Molly*, listen to me."

I stop my frantic pacing, turning to face my friend.

"I'm going to be right there with you. We've gone through your statement a thousand times; you know what you need to say. I'll put a stop to any question that doesn't fall in that script, and if at any time you feel uncomfortable, just say the word and I'll get you out of there."

I nod.

"I really need you to pull yourself together before we go out there. Any sign of weakness and they'll be right on you. I don't care if you have to dig deep, find your poker face."

I straighten my spine as I bury everything deep inside my soul, closing boxes in my brain and locking them up tight.

"That's it. Take a deep breath."

I do as she says, inhaling deeply before letting out a slow, calming exhale. "Let's go."

Jordan and Dad are waiting in the corridor for us when we emerge from the toilets. Dad is stoic as Bridget preps him, nodding along as he takes it all in. Jordan doesn't take his eyes off me, but I can't bring myself to look at him for fear of unravelling.

"Ready in the auditorium," a voice crackles, coming from the radio on Bridget's hip.

"Copy that," Bridget says, and my lips tilt up as I remember the conversation Jordan and I had all those weeks ago in the physio room. He remembers too because he nudges me softly, causing my smile to grow.

Bridget pauses at the door, connecting her headset to the radio, giving us a final moment to compose ourselves. Then she pushes the handle, leading us through to the media room.

Keeping my mask in place, I look around the room as Dad enters first, then me, and, finally, Jordan. There's not an empty seat in here.

The chatter in the crowd dies out as we take our seats on the stage, separated only by a long table in front of us. Jordan picks up one of the water bottles, filling my glass and then his before passing it down to my dad.

The whole scenario is bizarre—Dad and Jordan are acting as though this is any other press conference, while I'm over here trying my best not to have a full mental breakdown.

"Hi, everyone," Bridget addresses the crowd from her podium at the side of the stage. "Please keep your questions short and to the point. We're here to discuss football and football only. Anyone who does not adhere to this will be removed immediately. Let's begin."

Multiple reporters silently raise their hands. Bridget points to one at the front of the room.

"Jeff Cane, *The Echo*. Can you tell us what happened the other day on the sidelines?"

"The ref failed to call a foul," Dad immediately responds. "It was dangerous. If the timing was out by a second or two, it could have ended his career. It was a blatant red for Pottsbark, but Jonny Stephenson ignored this fact, and Molly, with the best intentions, stood up for our player. During this exchange, Jonny displayed derogatory behaviour and bigoted opinions towards Molly, and she stood up for herself. In the end, she was booked and sent to the stands. You should know we've lodged an official complaint with the FA and, therefore, this is all I can tell you."

I take a drink of my water, my shaking hands causing ripples in the liquid.

Get it together.

After our complaint, I received an apology from the FA but not from Jonny himself. Unfortunately for us, our suspension is also still in place due to our reactions on the day. As much as Jordan tells me otherwise, I know I've let everyone down.

"Lionel Common, *The Gazette*. What about your reaction, Robinson? You were given a yellow for the incident with Molly Davison and then later in the game, you were booked again, resulting in you being sent off. I believe you had a physical altercation with the referee?"

"There's a long history of bias against our club by Jonny Stephenson. This in no way defends my act of violence but will provide context. He knows how close we are as a team, management included, and he knew exactly what to say to provoke a reaction from me after our earlier run-in. Before I could stop myself, I reacted. I'm disappointed in myself for reacting physically. Anyone who knows me knows that's not in my character, and moving forward, the incident will stay with me."

"What did he say to make you so angry?" Lionel pushes.

Jordan glances at me, but I don't meet his gaze, focusing instead on the water glass.

"It's not something I care to repeat," he says, putting an end to the question, and we move on again, but this time, the question is directed at me.

"Troy James, *Footy Daily*. Molly, since the incident, there have been various reports in the papers about your dating life. Would you care to comment on the rumours?"

My head snaps up as I look at the reporter who asked the question. "I'm sorry, I thought we were here to talk about football. Do you have a football-related question, or shall we move on to someone else?"

"There's no reason for you to be so dismissive, Miss Davison. It's a simple yes or no question."

"That's enough. Molly isn't answering that question," Bridget tells him. "One more comment and the conference is over."

The reporter stays silent, but there's something about the knowing smirk he gives me that rubs me up the wrong way. It's always the same—every time I'm involved in a press conference or a panel, even when I was a player, the men are always asked to elaborate on tactics or stats, whereas I'm asked my opinions on the designs of the strips or if there's any juicy gossip, as if that's the only input a woman could have.

"You want to know if Jordan and I are dating? That's the rumour, right?" I snap at him, red-hot anger radiating from every pore as I completely deviate from the script. I feel everyone tense up. Jordan, Dad, Bridget. But even that doesn't stop me.

Jordan covers the microphone with one hand and his mouth with the other so no one can lip-read. "Molly, don't react to it. That's the story he wants."

I'm done with the double standards. I'm done with these arseholes looking at me and only seeing me as some feeble girl. I'm the assistant coach for a team that, let's face it, belongs in the Premier League. I'm more than just a pretty face in the dugout. If they gave me a chance to show it, they'd see that I know what the fuck I'm talking about, they'd know that I understand more about this sport than most of the men in this room combined.

"Why didn't you ask Jordan that question?" I ask, ignoring Jordan's warning. "If it's a question you so desperately want to know the answer to, you could have asked him a few minutes ago."

"Because I'm asking you," Troy says, calmly holding out his Dictaphone.

"Why me?"

"It's not important," he argues back, making me angrier and angrier because he can't even bring himself to say the words.

"Because I'm a woman and the topic of who I'm dating is the most important thing in the world? Fucking hell, next you'll be asking who I'm wearing, won't you? Ask a relevant question next time, for example, ask me what it means to me to be the first-ever woman to be nominated for the best up-and-coming coach award at the North East Sports Awards. Or better still, how did it feel to break the record for the longest run of games without conceding a goal? Those would be better questions than asking about my romantic endeavours."

Before I can do more damage than good, Bridget leans over me and switches off my microphone. I stand and exit the stage, not bothering to wait for Jordan or Dad to lead the way before I tear through the doors into the corridor that leads to my office.

"*Molly.*" I'm almost there when Jordan calls my name down the hallway, catching up with me quickly with long strides.

"Don't give me a lecture, please, I know that was uncalled for," I snap, pushing open the door to my office with more force than necessary.

"I wasn't going to. The guy was wrong to push like that, and you're right, his question had nothing to do with football." He shuts the door behind us, locking it before pulling me into a hug. "I followed you to make sure you're okay."

Letting out a long exhale, I relax into his hold. The brush of his hands on my back slowly knock down the already crumbling walls I'd built around me in preparation for the press conference. His hold tightens when I let out an involuntary sob.

"It's so hard. I just want to be taken seriously."

"I know, Molly." He dries my tears with the pad of his thumb and kisses me sweetly on the forehead. There's nothing more he can say.

Chapter Thirty-Six

Jordan

"You doing okay?" Brooke asks as I glance impatiently at the door for the thousandth time since we arrived at the North East Sports Awards, swirling my untouched drink in my glass just for something to do.

Molly and I decided to arrive separately. I would have loved to walk the red carpet and pose for photographs with her, but I know it's for the best, especially since the press conference brought so much extra unwanted attention to us, focusing on the fact that neither of us denied our relationship.

Although Molly is doing her best to ignore the attention, every now and then, I'll catch her googling our names to check what the papers are saying. Some of it is positive and many Wearside fans are openly "shipping" us, whatever that means. But a lot of it, as Molly predicted, is bad.

"Yeah, just a little stressed. Something is up with Molly and she's hiding it from me."

"Have you asked her about it?"

"Yeah, a few times, and she just tells me she's fine, but we all know that fine doesn't actually mean fine."

"Just give her some time, you know what she's like, she probably just needs to think it through in her head before she says it out loud."

Since we got back together, we've spent every night in each other's beds. But since the press conference four days ago, I've only seen her at training or hanging around the club. She insists that everything is fine and that it's sensible not to risk being spotted together. But I don't like it one bit.

As though I'm tuned into her every move, I look up from my glass the moment she appears in the doorway to the ballroom and my stomach does a summersault waiting for her to notice me. She pauses at the entrance, her eyes scanning the various tables, and when her eyes land on me, her face lights up with a beaming smile that takes my breath away.

She looks absolutely gorgeous, wearing a black floor-length satin gown with thin straps, a deep V showing off her perfect cleavage. It has a double split in the front that stops at her waist, and I have no idea how it's staying in place without flashing everyone in here. I simultaneously want to show her off and hide her away.

I do my best to recover as she makes her way over, letting her parents schmooze some people I couldn't care less about, but instead turn into a bumbling idiot trying not to make it obvious I'm having X-rated thoughts about fucking my coach.

"Wow," Bailey says as Molly greets him first. His jaw is slack as his eyes drop to her chest, so I shove it closed, hard. "Ow. Sorry."

"Eyes off, she's mine." I laugh, but I'm only partially joking.

"Yeah, that's on me. I apologise." He holds his hands in an amused surrender, backing away from her.

She greets Aaron next, who places a dramatic hand over his eyes as he gives her the quickest hug known to mankind. He backs off, giving me a cheeky smirk. "Don't want to get in trouble now."

"Fuck off," I say with a smile, shoving him into a seat so I can get by.

I lean in to hold her, placing a hand on her waist and kissing her cheek, loving the way her body reacts so differently to me than the others.

"You look beautiful." I drop my eyes, appreciating every curve of her body in that fucking dress as I try not to come in my pants at just the sight of her. Goosebumps cover her chest, and I can see her nipples harden through the sheer fabric.

"And you look very handsome," she says, brushing her hands up my lapels.

After what is probably an inappropriate length of time for a boss and employee to hold one another in a candlelit room, I reluctantly step away.

"Piña Colada," Brooke says, handing her the cocktail I ordered in preparation for her arrival.

"Thanks." She smiles at me, her sultry red lips pulling up at the corners as her eyes twinkle, and takes a sip. I almost combust when she lowers her glass and licks the cream from the corner of her mouth. My pants become tight as my body reacts to her just in time for her parents to walk over.

Great.

Without hesitation, I drop to my seat next to Aaron, pulling in close to the table.

"Oh, tonight is going to be fun." He tips his glass to me in salute before standing to greet Coach with a handshake.

I hate him so much in this moment.

"It's lovely to see you, boys." Molly's mam makes her way around the table, giving us motherly kisses on the cheek before taking the seat next to her daughter. Brooke sits on Molly's other side, followed by Natasha and Luke, and I sit exactly opposite her between Bailey and Aaron, which I fear may have been the wrong choice.

I place my napkin over my lap as I distract my brain with unsexy thoughts.

Like Coach murdering me when he finds out I fucked his daughter in the physio room while he was in the building.

Or Coach murdering me when he finds out we've been lying to him for years, keeping our relationship a secret.

Or Coach murdering me when he finds out I've been sneaking across his back garden to… well, I think we get the gist.

Jesus Christ, I need to get a grip.

That's easier said than done when my phone lights up on the table with an incoming text from Molly.

Molly: Do you want to see how smudge-proof my new lipstick is?

I smile as I start to type back. If we've learned something in the past few months, it's that we get off by hooking up in risky places. Hooking up here is probably the riskiest of all, and fuck, the idea turns me on to the point of pain.

Jordan: Find us a dark corner and I'll make it my mission to kiss it off.

Molly: I wasn't talking about kissing…

I look up, my mouth gasping open. She picks out the cherry from her cocktail, popping it in her mouth, eyes on mine as she licks the cherry clean of cream, twirling her tongue around it before sucking the fruit off the stem.

Holy. Fucking. Shit.

All the blood in my body, especially from my brain, rushes south, throbbing in my pants. I thought I was hard before, but I was wrong. A carefully placed gust of wind could make me come right here, in front of everyone.

This is torture. I hate her and love her and want to shove my cock in her mouth at the same time.

Jordan: The only coherent thought running through my mind is seeing you in that dress on your knees.

Molly: Want to know a secret?

Jordan: I don't know… Do I want to know a secret?

At this point, I don't know if I'll survive the secret.

Molly: I'm not wearing any underwear

Another message dings immediately after with a little picture icon next to it. My thumb hovers, terrified to open it. Terrified and very excited. I look from my phone to Molly and back to my phone again.

Fuck it. I open the picture and stare at it, doing everything possible to keep my jaw from hitting the floor.

It's Molly, standing in her bedroom mirror. A bedroom mirror that I have fucked her against and also used to watch me fuck her.

I think I might be beyond help now.

She's holding the dress to the side, showing just how high those slits go, and judging by the bare skin of her hip that I will be trailing my tongue over later, she's telling the truth. She's not wearing any underwear.

I know I've already said it, but… holy fucking shit, my mouth is actually watering.

A noise that sounds remarkably like a moan leaves my throat, and I almost drop my phone in a rush to hide the screen as everyone, including Molly's fucking parents, turns to look at me.

"You okay, Skip?" Aaron asks from next to me.

"Yeah, just thought I left my iron on. Better text my mam to go and check." I pick my phone up but don't trust myself to unlock the screen and have these two idiots see what's really going on.

"Didn't you pick up your suit from the dry cleaners this afternoon?" Bailey asks.

"Yes," I say through gritted teeth, begging him to shut the fuck up and change the subject, "but I had to iron it again."

Thankfully, Bailey and Aaron take the hint and drop it, leaving me to return to my text conversation with Molly under the ruse of texting my mam.

Jordan: Now all I can think about is you wearing that dress and me dropping to my knees to devour you.

"So, Jordan"—my head snaps up to look at Molly's mam—"Molly tells me you've found premises for your coaching academy?"

"Oh, yeah. I went down there to sign the paperwork last week, and the building work is starting in a month or so."

Molly's smirking.

Why is she smirking?

Why...

Oh, for Christ's sake. She's smirking because I just said "I went down" to her mam.

Someone kill me now.

"Oh, that's wonderful." She leans forward, brushing Coach's arm and bringing him into the conversation. "You're going to make a lot of families very happy. You should be proud."

"Thank you." I scrub the back of my neck, offering a shy smile. "It's the least I can do for those kids. I wouldn't be here now without that chance, so I want to pay it forward any way I can."

"We're all excited to see what you achieve, son," Coach tells me proudly. "You'll have my support for as long as you need it."

It means a lot coming from Coach, and I'm choked with emotion as the weight of his words settles over me.

Before I can respond, the room falls to a hushed silence as the evening's hosts make it to the stage.

Chapter Thirty-Seven

Molly

"And the North East Sports award for best up-and-coming coach goes to…" Steph Mead, eighties legend and former Wearside Women and England captain pauses for dramatic effect, anticipation falling heavily on my shoulders. "*Molly Davison.*"

I'm stunned into complete silence as my name echoes out of the speakers. Although I can see people clapping and cheering as they get to their feet, the blood rushing around my body creates a vacuum blocking out all sound. I look at my friends and family, taking in the scene playing out in front of me in slow motion as though I'm having some out-of-body experience.

Did they…?

Me, really?

Of course, I hoped I would win tonight, but did I think I'd really take home this award? Never in a million years, which is why I let myself have three cocktails on an empty stomach.

But I've done it. I've won. And… fuck, I have to give a speech.

"Oh my god." My brain finally catches up with my body, and, on autopilot, I stand from my seat, my hands trembling as both my parents pull me into a hug. I see their mouths moving, but I don't hear a single thing they say, as I'm too busy trying to hold myself together.

This is the validation I've been craving. Proof that I'm doing a great job. That people believe I'm worthy.

I make my way around the table, toward the stage, stopping only when I reach Jordan. It all feels like a blur, as though none of this is real and I'm about to wake up from a dream. He opens his arms for me.

I wrap my arms around his neck, pulling him close. "I did it," I say as tears prick my eyes. "I really did it."

"I love you, Molly. I'm so, so proud of you," he whispers in my ear, his hand curved around my ear to avoid people lip-reading. When I pull back, I gaze up at him. What I wouldn't give to kiss him right now. To share this moment with him publicly as my boyfriend.

"Go on up there and make history."

With newfound confidence, I hurry to the stage, where Steph waits with a giant glass trophy that is going to look fabulous in the club's trophy cabinet.

"Well done," she says, handing it over before hugging me. "You'll inspire a lot of young women today. We're all so proud of you, but I hope you remember to be proud of yourself."

"Thank you," I tell her, choking on my emotion as the weight of the trophy settles into my cradled arms.

I turn to the podium, and that's when the severity of the situation hits me as I stare out into hundreds of grinning faces. Everyone is on their feet clapping and cheering for me, but there's only one face I see out there, only one that matters to me right now. Jordan's.

"Wow," I say into the mic, a little breathless from the excitement as I take a good look at my award. "Thank you."

I blow out a long breath as I try to curb my emotions enough to get through my unplanned speech.

"This time last year, if you had told me I'd be here accepting this award as assistant coach of a men's side—and not just any men's side but the team I've supported since birth—I'd have laughed in your faces."

Press are gathered at the back of the room and a TV camera is pointed up at me from directly in front of the stage. I clear my throat as I prepare to open up like I never have before... on my own terms.

"I've never spoken about my accident publicly, but I was in a really tough place when I walked through that door on my first day, and this club saved me. I was battling depressive tendencies I never wanted to admit to having. I kept it from everyone because if I admitted it out loud, I felt like I would have to address it, and I wasn't ready for that. Working with this team as well as the academy girls, I've found my passion off the pitch, and I'll be forever grateful for my team. My mam and dad and my cousin Brooke have been my support from day one, but my family is huge now. Bailey and Aaron, you're truly the best fake little brothers I could have ever dreamed of having, and, Jordan..."

He beams up at me with pride, and oh how I wish I could declare my love for him.

"You're my best friend. I couldn't have done any of this without you, and not just because your performance and stamina are fucking incredible this season but because you enrich my life in so many ways, on and off the pitch."

He laughs out loud at the double entendre behind my words.

I look out at the room again, taking a deep breath as I notice all those people who doubted me in the beginning on their feet, just like Jordan predicted, applauding me.

"A lot of you in this room doubted me when I joined this club, a lot of you still do. In my first few months, I was trashed and verbally abused online and in person. I remember it all vividly, and though I'll never forget it, I forgive you. Because holding this grudge won't help me. Instead, I promise I'll redirect that energy to support others like me. I may be the first woman to coach a men's pro side, but mark my words, I won't be the last. So, get used to seeing lasses on the pitch and in the dugouts because we are here to stay."

Brooke cheers loudly, and as I turn from the podium, the music plays, signalling my exit from the stage.

A runner wearing all black and wearing a headset points to a heavy-looking door in the shadows. "Make your way through that door and along the passageway. You'll come to another door at the end that'll bring you back into the ballroom. We'll engrave your award and bring it out to you soon."

"Thank you," I tell her before venturing into the dimly lit corridor, the heavy door closing with a thud behind me.

"Nice speech." A familiar figure appears in front of me. The hairs stand up on the back of my neck as he looms in the distance. I look over my shoulder, wondering if I could make it back to the stage, but the sound of his footsteps approaching brings out that freeze reflex again. I watch every deliberate step he takes towards me, closing the distance between us.

"Thank you."

Mike Rogers tilts his head with a satanic smirk. My heart slams in my chest, and I'm almost sure he can hear it.

"I didn't expect to see you tonight," I add.

"Thought I'd stop by," he answers coldly. "Question, do you think you'd still have got this award if they knew you were fucking Jordan Robinson?"

"I don't know what you're talking about," I lie, fumbling at the spite in his words.

His eyes drop to my chest before following the curve of my hip to the slits in the dress. I wore it to impress Jordan because I thought it would be exciting to turn him on and find a place we could be alone, and for a while, I felt gorgeous and sexy, but having Mike's smarmy gaze on me now makes my skin crawl. I cross my arms over my chest in an attempt to hide my body, but it's no use—I know how revealing the slits are.

He chuckles darkly. This is all a game to him, and I'm playing into his hand.

"Come on, it's obvious. He's like a little lost puppy, trailing around after you wherever you go. No wonder he's performing well if he gets to stick his dick in you. Wouldn't surprise me if that's the reason Bailey and Aaron are performing well too. Do they get to share? Am I the only one he won't allow near you?"

Choosing to ignore his accusation, I reply with a shaky breath, "What do you want from me?"

"You know…" He looks down at his shirt sleeves as he rolls them up one by one. An anxious chill scatters down my spine, turning my blood to ice. "Dating a player can be seen as a conflict of interest; after all, Jordan is on the starting eleven each week. When the world finds out you're fucking, they'll question why he gets such good starts, especially since he's approaching the end of his career."

"He's the captain and has the best track record on the team. He holds the record for most goals scored for England and Wearside. He's good enough to be in the starting eleven each week." A lump forms in my throat. I hate this. I hate how small I feel. I hate how he makes my hands tremble with every step forward he takes until, eventually, he's right in front of me.

"Doesn't matter though, does it? Because if I tell the world, I'll be the one controlling the narrative." He grabs my chin firmly between his fingers and thumb, and I let out a squeal as he forces me to look at him, tears immediately springing to my eyes.

I jump as loud music begins to play out in the main room as the DJ begins his set. Even if I were able to scream for help, it would be no use. No one is close enough to hear me.

But that begs the question, why did no one else go through that door before I did? It didn't strike me as odd when I was sent this way off the stage, but now I think about it... I'm the only one to have been sent this direction and not allowed off the stage the way I came.

Mike did this. He designed it so I'd come this way.

Regaining some control over my body, I shake him off me. "Why did you lure me here? What is it you want? You want to hurt me? Because one look at me out there, he'll know and he'll come for you. And when Dad finds out, you'll be done."

He chuckles, rubbing his hand along his jaw as he thinks. "Break up with Robinson."

"No," I say firmly. And that one word has just confirmed we're together.

"You're lucky. Since you've just won that little award, I don't think I can afford to fire you just yet, but what I can do is bench Jordan so he ends his career watching from the dugouts instead of on that field."

No. No, he can't. Fuck, can he?

"You can't do that," I argue, though I have no idea what he can and can't do when it comes to the team.

"I think you'll find I can." He scowls. "Oh, and when the press and the fans ask why I've benched Jordan, I'll tell them it's because he'd rather get his dick wet than play for the team he claims to love so much. Do you think you'll be respected then? All that hard work to build your reputation will go up in flames with just one phone call from me."

"Please don't," I beg. "He doesn't deserve that. Not after everything he's given to this team. To this club. To you."

The corners of his mouth tilt up as he narrows his eyes at me. "Then dump him, and you both get to carry on as if none of this ever happened. You keep your job and he gets his dream retirement."

"Okay. Fine. But not tonight, not here."

"Tomorrow," he says, grabbing my wrist and leaning in, bringing his face close to mine. "I want confirmation."

I take a sharp inhale of air, my body shutting down completely as he kisses my cheek. Nausea crawls up my throat at the thought of his lips touching me, but thankfully, I keep my tears at bay.

Backing away, he watches me with that same evil look on his face. It's only when he's left the corridor that I let myself breathe, and even then, it comes out more like a sob as the memories of his lips pressing against my skin linger.

Chapter Thirty-Eight

Jordan

Returning to the table, Molly smiles and sits down. As her award is the final one of the night, the party is in full swing with the DJ already ten minutes into his set and a congregation of people on the dance floor.

She makes small talk with Brooke, who darts a look towards me, clearly noticing the shift in Molly's behaviour since she came back from the stage. When the runner brings her award to the table, engraved, she passes the glass sculpture around, and everyone oohs and aahs as they look at it, but she doesn't seem excited at all.

I watch her carefully. The excited smile she had when her name was called is now stilted, fake, and her eyes look exhausted. What the hell is she hiding?

Doing my best to ignore the tension, promising myself I'll get to the bottom of it when we're alone, I return my attention to Aaron and Bailey. I barely hear a word they say, keeping my eye on Molly at all times.

"Can you take me home?" she asks me half an hour later. "I'm exhausted."

"Yeah, of course. I'm ready when you are."

Her forced smile sends off alarm bells in my mind. But at least she's coming home with me tonight. I can cling on to that.

"I'll say goodnight to my parents and meet you out by the car," she tells me before disappearing into the crowd.

I don't bother saying goodbye to anyone; instead, I head straight for our car, telling the driver Molly will be right out, and a few minutes later, she's hurrying down the stone steps to our limo.

She climbs in the back of the limo ahead of me, and I give the driver my address, telling him to come back here after for Bailey, Aaron, and Brooke, who shared the ride.

Once we're safe behind tinted windows, I slide shut the privacy partition, blocking out the driver, then turn to her.

"Molly, what's going on?"

"I'm just tired." No, if she was tired, she'd have her arms wrapped around my bicep and her head on my shoulder fighting to keep her eyes open. She shifts her gaze to the side unable to meet my eyes that have been locked on her all night, leaning over and pulling a bottle of water out of the cooler next to her before taking a sip. She's not fooling me.

"Molly, talk to me."

For a moment, I think she's about to put me out of my misery. She tosses the bottle to the seat next to her before turning back to face me, sliding closer. But instead of talking, her mouth is on mine, meeting me with warm frenzied kisses. After four nights apart, I kiss her back eagerly, allowing my hands to slip inside the split of her dress, finding her bare, just like she told me earlier.

She climbs over my lap, gasping against my mouth as my hands grip her, digging into the soft flesh as I pull her close.

I part my lips, granting her access and allowing her tongue to brush against mine. I would put a stop to this, but with every second that passes, I feel her relax against me, losing some of the tension she's been carrying. With a hand in her hair, I pull her in closer, letting her feel the hard-on I've been sporting since the second I laid my eyes on her tonight.

"Jordan," she gasps as I move along her jaw to her neck, grinding up into her.

Leaning back, her hands fumble against my belt and waistband as she frees my aching dick.

"Babe." My train of thought vanishes when she drops to her knees on the floor of the limo in front of me, licking her lips.

"Lie back," she orders, and because my brain is a little hazy from all my blood rushing south, I do as she asks with no protest, sliding forward in my seat and propping myself up on my elbows. This is the exact scene I pictured in my mind, and fuck, it's even better than I could have ever imagined.

She doesn't take me into her mouth right away, but pulls down the straps of her dress, exposing her perfect, pebbled nipples. I reach for her, brushing the pads of my thumbs over them as she arches her back with an aroused sigh. Rising on her knees slightly, she leans forward, pushing her breasts together around my straining cock. She looks up at me innocently before sliding up and down my swollen length.

Holy shit. This is… this is amazing.

I move my hips up and down, meeting her movements and slowly fucking her tits, loving the feel of her soft warm body pressing against me. All the while, I keep the pressure on her nipples. I rub them, tweak them, tug on them with my forefinger and thumb as she lets out a small series of gasps and moans. Just when I think nothing could feel as good as this does, she sticks out her tongue and bows her head, licking the tip of my cock.

I stutter at the contact, and she smiles. Lowering her head further, she slides down my body, taking me into her mouth in one long slow suck, her cheeks hollowing out as I lose all control and give in to her.

She sucks and licks and grazes her teeth over the head of my dick and down the shaft, driving me crazy with every stroke of her fist wrapped around my base. All rational thoughts have vanished now and been replaced with one thing: the sight of her in that dress on her knees sucking me off.

"Ah fuck, Molly," I groan as I pull her long dark hair away from her face, holding it in my fist. "You look so good, babe. Like every wet dream I've ever had."

Her moan of appreciation vibrates throughout me as I feel the first spark of my orgasm building. Her eye contact and the sounds she makes as she takes me deeper and deeper into her throat drive me closer and closer to the edge, and I need more of it.

"Touch yourself. Make yourself come," I order her.

When her hand disappears under her dress, her eyes roll back as she plays with her clit. I can barely think straight, but I know she'll be wet, I know she's tight.

Even as I watch her hand work against herself, she's relentless on me too, twisting her fist around the shaft that doesn't quite fit in her mouth, alternating between sucking my dick and pulling my balls into her mouth until they're tight and ready to uncoil. In the past, I'd probably be embarrassed by how pathetically quick my orgasm builds, but Molly… she sees it as a badge of honour, knowing how easily I fall apart for her and only her.

Her soft whimpers turn into thrashing moans as her body tenses between my knees, shuddering against her hand as her orgasm hits. I can barely hold back until she's finished, the sight of her coming as she sucks me finishing me off too.

"I'm going to come," I warn as my spine tingles and stomach tenses. I gasp as she takes me out of her mouth just as my white-hot pulsing orgasm hits and I burst onto the soft skin of her exposed breasts in long spurts.

"Fuck," I groan as I watch her drain me, her hand continuing the low strokes, drawing everything out of me with slow, intentional movements. As I come around again, Molly moves back to her seat, looking down at her skin as she massages my cum into her breasts.

"Well, that was worth ruining a satin dress for." She grins over at me as she puts herself back together.

"Fuck, I'm so sorry," I say, looking down at her stained dress. I fucking love that dress too. "Here." I pass her my jacket to cover up, tugging her back onto my lap as I kiss her tenderly.

A few minutes later, we pull up to the gates, and I tap the app on my phone, letting the driver through. We don't speak as the car slowly comes to a halt outside my door. She looks down at me, an unreadable expression on her face that gives me an uneasy feeling in the pit of my stomach. I push it away, stepping out of the limo and holding my hand out for her.

Thankfully, she takes it, weaving her fingers in mine as we thank the driver and make our way up the steps to my door.

"I know what you did there," I tell her as I slide the key into the lock, turning it to open the door.

"I don't want to talk tonight, Jordan. I promise, tomorrow we'll talk, but tonight, I just want to be with you. I want you to wrap your arms around me as we make love and then I want to fuck, hard, until I forget everything else in this world except you."

I lead her in, flicking on a lamp on the side table and locking the front door behind us. "I can do that."

Putting aside my insecurity feels nearly impossible, but I know I have to listen to her needs. I take her in my arms and hold her tightly to me. I don't crush my mouth against hers like I want to; instead, I place small, delicate kisses over her skin until I reach her mouth, where she meets my soft kiss.

She opens up to me almost immediately, letting my tongue inside her mouth as I push her towards the nearest wall, pinning her against it. Her breath hitches as she stares up at me, her head tilted back.

"Where do you want it, Molly? Up against the wall or in our bed?" I ask, tracing my hand down over her stomach, across her hip, then snaking inside her dress once more. I nudge her feet apart with my foot, widening her legs as I brush my fingers over her already-soaked clit and tease her entrance.

She whimpers at the contact, grinding against my hand involuntarily. "Take me to bed."

She gasps as I push my finger deeper into her wet heat, a tease of what's to come.

In a flurry of movement, I have her in my arms with her legs crossed at the base of my back and carry her up the stairs until I'm holding her by our bed, kissing her as I tenderly stroke her head.

In a matter of seconds, I have her naked and spread out on the bed in front of me and watch the heavy rise and fall of her cum-soaked chest.

I undo my tie first, throwing it onto the floor before rolling up my sleeves.

"I love you, Molly," I tell her, leaning over her as we kiss, her mouth moving determinedly against mine.

"I love you too," she says, but even though I know she does, there's something hidden in her words. "You know I love you so much."

I make my way down her body, sucking her perfect pink nipples as she arches her back, fisting the pillow beneath her head. My fingers glide through her folds as she moans softly.

"Oh god," she says as I pull them into my mouth, looking up at her as I lick away her juices.

Giving her more, I watch as I slide my fingers inside her, stretching her around me as though she were made exactly for me in every way possible. I lean back to look at her, her perfect centre glistening for me. She lowers her hand to spread herself wider, opening herself up for me. I lower my mouth to her, and her breathing catches when my tongue laps against her slowly.

"Oh, Jordan. Yes. *Fuck.* Yes." She pants and cries out as her hips grind against my face, matching each thrust of my fingers as she grapples with the bedding in her white-knuckled fists.

"I'm so close," she cries. "Jordan, yes. Oh fucking god yes." She cries as our movements quicken. "*Oh fuck.*"

Her entire body tenses as her orgasm hits, her walls spasming and clenching around my fingers as she writhes against my face.

"Oh god," she breathes, looking down at me through her sex-hazed eyes. "That was something else."

"It certainly was." I stand, remove the rest of my clothes, and join her in our bed.

"Make love to me, Jordan."

Chapter Thirty-Nine

Molly

I stretch out in the king-size bed that smells just like Jordan, inhaling his masculine scent and imprinting the memory into my aching soul. His side is still warm, so he can't have gone far.

I silently climb out of bed as I look around the room that has gradually become mine too. As I tiptoe around the room, the smell of coffee wafts up the stairs through the open bedroom door, so I know I don't have much time before he makes his way back up here.

Going to the wardrobe first, I grab the duffle bag I used to bring my clothes over here and take it straight to the chest of drawers across the room, scooping out my clothes and shoving them in the bag. After my drawer is empty, I grab my book and my phone charger from the bedside table, throwing them in before hurrying to the bathroom. Within a few minutes, everything is packed and I'm walking across the upstairs hallway when something stops me.

I pick up the frame from the shelf at the top of the stairs. The tears that spring to my eyes quickly spill over my lashes and onto my cheek. It's the picture I sent him of me in Portugal, smiling over my shoulder with Jordan's name printed across my back as he trains in the background.

Swiping away my tears, I throw that in the bag too.

I'm going to miss this whole life we've started to build together.

As I make my way downstairs, I hear Jordan singing along to the radio in the kitchen, and my chest constricts, my stupid heart already sensing the heartbreak it's about to endure.

Stopping by the front door, with one hand I tug on my trainers and the other I pull out my phone and text Brooke. There is no going back now.

Molly: Come pick me up at Jordan's place. ASAP. It's urgent.

Before I put my phone away, a text comes through, but it's not from Brooke. Bridget's name pops up on my screen with a link to an article. Just reading the headline has my blood running ice cold.

Devoted captain Jordan Robinson stands by his rumoured girlfriend's side as she wins a prestigious award.

I'm still scanning over the article when I walk into the kitchen. When I look up from my phone, the tears start up again. Jordan stands with his back to me, wearing nothing but his boxer briefs as he hums an unknown tune to himself. My gut reaction is to run to him, seeking comfort in his warm embrace. He hears my footsteps and turns to face me.

"Oh fuck, what's wrong?" Jordan's face morphs into one of pure shock, a coffee cup in each hand. I don't blame him—I'm a weeping mess dressed in pyjamas and trainers, carrying my belongings in a duffle bag that I haven't bothered to zip up.

I shake my head, flinching away from him as he practically throws the mugs back onto the countertop and rushes to me. There's no way I'll get through this conversation if he's touching me.

He looks at me with a hurt expression I don't think I'll ever forget or forgive myself for.

"Are you going somewhere?" His voice is alarmingly flat as he looks me up and down.

"We need to talk." My voice breaks as more tears fall. All I want is to run into his arms and have him comfort me and tell me everything is going to be okay. But I can't deny that this article, although it's breaking me apart, has come at a convenient time.

I swipe at my tears, angry at my emotions for betraying me when I need to be strong. I'm doing this for him so he gets to end his career on his terms, not being punished for falling in love with me. Not only that, I'm doing it for me too, to protect the reputation I've worked so hard to build over the last six months.

"Molly," he says, neither a question nor a statement, but somewhere in between. Worry etches between his brows.

I dig down deep and build a fortress around me. "We need to break up," I say, using all the determination I have to keep those defensive walls in place. It feels as though I've built the walls with sand instead of cement. Cracks show quickly, but I do my best to keep them together. When I get home, then I can break down again. I just have to get through this conversation.

"What are you talking about?" His voice is even, as though he's using every ounce of self-control he possesses not to react, but I can see the shock in his eyes.

"I'm breaking up with you," I repeat. This time, it sounds marginally more confident.

"No." He reaches for me again. I step backwards, just out of his reach, and he looks stricken, as though I may as well have slapped him around the face. "You aren't just going to end our relationship in one sentence."

I hand him my phone. He looks at it confused before taking it from me and looking at the screen.

"That headline should be about me winning my award. It should be about my career, about my achievements." My breath shakes.

"*Devoted captain Jordan Robinson stands by his rumoured girlfriend's side as she wins a prestigious award*," he reads before bringing his eyes up to meet mine. "Molly, for a start, that's the worst headline I've ever read."

I snatch my phone back and continue to read.

"*Of course, it's not the first time Davison has been linked to the star striker who last month broke the record for most England goals scored. Robinson, who retires after eighteen years of professional football at the end of the season, was spotted standing up for his rumoured girlfriend in front of 46,000 fans at a recent home game in a move that fans of the couple are calling 'boyfriend goals'.*"

"That's a bullshit article." He rubs his palm across his jawline and grips it tight.

"*But now, a new photograph has come to light showing the very same Molly Davison and Jordan Robinson enjoying a cosy date together four years ago. Waitstaff recall the pair looking very close and in love as they dined together in a cosy jazz bar in Covent Garden before passionately kissing in the street as they waited for their taxi.*"

I turn the phone to show him the photo in question. It's undeniably us, with our hands roaming all over each other in a busy London street.

"In this article, I'm nothing more than a damsel in distress or a desperate horny woman digging her heels into you. You're the hero with a decorated career, protecting me from villainous referees." I throw my hands out, giving in to my frustration.

"Molly, we don't need to break up over this. You're overreacting. We can go down to the club and see Bridget and sort this bollocks out."

"I'm *not* overreacting. I'm sorry, Jordan, but this… us getting together. It was a mistake. I'm sorry, but I need to go." I hoist my bag over my shoulder and move towards the door. With every step I take, a part of me breaks off.

"*Fuck.*" He drags his hand through his messy bed hair. Unfortunately, he doesn't make this easy and follows closely behind me. "Don't do this. I can't lose you again."

God, I hate that I put that strain in his voice.

"*I don't want to sort this out,*" I shout. "I should have listened to my gut all those months ago. I know that working together now isn't going to be fun, but it's something we're going to have to do, so please just listen to me when I say it's over."

We stare at each other for a few minutes, tears in both our eyes as the pain I know he's feeling too spreads throughout my body.

This time when I walk away from him, he doesn't stop me or even try to follow me. I yank open the front door, letting it slam shut behind me as I jog down the steps just in time to see Brooke's car pull up to the door.

Aaron gets out of the front passenger side. "Hey…" His eyes widen with alarm as I push past him, sliding into the seat, slamming the door on him, turning away from the window to clip in my seatbelt.

"What the hell is going on?" Brooke pales as she stares at me. "Are you okay?" And just like that, her words open the dam that was holding back my tears.

"Can you drive, please? I don't want Aaron to see me like this," I beg as a sob heaves from my chest, followed by another and another until I'm hyperventilating, fighting to pull air into my lungs.

"Shit," she says, pulling out of the gated driveway. "What's happened?"

I shake my head and bury my face in my hands. A little way along the road, I feel the car slow and come to a stop, and when I look up, I see she's pulled over into a nearby park, finding a spot away from the view of the road.

Pulling on her handbrake, she leans across and wraps her arms around me, doing her best to comfort me, but I'm too far past that now.

"We b-broke up," I stammer through the tears that flow with no end in sight.

"You broke up?" She jumps back, her eyes wide. "Why?"

"I ended it." Another sobbing fit ensues.

"Okay, maybe things aren't that bad. If you calm down, maybe you can talk to him. I'm sure whatever is happening, you'll be able to work through this."

Doesn't she realise I don't need her to jump into problem-solving mode? I just need her to be here for me and hold me together as my life falls apart.

"*Brooke, drop it.* It's what I want."

"Then tell me, why are you so hysterical?"

"Brooke, take me home," I say, ignoring the question. It's pointless trying to lie to her and I don't know if she'll look at me the same if I tell her the truth.

She relents, turning the key in the ignition as the car roars to life again.

The rest of our journey is in silence. And if I could go back to this morning before I left, I'd do it all again if it meant saving Jordan's career.

Chapter Forty

Jordan

I don't know how long it's been since Molly left, but an incessant banging on my door breaks me from my trance. I lean back against the wall, legs stretched out, panting as the adrenaline leaves me and grief threatens to overwhelm.

For a while, I stood staring at the front door, waiting for her to come back. When it sank in that she wasn't going to, I made my way into the kitchen, which is where most of the damage is. Glasses, plates, and anything I could get my hands on were hurled through the air, colliding with various hard surfaces and shattering like my heart.

"It was a mistake," she said.

So why don't I believe her? Why do I have a sinking feeling that there's more to this than she gave me?

The knocking continues, but I ignore it. There's no way it's Molly, and I'm not in the mood for company right now.

"Go away," I call out.

I hear a key turn in the lock and the door click open.

"Go away," I repeat, quieter this time as I lean forward and put my head in my hands.

"What the fuck has happened here?"

I look up at Aaron standing in my kitchen doorway, his eyes wide. He pushes broken glass and crockery aside with the toe of his shoe as he crosses the room, the fragments scraping against the tile. He turns on the spot, looking at the damage scattered across the floor before he turns his attention back to me.

"Are you okay?" he asks, stepping over my outstretched legs and sitting next to me.

"No." I can't process anything right now other than the fact Molly has left me. And fuck knows I can't bring myself to say that out loud.

He reaches out a hand and gently takes hold of mine. He lifts it to inspect a particularly nasty-looking gash on my hand that I didn't notice. Even now, I can't feel it. Maybe the pain is too minimal compared to the overwhelming hurt of losing Molly.

"Fuck," he mutters. "Get up."

I let him tug me towards the sink and hold the wound under the cold water, then he hands me a clean tea towel to stop the bleeding as he searches for my first aid kit, eventually finding it beneath the sink. He works in silence, cleaning the wound with an old bottle of vodka from my freezer before applying strips to close it. He starts to roll a bandage around my hand.

"She left me," I whisper.

"I know, Skip, Brooke called me just before I came in."

I've never seen Aaron look so caring. It's usually me taking care of him, bandaging him up when he's hurt himself or gotten into a fight after hitting on someone's girlfriend on a night out. I've lost count of how many times I've helped him ice a black eye. The only reason I even have the wound closure strips is because I had to stick his eyebrow back together once.

"She told me she picked Molly up earlier and she was hysterical."

"She didn't seem hysterical when she left. She didn't seem hysterical when she told me our relationship was a mistake," I snap, snatching away my hand to finish bandaging myself, tying it in a knot so tight it pinches my skin. "She walked out on me without a second fucking glance, without trying to talk things through."

Aaron lets out a patient sigh, then turns and grabs two crystal whisky glasses I had the sense not to toss across the room and a bottle from the cabinet. Placing them on the countertop, he pours two generous glasses and hands me one. The first sip burns, but I take another long mouthful, draining the glass.

"Come on, Skip. That doesn't strike you as odd?" he asks calmly, refilling the glass, not bothering to point out it's barely ten a.m. "Last night, she seemed fine, and now she's done?"

I take another sip, the burn clearing some space in my brain to think.

"She blamed it on some article online… but I don't know. She seemed weird after she got her award, like she was pulling away. Then when we got home…" I pause, not wanting to talk about our sex life with Aaron. "It was like she was saying goodbye. I think that article was a convenient excuse."

"Then, go and fight for her," he tells me as though it's that easy.

"I'm not going to do that, mate." I shrug, looking down at my glass and swirling the amber liquid.

"Why not?"

"Because whether it was just a convenient excuse or not, she's right. That article was about her achieving one of the most celebrated awards in sports, and the journalist focused on me, on my achievements." I pull up the article and show it to him. "They referred to her as 'my girlfriend' when it was her night, her award. She deserves the chance to shine."

Aaron's eyes move from the article to stare into mine. "Do you love her?"

"Of course I do. But there's that saying, 'if you love something, set it free', right?"

"Even at the cost of both of your happiness?"

I ignore the question, looking around the room before I drain my glass. "I'm going to clean this mess up."

"I'll get the brush."

Chapter Forty-One

Molly

The sight of the message on my screen a week later makes me sick to my stomach and my skin crawl. I don't want to know how Mike got hold of my personal phone number and hope to god he doesn't use it again but I can't ignore the fact his message provides a little relief. Relief that Jordan's career is safe and he gets to end it on his terms. That's what all this is about, right?

News of the break-up spread quickly among our friends. Of course, they're all concerned—my actions seem random and illogical because I've not told anyone the whole story, focusing instead on the lie I concocted. If I tell that version of the story enough, I'll eventually start to believe it myself, I'm sure.

Continuing to work is mentally draining, and with this being my first day off, all I want to do is sleep all day, but of course, things never go as planned. It's not even nine a.m. when my doorbell rings and I'm forced to drag myself out of bed.

"I'm coming," I call out as it rings for the third or fourth time. "Just give me a fucking second," I add, this time under my breath, before pulling open my door to reveal Brooke and Aaron standing wrapped in thick coats as snow falls around them.

"Hi?" I say, trying to pull myself together as I rub my tired eyes. "What are you doing here?"

"We came to talk to you," Brooke says, her eyes falling on the shirt I've worn to bed all week. Jordan's Wearside shirt, the same one I stole from our first match. The same one I've worn to every single match since.

"We're worried about you," Aaron confirms, looking at me as if I've just climbed out of the depths of hell. "We're worried about both of you. You and Jordan."

"Can we come in?" Brooke asks.

I don't have the energy to argue with them today, so I move aside. "Yeah."

I leave them to shrug out of their coats and hang them on the pegs by the door as I make my way to my kitchen to put the kettle on. Even though they're still in the hallway, I can hear them whispering urgently to each other, which is eventually drowned out by the boiling kettle.

For one day, I would have liked to wallow in my sadness alone. Should have known that was an impossible ask.

Throughout the week, Jordan and I haven't been able to look at one another. In training sessions, one of the other coaches has taken over for me if there's anything I've needed to say or bring up as we all skirt around the massive elephant in the room and attempt to hide it from Dad even though I know he's probably already read that article. He just hasn't said anything about it. It's making me even more fucking miserable than I already am.

Dozens of times, I've almost broken and told Jordan the truth, but when I watch him play, I'm reminded why I can't tell him.

"Tea or coffee?" I ask as Brooke and Aaron come into view, standing on the other side of my breakfast bar.

"Coffee, please," Aaron says.

"I can make them," Brooke says, about to step closer.

I huff out a sigh. "I can make three cups of coffee, Brooke."

Aaron tenses his jaw, holding something back as he looks between his best friend and me. Brooke shakes her head ever so slightly at him, and he reluctantly drops it.

I continue to make the coffee, taking my time adding the milk before sliding the mugs over the breakfast bar. I take a seat on one of the bar stools as the pair of them take their seats too. The pendant light hangs between us over the breakfast bar, and although it's not switched on, I feel as though I'm in an interrogation.

"Sorry," I say. "I shouldn't have snapped."

"That's okay, you're going through stuff," Brooke says, her voice soft and sweet.

"No, it's not okay," Aaron says, crossing his thick arms over his chest.

"You don't need to worry about us," I say. "Jordan and I didn't work out. We're just trying to figure out a way to coexist until the end of the season."

"Really? Don't need to worry? Try telling that to the rest of the team. Your break-up is affecting everyone, no matter how well you both think you're handling this," Aaron snaps, finally breaking, and I wince at the harshness in his voice. I've never heard him talk this way to anyone, never mind me. "Everyone is walking on eggshells around you both, not wanting to accidentally set one of you off or say something in front of Coach or make it even more awkward than it already is." The anger rolls off Aaron, leaving a heavy ball of guilt in my stomach. He and the lads have been stuck in the middle. I guess I just didn't realise how much it's affecting them all.

"And then there's Jordan," he continues. "I had to pick him up from the floor last week and patch him up because he destroyed every single smashable thing in his kitchen and hurt himself doing it. I'm the one that usually needs taking care of, sometimes Bailey, but *never* Jordan." He combs his fingers through his long hair, pushing it back from his forehead as he studies me with a firm gaze. "He's a fucking mess. He knows there's something more going on with you that you haven't told him, he knows your excuse was bullshit, but he won't do anything about it because although you're a terrible fucking liar, he can tell you've made up your mind."

"Talk to us, Molly," Brooke says comfortingly as silent tears fall heavily from my eyes. "Why did you end it?"

"It doesn't matter why I did it," I say, my voice barely audible. "All you need to know is that I had to."

Brooke shoots a pleading look at Aaron, who straightens up in his seat, preparing to go in for another round. I hate this good cop, bad cop thing they're doing and I don't know how much longer I can cope with Aaron judging me like this.

"What does that even mean? You didn't have to do anything. You obviously don't want to break up with him. Anyone can see that you love each other and you belong with each other. I just can't see for the life of me why you'd do this to him. You've broken him, Molly. How could you put him through all this pain in the most important season of his life?"

That's what breaks me. The accusation and bitterness in his voice that I did this to Jordan on purpose tears open the wounds that haven't even had the chance to heal. The accusation that I've broken his heart as some sick game for my own entertainment.

"How could I do this to him?" I yell, finally losing it. "Can't you see I'm doing this *for* him? I'm trying to save his season so he can go out on his terms." My voice falters as more tears bubble to the surface.

Aaron opens his mouth to argue, but Brooke stops him with a hand on his chest.

"What do you mean 'his terms'?" she asks, her brows pulling together in confusion.

"I can't do this." I hang my head back, focusing on my ceiling as tears pour out of me. Whatever is left of those poorly constructed walls I built to protect myself crumble away completely, leaving a shell of a woman behind.

"Whatever is going on, don't do it alone. Please. Not this time." The sound of my cousin choking on her emotion is sobering.

I don't want to do it alone. I don't want to hurt Brooke. I don't want Aaron to think I'm a terrible person. I don't want to make this difficult for our friends.

But if they knew the reason, they'd understand.

"If I didn't break up with him, Mike was going to ruin the both of us." I lose all strength in my body as my shoulders slouch.

"Mike Rogers did this?" Aaron says, dropping the bad-cop attitude. "Molly, you need to tell us everything."

Chapter Forty-Two

Jordan

Aaron: S-O-fucking-S. Need to speak to you all ASAP. Jordan's house in 5 minutes.

For fuck's sake.

Since Molly broke up with me, my friends have been relentless. If it's not texts in the group chat asking how I am, it's phone calls asking to borrow random shit or showing up on my doorstep unannounced to check in on me. But even for Aaron, who has been known for his dramatics, this message seems odd.

Jordan: Now's not a good time because…

Because what?

I've used napping as an excuse eight times this week, having a long hot soak four times, I can't say I'm not home, as everyone knows I've not left the house unless I've been at work…

> **Aaron**: Non-negotiable. It's about
> Molly and it's important.

Molly.

My pulse spikes. Is she in trouble? Is she leaving the club? Why else would he be calling a group meeting with such short notice? I can feel myself spiralling out of control when a moment later, my doorbell rings.

Kieran and Bailey, along with Bailey's twin eleven-year-old daughters, stand on my porch steps just as Aaron appears. He rips down our shared driveway in his Audi as if he's broken every speed limit between wherever he's come from and here.

Aaron takes the steps two at a time, barging in and leading the way through my house to my kitchen without uttering a word. Rummaging around my cupboards, he pulls down four mismatched glasses and a bottle of whisky, planting it in the middle of the kitchen island, where we gather.

"Okay, girls, Dad needs to have a grown-up conversation," Bailey says as Aaron pulls the cork stopper from the bottle. "Can you remember how to set up the TV in Uncle Jordan's movie room?"

The girls nod before excitedly running off in that direction, seemingly oblivious to the tension growing here.

"Sit down and take a drink." Aaron pushes a glass towards me. I look down at it, not sure I can stomach a drink right now. "Trust me, you'll want that when I tell you what's happened."

Aaron takes a deep breath and downs his own drink before he begins. "Mike Rogers threatened her."

"He did fucking what?" The words are out of my mouth before my brain can fully process the extent of what Aaron said. I push my hands on the marble, standing so quickly my stool flips back, landing on the floor with a clatter. "I'm going to fucking kill him."

"What do you mean he threatened her?" Bailey asks as Kieran picks up my stool.

"Sit down, Skip. I know you'll want to kick the living shit out of him, and so do I, but this is serious, and how we handle it is important," Aaron tells me, and I give in with a sigh.

"We all know Mike is a rich and powerful man, with way more wealth and influence in this industry than we have," Aaron says sternly, his eyes planted on me. "He cornered her after she left the stage. He told her he knew about you two and that if she knew what was good for her, she'd break things off with you. He threatened to bench you for the rest of the season if she didn't end things, and when the media would ask why you'd been benched, he planned to tell them exactly why in the hopes it would turn the fans against her."

My blood boils in my veins as the unrelenting urge to throw more stuff takes over me. The worst part is, I should have seen this coming. I saw how he reacted out on that balcony—he hated that I stepped in, I could see it in his dead eyes as he watched us leave.

"So, what can we do?" I ask Aaron through gritted teeth. "If I can't kill him, we need to do something."

"I have a plan, but we need to agree on it as a team because it'll affect more than just us if we go ahead with it."

Chapter Forty-Three

Molly

I start taking my coat off as I walk down the corridor to my office. Fridays are my favourite day of the week to work. There is no training and I only have a few scheduled meetings, so it means the place is usually quiet apart from the occasional player coming in to use the gym or see their physio, and even then, I'm normally left alone to prepare for Saturday's ga...

I freeze in the doorway to my office, my coat hanging off one arm and my scarf twisted around my neck. Jordan is leaning back in my desk chair, his heels resting on my desk and his legs crossed at the ankle. My heart stumbles over itself, completely unprepared to deal with the emotions that threaten to drown me. Almost like it's second nature, my eyes track the length of his body, from his feet all the way up until I meet his eyes. He looks good, as though he's finally gotten a good night sleep, which is more than I can say for myself. But as he sits there, watching me carefully, he gives nothing away.

What is he doing here?

He gets to his feet and closes the distance between us. My feet refuse to move, my brain and body unable to function.

Every time I've seen Jordan since we broke up, I've had days to prepare. I rebuild those shabby walls around me enough to get through the interaction, and when I get home, they crumble away again and I let myself feel.

Right now, I'm not prepared at all, and worst of all, I don't have those walls up to protect myself.

He leans past me, his familiar masculine scent surrounding me, pulling me in to him like a magnet as he closes the door and locks it.

"Jordan," I say, my voice sounding way breathier than I intended. I'm not strong enough for this.

"Yeah, Mol?" he asks as he untangles me from my scarf and pulls off the rest of my coat, hanging them on the coat rack by my door before returning to stand in front of me.

"What are you doing here?"

He backs up towards my desk, and when I still don't move, he slides his hand down my arm to take my hand. My heart skips as he pulls me to him, making me stand between his thighs.

"I'm here to tell you that I'm about to do something you're probably going to say is reckless and irresponsible."

I study him through narrowed eyes. I don't like the sound of this. "What are you talking about? What are you going to do?"

"I'm also here to tell you we aren't breaking up," he continues, ignoring my question. "I didn't fight for you before, Molly, and I lost you for three painful years. I'm not going to let that happen again."

"Jordan—"

"I know about Mike and what he said to you."

My chest tightens and a slow heavy breath escapes me in a quiet sigh. "What?"

None of this is making any sense. Especially not as he weaves his fingers in and out of mine as though we're having a conversation about what we should have for dinner.

"Aaron told me."

And he's still here, fighting for us. But can't he see it's pointless?

"If you know, you should understand. You coming here, telling me things aren't over won't change anything. It'll just hurt us more." I pull out of his embrace, annoyance surging through me as I pace around my office, wrapping my arms around myself in an attempt to keep it together. "I won't be the reason your career ends with you on the bench."

"Once again, you didn't include me in your decision. You didn't ask me, Molly. You didn't ask how I feel about it, just like the last time you ended things between us." He stands, closing the distance between us again, but this time, he doesn't touch me. "Fucking hell, I thought I made it clear to you that I'm in this for life, and that means working through things like this together."

"Football *is* your life," I shout. If Mike gets wind that he's here saying this to me, everything will come crashing down. "You deserve to have the ending you've always dreamed of."

"Football might look like the most important thing to us from the outside, but you know more than anyone it's not. It's about the people and the relationships you develop as part of a team. Do you think I'd still be here if I didn't have Aaron, Bailey, Kieran, or your dad? Do you think I'd still be here without Bridget digging me out of more sticky spots than I can remember or Phil battling through my many hamstring injuries as if they're his own? Do you really think I could have gotten through this season without *you*?" His voice softens as our eyes meet. "Because I'm telling you now, there is no way I would have got this far if you had never come home. You didn't look at me and write me off because it was my last season, and I know Joey told you I'm a lost cause, but you didn't believe him. You saw something left in me, you pushed me, helped me develop and refine other skills no one else had picked up on." I blow out a slow breath as tears sting my eyes and tingle inside my nose.

This time when he reaches for me, my resolve is weaker and I don't move away. I let him caress my cheek as his eyes connect with mine deeper than they ever have before.

"The ending I dream of is one where you're standing at the sideline, smiling that beautiful bright smile of yours I love so much as the final whistle of my career blows. If it's me sitting on the bench or playing out on the pitch, I don't care as long as you're there with me, standing by my side as I close this chapter and open our next one."

My heart stutters as he makes his way to my hair, tangling his fingers through the loose strands. With his free hand, he tugs my waist to him until our bodies are aligned.

I look up at him, his vulnerabilities plastered across his face as he begs me to stand by his side.

"What do you say, Molly?"

A tear slips down my cheek as I nod, followed by others until he's just a blurry shape in my vision. I stand on my tiptoes, pressing my lips against his as the tension and heartbreak I've been carrying melt away.

"I love you, Jordan."

A relieved breath falls from his lips. "I love you too, Molly. And as much as I'm very much looking forward to reuniting properly, I actually have a team meeting to get to."

I pull back to look at him, keeping my arms on his shoulders. I tilt my head, my brow furrowing as confusion passes over my face. "What are you talking about? There's no team meeting today."

He smiles as he dries my tears with his thumbs, keeping my face between his palms as he leans down to kiss me one last time. "Oh, I think you'll find there is. Look at your calendar." He grins. "And once we're done with that meeting, we're going to go home, to our home."

Chapter Forty-Four

Jordan

Aaron squeezes my shoulder tight as he sits by me in the front row of the packed auditorium, leaving a seat free between us for Molly. He glances at my fists clenching in my lap. "You going to be okay here?"

I release my fists, wiping my palms on my thighs before nodding. "Yeah," I say, shaking the tension out of my shoulders. I could go toe to toe with Anthony Joshua with all this adrenaline surging through my veins.

"We all want to kick the shit out of him, okay. But we need to do this right, so stick to the plan. We've got your back." He glances at his watch, then looks over his shoulder to where people are still squeezing into the room.

Following his gaze, I look around at everyone gathered here. I only counted on our squad turning up today, but whispers clearly spread quickly among the women's and the under-twenty-one squads and they're equally protective over Molly. I even spot some of the staff from the cafeteria and the marketing department in the crowd as well as other members of the coaching staff. Everyone has turned up for her, and I couldn't be more grateful.

"Bridget's just text to say they're on their way," Bailey says, joining us and taking the seat on my opposite side.

This is it.

My heart is lodged in my throat as I wait, but thankfully, the wait isn't long. Bridget enters first, her posture straight as she leads the small group through the lower-level door by the stage. The same door Molly, Coach, and I entered through for that shitshow of a press conference.

Holding her arm out, she directs Molly, Coach, and the co-chairmen Jason and Mike into place at the front of the room. They're obviously confused at what's going on here. It's not every day the team captain calls an urgent meeting and shows up with an army of support.

I meet Molly's eye, giving her an encouraging smile.

"What is this?" she mouths at me.

"Do you trust me?"

She nods before looking at her dad.

"What is going on here?" Coach asks.

"We called this meeting to tell you that we're going on strike," I say to Coach, and if looks could kill, I'd be dead right now.

"What are you talking about? Who is going on strike?" Coach grits out, the vein in his forehead fit to burst.

"We all are," Bailey says, looking Coach in the eye defiantly.

Mike's lip curls, his voice sharp and laced with disgust. "If this is about money—"

"This is a mutiny." Aaron stands, glaring at Mike.

"A mutiny?" Coach seethes, rubbing his fingertips in circles around his temples. "A fucking mutiny?"

"Against Mike Rogers," Kieran confirms calmly.

"Why?" Jason asks. He's the only person in the room who seems utterly confused rather than mad. He knows we wouldn't do this lightly.

I stand beside Aaron. "Molly Davison is the best thing that's happened to this club, and when someone tries to blackmail her, we don't take that lightly. She's a part of our family and we all love her very much, although in my case, it's different because I've been in love with her for a very long time." I'm talking to Jason, but I'm watching Molly. "And I'm not naive enough to think you all don't know that by now."

"Mike, would you like to tell your side of this story, or should we continue?" Aaron asks, crossing his thick tattooed arms over his chest.

Mike looks as though his brain is malfunctioning as he puts two and two together.

"Mike?" Jason prompts his business partner.

"It's against club rules for a player to date a coach. I simply reminded Miss Davison of this."

"No, it isn't," Claire, our HR manager, says from the far corner of the room. "There is no such rule."

"It's a conflict of interest," Mike argues.

"So, tell me, Mike," I say, "if it's a conflict of interest for me to date Molly, why doesn't that apply to you? After all, you did try and force yourself on her at the charity event a few months ago, remember?"

"I—"

"And if it's a conflict of interest, why didn't you go through official club channels instead of ambushing her in a dark corridor and threatening to sell lies to the media about our relationship? Why did you threaten to have me benched unless she broke up with me?"

"Molly, is this true?" Coach's face crumples as he looks into his daughter's eyes. The anguish written on her face is enough to confirm it.

"This is fucking bullshit. You can't prove that I said any of that. It's her word against mine, and who do you think the papers will believe?"

"You were wearing a microphone. Sure, it wasn't connected to the main speakers, but it was still recording, and we have a copy of the tapes. Multiple copies actually." The mic-drop moment I've been looking forward to. Our final card.

He looks at me, shock etched on his face as his house of cards comes toppling down.

Coach steps beside me in solidarity, turning to look at Mike, his arms crossed tightly over his chest. I've seen Coach angry before, but never like this with steam practically shooting from his ears and nose and a slow rumble building from deep inside of him.

"We pay you to play. If you don't play, then we don't pay," Mike says, desperation in his voice.

"Actually, they're all under contract; we have to pay them," Claire argues.

I hold my hand out for Molly, and she takes it, allowing me to pull her into the seat next to me, tears brimming in her eyes as she looks at everyone surrounding her.

"What are your conditions?" Jason asks.

"We want Mike removed from the board," I say.

"I own fifty-one per cent of this club; you can't remove me from the board."

"Fine, then we'll be releasing those tapes to every single news outlet in the UK. How do you think that'll turn out for you?"

"Actually, Mike"—Bridget steps up—"as of this morning, you don't own any of this club. Your shares were held by your smallest company, Rogers Holdings, which, since your divorce was finalised this morning, actually belongs to your ex-wife."

Mike pales at the realisation that he's lost all control.

I do everything to hold back a laugh that "clever" Mike made one of the silliest decisions of his life.

"Go clear out your shit, Mike," Jason snaps. "You're done."

He weighs up his options before storming out of the auditorium in a cloud of anger and disbelief as the rest of us celebrate as if we've just won the league.

"I can't believe that just happened," Molly says, diving into my arms and kissing me hard. I pull back as our friends fight to hug her too, followed by Jason and, lastly, her dad.

I stand up taller, gathering all my courage to face Coach, regretting that I didn't fill him in on any of this beforehand. "I'm sorry we didn't tell you about our relationship. Molly's career is important to both of us, and after everything she's been through to get to this point, we didn't want anything to jeopardise that. But you should know I love your daughter and I'll do anything to protect her."

"Son, you seriously think I haven't known about you two this entire time?" Coach laughs.

"What?" Molly's head bounces between me and her dad as though I've got a clue what he's talking about.

"Neither of you would be cut out for espionage, that's for sure. You know we have motion sensor CCTV in the back garden, right? Every time you sneak in and out, the bloody app alerts me."

"Oh my god." Molly's face burns red. "Why didn't you say anything?"

"Because I understand why you tried to keep it under wraps. Whatever you both decide to do, if you decide to share your relationship with the public or not, you'll have my support." Coach wraps his arms around his daughter and kisses her softly on the head. "I'm just glad you're both happy." He shakes my hand before walking away to join the others.

"Oh my god, I'm mortified." Molly's expression is a picture.

I'm still smiling when I bring my mouth to hers, revelling in the kiss we started back in her office. She parts her lips with a sigh, not caring that we have an audience as we get lost in one another. It's only been ten days since we were last together, but ten days more than I like.

"So, shall we go and get some lunch?" Aaron asks.

"We were actually going to go home," I tell him without taking my eyes off my girlfriend. "We have some making up to do," I add with a wink.

"Seriously, you'd rather go home and have filthy sex than come out with us?" Aaron laughs.

"When we are the ones who got you guys back together?" Brooke says, appearing at Aaron's side with Bridget not far behind her.

"I think you'll find I orchestrated this whole meeting." Bridget props her hands on her hips. "Your idea was to ambush him in his office. I added the flair."

"We'd love to get lunch, wouldn't we, Jordan?"

I groan dramatically, and Molly laughs.

"There is plenty of time to go home and make up properly. But for now, I want to show off my boyfriend in public. I don't want to hide away anymore."

Epilogue

Jordan – Six Months Later

"Molly, would you like to lead?" Coach asks as Molly stands front and centre in the dressing room at Wembley Stadium. It's the play-off final, and the winner gets promoted into the Championship. What a game to end my career on.

Molly presses a button on the laptop, and an image fills the big screen beside her. There's a mixture of laughing and "awwws" as Coach hides his face in his hands with a groan.

"This is me," she says, pointing at the five-year-old version of herself on the screen in her Wearside FC kit. "And this is my dad."

"Nice pornstar tash, Coach," Aaron teases good-naturedly.

"It was the nineties," he defends himself.

Molly laughs before turning back to us.

"I want to start by explaining to you what this club means to me. I've supported this team since the day I was born. Being a Wearside fan hasn't always been easy—there have been a lot of ups and downs for the club—but as you can see, I always had a smile on my face when I was at this stadium."

A series of pictures play on the screen of Molly at various matches and events at the club with her dad.

"I started my career with the women's team when I was sixteen." Her voice breaks slightly with emotion, and a lump forms in my throat. "I discovered a lot about myself playing football. I developed my skills and learned how to be the best player I could be. But that's nothing compared to what you boys have taught me."

The room is silent as she paces while pictures of our time training and hanging out together flit across the screen as she talks.

"When I took this job, I'll be honest and tell you I took it because my dad was worried about me. I really didn't think I'd stick it out because nothing else I had tried since my accident had stuck. I was broken, I was hurting, and I was lost. You all know the mental strain an injury can put you through. Add in the fact it ended my career, well, it was devastating. I wasn't ready for the end.

"When I walked into that dressing room at the start of the season and looked at all your beautiful faces"—laughter fills the room again—"all of a sudden, I was that little girl again. I was excited about my life again. I couldn't wait to get up in the morning and come to work. You boys brought me back to life."

She pauses, taking us all in as we feel the weight of her words.

"Out there at this very moment, there are thousands of young people just like I was. They're wearing your names and numbers on their backs ready to sing their hearts out for their favourite players. So, let's go out there and give them a match that will inspire the next wave of footballers."

Everyone is on their feet on the benches clapping and cheering as she comes around to embrace us one by one.

Aaron leads the chant of "we love you, Molly, we do", which has become a stadium favourite, and the noise in the room is deafening.

When she reaches me, she wraps her arms around my waist, sliding her warm palms against my back, and looks up at me.

"That was a great speech." I grin down at her.

I take her face in my hands, but before I can kiss her, she asks, "How are you feeling?"

"Sad, excited… ready."

"You're going to be amazing, Jordan."

I lean down and kiss her softly. This time, the room erupts into wolf whistles and a dramatic groan from Coach. Molly doesn't stop kissing me though; if anything, she kisses me harder. When she pulls back, she's grinning.

"Okay, let's go win this," Coach shouts, keeping the energy up as we file out of the dressing room towards the tunnel.

Five minutes remain of my career playing professional football.

I want to savour every second; however, my thirty-four-year-old body is reminding me why it's time to retire. It feels as though I'm closer to a hundred with each kick I make. My muscles ache after eighty-five gruelling minutes of playing against a tough side, but one look at the dugout, at Molly giving me an encouraging thumbs up from the touchline gives me a boost of energy. Five minutes—that's all I need to do.

As the opposition get ready for their throw in, it's now or never if I want to score one final goal for Wearside.

This is it.

I get in position, marking the closest defender to me, ignoring him as he grapples with me, trying to push me aside. When the ball is played, it lands at the foot of one of their other players, who turns to take the ball up the line. Without the looming pressure of injury taking me out of future games hanging over me, I don't hold back when I sprint after him, catching up quickly and going in for a hard tackle.

"Fuck," he whines as I drag the ball back and turn, lifting my head for a glance at where I hope Aaron is. I smile as I see he's there.

I cross the ball to him and sprint up the pitch to get into position in the box, ignoring the way my legs protest with every step. Aaron's head flicks towards me as he hits the ball hard, but the ball's direction is ever so slightly off. I almost let out a huff, the feeling of defeat and that I've let everyone down looming hard. I've had an entire game to get a goal. An entire ninety minutes to get just one goal. Which, I know is not as easy as it sounds. But everyone has so much hope in me…

The ball rebounds off a defender with a loud thump before flying straight towards me on an unexpected trajectory.

My eyes widen.

I can't let this goal get away.

With a deep grunt and zero care for my physical wellbeing, I leap into the air, lifting my leg high enough that when the ball reaches me, I throw it back, kicking the ball over my head towards the goal.

I land on the ground in a heap, tilting my head back just in time to see the ball whoosh against the back of the net.

It's in.

Holy fuck, I actually did it. My hands spring to my face, covering it as tears begin to fall and roll down my temples, onto the grass.

I did it.

The referee gives three sharp blows into his whistle, signalling not just the end of the game, but the end of my lifelong career with Wearside.

I stretch my arms and legs like a star and watch as the crowd are on their feet, their roar so loud that people on the other side of the river will be able to hear it. I'm tired, sore, and aching, but that's all in the back of my mind as I soak up the noise around me. It's the complete opposite of last season.

Aaron reaches out a hand, pulling me to my feet and hugging me tightly as each of my teammates joins the group hug.

"A bicycle kick for your final goal? Skip, you're a fucking legend." Tears are brimming in his eyes as he leans back, slapping me on my chest.

"Proud of you, Skip." Bailey's comment is simple and refined, yet still packs a punch to the gut that has a lump forming in my throat.

Pulling myself together a little, I congratulate each and every one of my teammates for a fantastic season. I know without a shadow of a doubt they'll continue to do well next season without me.

As the backroom staff and press cameras join us on the pitch, I turn to look for Molly. I immediately see her sprinting towards me, her long dark ponytail swishing behind her and a giddy smile on her face.

"Go on, Skip." Aaron laughs, slapping my chest as he's joined by Bailey.

"Good luck," Bailey adds.

Molly reaches me, launches herself into my arms, wraps her legs around me, and peppers excited kisses all over my face. "Oh my god, that was amazing. I'm so, so, so proud of you."

"It's all thanks to you, Mol." Without breaking apart, I slowly lower her to her feet and pull her close to me by her waist so our bodies are pressed together.

I thought I was nervous before the game, but my palms aren't just clammy from the physical exhaustion of the game and my heart is hammering just as hard as the butterflies I get every time I look at her as we stand in the centre circle, fifty thousand people surrounding us who have no clue what I'm about to do.

"You're in for such a treat when we get home," she teases. "Best night of your life, I swear."

"You have no idea, Mol."

"What do you—oh my god." The words whoosh out of her as I drop to one knee and untie my boot laces, freeing the ring that's been there the entire time, holding it between my finger and thumb. I take her left hand in mine as the stadium erupts into celebration once again when they realise what's happening.

"Oh my god, is this real?" Tears spring to her eyes as she looks down at me, and I nod, unable to keep a grin from tugging at my lips.

"Molly Elizabeth Davison, you are the best thing that's ever happened to me. You came back into my life when I was lost and lonely and showed me so much compassion and joy and love. Christ, I don't know how I got you to fall in love with me, and I definitely don't deserve you, but I'll spend the rest of my life trying to be half the man you deserve. Will you marry me?"

Her right hand flies to her face as she chokes on an excited sob. She stares at me through wide eyes as though she doesn't quite believe what's happening, then nods rapidly multiple times. "Yes. Yes, I'll marry you."

An overwhelming sense of emotion hits me when I slide the ring onto her finger. We made it. After all we've been through over the past four years, she's finally going to be my wife. Sooner rather than later hopefully.

My incredible fiancée looks down in awe at the ring. "This is beautiful." I had it designed especially for her—a large emerald cut diamond with a border of smaller diamonds surrounding it. She swipes her tears away so she can take a better look.

I stand quickly, lifting her into my arms again. "Not as beautiful as you."

This whole thing with Molly feels like a dream, but when she tangles her tongue with mine and my body wakes up in response, I know it's real.

"Holy shit, that was the most terrifying moment of my life." I laugh as though I'm joking, but I mean it. As she kisses me again, her tears are flowing freely and my cheeks are wet too. "I was more nervous to ask you to marry me than I was to play the game."

"I'm so proud of you, Jordan. Look at what you've achieved today. A hat-trick and a fiancée. And if we're really lucky, we'll be pregnant by the end of the night." She winks, but hey, challenge accepted.

"This is just the beginning, babe. I'm so ready for what comes next so long as I have you."

"I love you so much."

"I love you too, Mol."

The crowd erupts into yet another loud cheer before chanting Molly's song, but when her sparkling eyes gaze lovingly into mine, it feels as if it's just the two of us standing in the middle of an empty Wembley Stadium.

Acknowledgements

A Wearside Story has been a labour of love since 2022 and I can't believe how much the story and these characters have grown and evolved over time.

I want to give a huge thank you to Cassandra and Lauren from Cahill Davis Publishing for nurturing me and helping me bring so much added depth to the world of Wearside FC.

As always, this book wouldn't have been possible if it wasn't for my family and friends and the support and patience they have when I'm on a deadline and not questioning me when I stare off into space having a conversation with the imaginary people that live in my head.

Finally, to my author and reader friends, Chels, Carrie, Jess, Louise, Laura and Melissa. Thank you for all of your words of encouragement and always being on the other end of a message. I love you all so much!

About the author

Ellie White was born and raised in Sunderland and is a proud Mackem!

She lives in Houghton-Le-Spring with her husband and two young children. She supports Sunderland AFC and is a lover of chocolate, rom-coms, musicals and Formula One.

If you've enjoyed this book please leave a kind review online, not forgetting to tag her. It doesn't have to be much, just a few words will do; it will make all the difference!

Follow her on Instagram @elliewhite_writes or search for her on Facebook, X (Twitter) and TikTok to stay up to date with new releases.

Other books

<u>Playing for Real – A Wearside Story, Book 2</u>

An open door, best friends to lovers, fake dating romance that follows Aaron Milburn, Wearside FC's rumoured new captain and Brooke Davison, captain of Wearside Women and the England Lionesses.

A drunken mistake means Aaron has a tough choice to make. He needs to clean up his act or he'll lose out on the captaincy and Brooke might just be the person to help him. As they embark on a plot to improve Aaron's reputation, they decide to fake a relationship, although the embers that lay the foundation of their friendship.

<u>Playing for The Win – A Wearside Story, Book 3</u>

An open door, forbidden love romance that follows Bailey Airey all the way down under, to compete in TV show Celebrity Jungle Survivor.

When Bailey is stranded at the airport, his flight to Brisbane cancelled, he tries to pass the time in the airport lounge with a brunette he's seen many times but never formally met before.

Courtney Sanderson is the world's biggest pop star right now but also the girlfriend of Bailey's former friend and on pitch rival, Mark Rice. When Courtney offers to take Bailey with her to Brisbane on her private jet, spending three weeks in the Australian jungle fast becomes the least of Bailey's problems.

<u>Playing for Forever – A Wearside Story, Book 4</u>

An open door, brother's best friend, married in Vegas romance that follows Bridget O'Leary, Wearside FC's press officer and head of marketing.